Jules Verne, Edward Roth

To the Sun?

A Journey Through Planetary Space

Jules Verne, Edward Roth

To the Sun?
A Journey Through Planetary Space

ISBN/EAN: 9783337128012

Printed in Europe, USA, Canada, Australia, Japan

Cover: Foto ©Andreas Hilbeck / pixelio.de

More available books at **www.hansebooks.com**

TO THE SUN?

A

JOURNEY THROUGH PLANETARY SPACE

FROM THE FRENCH OF

JULES VERNE

AUTHOR OF "OFF ON A COMET!" "FROM THE EARTH TO THE MOON," AND "ALL AROUND THE MOON"

BY

EDWARD ROTH

With Thirty-six Full-page Illustrations

PHILADELPHIA

DAVID McKAY, PUBLISHER

23 SOUTH NINTH STREET

CONTENTS.

ix

LIST OF ILLUSTRATIONS.

ix

TO THE SUN?

CHAPTER I.

THE CHALLENGE.

"CAPTAIN, it does not suit me to surrender."

"I regret it extremely, my dear Count; for my own case is precisely similar."

"You are in earnest?"

"Never more in earnest in all my life."

"But I was first on the ground, Captain."

"My dear Count, in certain circumstances precedence can never be conferred by priority."

"Captain, words are tiresome."

"Count, I never liked them."

"Let us end this argument, Captain."

"I shall be delighted, Count."

"The sword is a splendid logician, my dear Captain."

"The pistol is hardly inferior, my dear Count."

"Accept my card, my dear Captain."

"Oblige me by a like favor, dear Count."

13

The words had been rapid, delivered in regular cut-and-thrust style; but the exchange of cards was quicker, if possible. The adversaries glanced at them with a ceremonious bow, and prepared to depart. The Captain's card bore

Cap. Hector Servadac,

Staff Officer,

MOSTAGANEM.

The Count's,

Count Wassili Timascheff,

Steam-Yacht DOBRYNA.

"When and where are the seconds to meet, Captain?"

"Two o'clock this afternoon, at the Staff Buildings, if you have no objections, Count."

"None whatever, Captain. The Staff Buildings are on the north side of the Place d'Armes at Mostaganem, are they not?"

"On the north side, Count. They can't be missed. I have the honor to bid you good-morning."

"The honor is mine, Captain."

Again the adversaries exchanged a most courteous salutation. They were turning away, when the Count suddenly stopped.

"Captain," he observed, "don't you think it would

THE CAPTAIN AND THE COUNT.

be just as well to be silent regarding the real cause of our meeting?"

"Exactly my opinion, Count."

"No name then shall be mentioned?"

"None whatever."

"But we must find some pretext."

"A pretext? Nothing easier. What objection would you have to a musical quarrel, Count?"

"Capital idea, Captain. I am crazy on Wagner — which, by the way, is true enough."

"And I on Rossini," answered the Captain, smiling: "which is anything but exaggeration."

With these words the gentlemen finally turned away, having once more exchanged a courteous salute.

The time of the year was the 31st of December; of the day, a little before noon. The place, the extremity of a little cape on the Algerine coast, between the towns of Tenez and Mostaganem, and a few miles north of the mouth of the river Sheliff.

The cape was sixty or seventy feet high, and the blue waters of the Mediterranean broke murmuringly on the rust-colored rocks at its base. The sun, hidden behind a dark cloud, could no longer bespangle every projection of the coast by his slanting rays. In fact, very little of the coast, or even of the sea, could be seen at the time. A dusky haze lay on both. This was, however, nothing

new.   For the last few months, strangely persistent mists
and fogs had been observed all over the world.   Every
one tried to account for them, but the best meteorolo-
gists acknowledged themselves vanquished.   Even on the
ocean, the fogs had been so dense that the mail-steamers
were obliged to be blowing whistles and firing cannon
continually, for fear of a collision.

Count Timascheff, hastily quitting the Captain, soon
reached a small four-oared gig that was awaiting him in
one of the numerous little creeks indenting the shore.
Hurriedly taking his seat in the stern, in a few minutes
he was on board a light-built steam-yacht which, with
main-sheet sail hauled in and foresail set aweather, was
lazily swinging at a few cable-lengths off shore.

The Captain, losing just as little time, quickly signalled
his Orderly, who had been waiting patiently at a few hundred yards distance, seated on one horse and holding
another, a magnificent Arabian, by the bridle.   In less
than a minute, the Captain was on horseback and making
rapidly for Mostaganem, closely followed by the Orderly,
who was nearly as well mounted as his master.   It was
half-past twelve as they galloped over the bridge lately
erected over the Sheliff by the engineering corps.   It
was fully a quarter to two when their horses, white
with foam and reeking with perspiration, reached the
Mascara gate, one of the five entrances giving admission
into the little fortified town.

At that time, Mostaganem, the second city in the province of Oran and headquarters of a military subdivision, could reckon a population of about fifteen thousand, one-fifth at least being French. It was a thriving, industrious community,— its confectionery, textile fabrics, mattings, and morocco leather work being particularly remarkable, and its exports to France of corn, cotton, tobacco, wool, cattle, figs, raisins and other fruits, quite considerable. Of the Roman port that in the old times had afforded such poor protection against the dangerous winds of the north and northwest, not a vestige now remained. A new and well sheltered harbor occupied its site, where ships could rest in perfect safety, and the numerous productions of the Mina and the lower Sheliff countries enjoy a most convenient outlet. It was on account of the favorable shelter afforded by this harbor that the *Dobryna* had ventured to winter on this dangerous coast. For the last two months the Russian flag had been floating from her gaff, while from her masthead fluttered the ensign of the yacht club of France, with the distinguishing signal M. C. W. T.

Captain Hector, without a moment's delay, made for the barracks, where he soon found a commandant of the Second Rifles and a captain of the Eighth Artillery, two faithful friends to be trusted for life or death. They listened with all becoming gravity to his request, but a

slight smile glittered in their eyes when he spoke of a musical discussion as the cause of the threatened encounter.

"We may probably arrange matters," suggested the
commandant.

"No arrangement is to be thought of," was Hector's
curt reply.

"A few modest concessions on either side would not
be unbecoming," observed the artillery captain. "Allowances could be made for difference in musical taste."

"No concessions! no allowances!" answered Hector,
testily. "Preferring Wagner to Rossini is a mortal
offence. Such a dispute the sword alone can settle."

"Particularly as a sword thrust is not always mortal,"
observed the commandant.

"And more particularly as a sword thrust is exactly
what I have made up my mind not to receive," replied
Captain Hector in a confident tone, that put an end to
all further discussion.

Having no time to lose, the two officers proceeded at
once to the Staff Buildings. Shrewdly guessing the
cause of the dispute, they never exchanged a word even
to each other on the subject. The cause of the duel
was not their affair. Their duty was simple enough —
to see the other seconds, and make all necessary arrangements to have the meeting come off with the strictest
attention to every punctilio in the Code of Honor.

THE CAPTAIN AND HIS FRIENDS.

This was no difficult matter, as they told Hector a few hours later. The Count, an aid-de-camp of the Emperor, — most Counts are, out of Russia, — had accepted the sword, the soldier's weapon; the place of meeting was a well-known spot under the cliffs, where the Count and the Captain had the interview already described, about two miles from the mouth of the Sheliff; and the hour was nine o'clock next morning.

"All right!" said Hector, in reply to these details. "Till to-morrow, friends, at nine o'clock." With these words, he gave their hands a warm squeeze and hastily left the city.

His friends, having nothing better to do, strolled leisurely over to the café Zulma, where they passed the evening playing piquet, smoking cigars, and sipping Moorish coffee.

For the last two or three weeks, the Captain, having charge of a section of the coast survey, had been obliged to change his city quarters for a hut near the shore, about five miles beyond the Sheliff. The requirements of his duty kept his days busy enough, but the long nights were so very lonely, that any other officer in the service except Hector would have found them intolerable. The Captain, however, never made a complaint on the subject, and probably even thought that there was nothing particularly worth complaining about.

He now rode back leisurely, but, though the evening
was getting dark, he soon pulled a scrap of paper out of
his memorandum-book and began to write something
on it with as much steadiness as his prancing Arabian
permitted. What he was trying to write, we have no
notion of concealing. It was not his will; far from it:
it was only poetry. He was getting up what he called
a *rondeau*, which he expected to recite with great effect
on his next visit to Oran, where about a month ago he
had met a beautiful young English widow, whose violet
eyes he had been dreaming of ever since. Having heard
her express enthusiastic admiration for Tennyson, and
noticing that her disposition was of a gentle, retiring
nature, he concluded that the road to her heart lay
through poetry, and to poetry accordingly he now devoted every spare moment. His success, however, had
so far by no means kept pace with his expectations.
Though he understood English very well, English rhymes
and above all English spelling he found exceedingly
puzzling. This evening, in particular, whether from his
interview with the Count or the unaccountable state of
the weather, he felt himself to be in anything but the
vein.

"No matter," he cried, gayly. "Let me stick to it,
and I shall do something. Any one could scribble
French verse, but English poetry from a Frenchman —

show me the woman who could resist that! not to talk of a young widow on the Algerine coast, where strangers are not as plentiful as mosquitoes. Let's see how much we've done so far!"

And he commenced :

"STANZAS TO THE HONORABLE MRS. CHETWODE,

IN REPLY

To her Charming Question, 'Why should we Love?'

"We love, my pensive saint, my Peri coy,
For love's sweet sake :
To barter gloomy thought for smiles and joy ;
To cure heart-ache."

"But here I stick. Since yesterday morning I can t think of another line. I like the swing of my verses; but if I don't do better this evening, I'm afraid I shall have to recast them in some simpler form. Halloo! Ben Zouf!"

"Present!" replied the Captain's Orderly, riding up quickly within easy talking range.

"Did you ever write any verses?"

"Never, Captain. In our school we never got beyond long division."

"I mean, when you were in England."

"I never made any English verses myself, Captain, and for a good reason. But I learned some very pretty ones while I was in London."

"Indeed! How was that?"

"You see, Captain, we lived near the Park. My orders were to have the General's horse ready every morning at the door at eleven o'clock. I was always there to the second, but the General seldom left the house before twelve. I never felt the hour tiresome. On the contrary. A few minutes after eleven every morning a neighboring door opened and out came a young lady in charge of two children on their way to the Park. She was a beauty, Captain! but she never cast an eye at me. I soon found out she was from the country, and that the reason why she looked so sad was the loss of both her parents. I then determined to write to her something highly respectful, but original and touching — but pardon me, Captain, I'm no doubt wearying you by my long rigmarole."

"On the contrary, Ben Zouf! I find your Britannic idyl charming; intensely interesting! Go on!"

"Well, Captain, I was recommended to see a journalist who writes poetry for the *Times* — the great London paper, you know. I did see him. He knew but little French, I knew but little English; still we soon came to an understanding. She was as beautiful as an angel — I told him to spare no pains, and I'd spare no money. I wanted to have something respectful, original, and touching, you know, Captain. Without something to touch the heart, poetry, in my opinion, is good for nothing."

"Quite right, Ben Zouf. The touchstone of poetry is its power to sweep the heart-strings! Pray, continue."

"The journalist told me he knew my wants exactly, and next day he proved it. The verses he brought were so fine, so splendid, so touching that I got them by heart at once, and have never forgotten them."

"Let us hear them."

Ben Zouf recited his verses in a voice quivering with emotion:

> "The rose is red, the violet's blue,
> I am thy sweetheart, fond and true;
> If you love me as I love you,
> No knife can cut our love in two!"

"Ha! ha! ha!" cried the Captain, in a roar of laughter. "Touching, original, powerful, is no name for your verses. Epic, grand, sublime they should be called. I hope you paid your poet well for such an effort."

"I paid like a prince, Captain!" answered Ben; "so at least the poet said when I slipped a half-crown into his hands. I was a poor man," added Ben, modestly, "but I adored originality. Give me originality, said I, and hang the expense!"

"Right again, Ben Zouf," laughed the Captain.

quickening his horse's pace a little, and resuming his soliloquy. "The English poet had about as much originality as myself—more I think—let me see if nis floral hint don't improve my dull lines."

He made the change, and then read aloud the improved version :

> "We love, my witching rose, my violet coy,
>   For love's sweet sake;
>   To barter gloomy thought for smiles and joy,
>   To cure heart-ache—"

But beyond this the Captain's poetic inspiration utterly failed to carry him. After another quarter of an hour's ineffectual efforts to compose a single line, he closed his memorandum-book impatiently, set spurs to his horse, and reached the hut shortly after dark, closely followed by his faithful Orderly.

CHAPTER II.

A T the date of the beginning of our story any one curious about the subject, by calling at the war office, Paris, might find the following record, in Register 1716, page 395:

SERVADAC (HECTOR), born July 19, 18—, at Saint Trelody, district of Lesparre, Department of Gironde.

PATRIMONY, 1200 francs a year.

IN THE SERVICE, 14 years, 3 months, 5 days.

DETAILS OF SERVICES: School of St. Cyr, 2 years; Staff School of Application, 2 years; in the Eighty-seventh of the Line, 2 years; in the Third Chasseurs, 2 years; in Algeria, 7 years.

CAMPAIGNS: Japan, Soudan.

POSITION: Captain of the Staff Corps, at Mostaganem.

DECORATIONS: Chevalier of the Legion of Honor, March 13, 18—.

Servadac was now thirty years of age. An orphan,

25

without family; of small patrimony; reckless of money,
but keen for glory; generous to a fault; like most Gas-
cons a little Quixotic; fonder of attack than defence,
but always ready for either; of preëminent courage,
though without the slightest scratch to show it; true
sprout of a chivalrous stock of ancestors, who never
seemed happier than when in trouble, the Captain
seemed to be one of those favored mortals that had
some kind fairy for a godmother, who predestined him
from birth for something altogether beyond the career
of ordinary humanity.

Physically, he was quite a good-looking young fellow. Five feet nine in height, of sinewy, graceful
limbs, curly hair as black as jet, perfect hands and
feet, silken mustache with a martial twist, of dark-blue
eyes gleaming with an honest look of fearlessness
and good-humor, the Captain seemed formed to please,
and we can say truly, always did please, though apparently seldom aware of it.

We must admit, however, that Servadac was not
overstocked with book learning. "We are no skulk-
ers," is a common expression among artillery officers,
and in the main they are correct. The Captain could
not say this. At Saint Cyr he "skulked" fearfully —
English being almost the only branch to which he devoted anything like real attention. At the Staff School

of Application, in Paris, his industry was just as indifferent — English "poetry" alone appearing to have
any charm for his few spare moments. Still, his wonderful facility for picking up odds and ends of information and rapidly assimilating them with little or no
trouble, had enabled him to quit the School and enter
on the Staff Corps with some credit, more, in fact,
than fell to the share of some of his comrades who
had been the most distinguished graduates of St. Cyr.
This shows the nature of the man — eminently practical, only slightly acquisitional. Besides sketching and
drawing with considerable skill, the Captain understood the art of horsemanship in an eminent degree.
To this day the young men at St. Cyr talk traditionally
of his marvellous feat in mastering *Le Gaillard, Uncle
Tom's* terrible successor, that had broken more limbs
and endangered more necks than any five horses together since the starting of the school in 1808.

His military reputation stood very high. He had
been several times complimented by name in presence
of the whole army for unusual fearlessness and presence
of mind. One instance of this kind will be enough
to record.

He was one day leading a company through the
trenches, before a besieged town, when he came to a
spot where the crest of the earthwork, struck by several

shells, had given way for a space five or six feet in length by one or two in depth. The soldiers, seeing that the mound was not high enough to afford sufficient protection against the bullets hissing around them like hail, naturally hesitated to dash past the opening. Captain Hector instantly took his course. Clambering up the earthwork, he threw himself across the breach, which his body exactly filled.

" Pass now ! " he cried ; " but be quick ! "

The company passed, a storm of bullets roaring over their heads, but not a man hurt, not even the Captain, whose preservation seemed little short of miraculous.

With the exception of two campaigns in Japan and Soudan, the Captain's services had been confined to Algeria ever since quitting the School of Application.

As already mentioned, he was now discharging the duties of Staff Officer at Mostaganem. Lately appointed to some topographical work on that portion of the coast between Cape Tenez and the mouth of the Sheliff, he had installed himself in a miserable little hut, a *gourbi* the Moors called it, where the accommodations were by no means luxurious. The Captain was not the man to complain about trifles. He loved liberty and independence dearly, with plenty of air and sunlight. These he had now to his heart's content, and these he thoroughly enjoyed, whether pacing the shore to measure his distances, climbing the cliffs to make his observations, or, mounted on his fiery Arabian, careering along the vast terraces of the Dahra to enjoy the ocean breezes and magnificent scenery. Such a life he was loath to exchange, and therefore he took no extraordinary pains to hurry through his work with more haste than was absolutely necessary. He even found time now and then to take a run to Oran, to show himself at the General's weekly reception, or to Algiers, where he never failed to appear at the Governor's grand monthly ball.

It was on one of these occasions that he met the beautiful Mrs. Chetwode, the lady in whose honor the famous "Stanzas," now in a state of incubation, had been undertaken. She was the widowed sister of a French gentleman's wife, whose delicate health had compelled herself and her family to spend their winters on the genial Algerine coast. Mrs. Chetwode was still young, though it was now more than four years since her husband had been lost in a sudden squall, while yachting off Sardinia. Several of the crew had perished, and Mrs. Chetwode had been in such danger, that for some time her recovery was considered extremely doubtful. The terrible catastrophe she had never forgotten. It made her reserved, pensive, almost melancholy. Her eyes seldom flashed with their old merriment, and the roses seemed to have fled her cheeks forever. All this rendered her only more attractive to Captain Hector. Her silence never wearied him. His exuberant spirits floated on more joyous wings, whenever he tried to dissipate her seriousness. These attempts, it must be remarked, were tolerably successful, and it was very seldom indeed that the Captain tore himself away without leaving the charming widow's eyes brighter and her lips beaming with a gentle smile. Still, as the closest observations had so far failed to detect the slightest sign of any marked preference in his regard, he had not yet been able to prevail on himself to ask the momentous question. He was aware that he had plenty of rivals, among others the Russian Count, the intimate friend of the lady's late husband — their yachting mania connecting them with a very strong link of mutual attraction. But the Captain did not know that this very circumstance had completely destroyed all the Count's chances — the beautiful widow, ever since the accident, entertaining an ineradicable horror of yachts and everything connected with them. On the contrary, the Captain dreaded more from the Count than from all the other rivals put together.

These were mostly Frenchmen, Germans, or Italians, who, if they spoke English at all, spoke it so absurdly that they often made the demure widow break out into little ripples of merry laughter at the identical moment when they counted on being most impressive. But the Count was a splendid linguist — equally at home in most of the languages of Europe. The lady herself often declared openly that she had never heard more elegant and stately English than fell from Count Timascheff's lips. Such an observation was, of course, all gall and wormwood to our poor Captain, who, though he spoke English rather indifferently, really understood it very well, and even prided himself on it as his greatest accomplishment. It was to countermine the Count on his own vantage-ground that he had undertaken the appalling task of addressing his lady love a poem in her own language — a feat which, if successful, would not leave the Count a leg to stand on. It was this great, but unfounded, dread of the Count's superiority that had also made him more desirous to measure swords with his rival in deadly combat than he would have been in almost any other circumstances. For the Gascon Captain, with all his hot blood and brave words, had not a particle of malice in his composition, and in his calm moments would readily forgive his bitterest foe.

Both belligerents, as we already know, though thirsty for each other's blood, had never forgotten that they were gentlemen. However the duel might end, the lady's fair fame could not be compromised. Her name had been religiously respected.

Captain Hector's only companion in the *gourbi* was our friend, Ben Zouf.

The Captain's man, in every sense of the term, Ben would not change his position for that of aid-de-camp to the Governor-General of Algiers. But the more utterly and completely devoid he was of ambition on his own account, the more keenly susceptible he felt it his duty to be on that of his master. The Captain's slow promotion he often growled about, and openly professed himself to be the bitter foe of partiality and ingratitude. The first thing he did every morning, before brushing his master's garments, was to see if a few grains of spinach seed had not sprouted up during the night in the shape of an epaulet on the left shoulder of the Captain's uniform.

The name *Ben Zouf* might make you imagine that he was a Zouave, or a Turco, or at least a native of Algeria. He was nothing of the kind. He was a full-blooded Parisian, and his real name was Lawrence. *Ben Zouf* was probably a whim of the master's, certainly not of the man's. Ben would no more think

BEN ZOUF.

of changing his name than of denying the place of his nativity. Than this we can think of no stronger comparison. For if any one ever was proud of his birthplace, it was Ben Zouf. This hallowed spot was not only Paris, but Montmartre; and it was not only Montmartre, but the summit of Montmartre, midway between the tower of Solferino and the Galette Windmill. Any one fortunate enough to be born under such exceptional conditions would have the right to be proud of his native hill and to look on it as the eighth wonder of the world. This at least was Ben's opinion, for in his eyes Montmartre was the finest mountain on earth, and the Montmartre district the finest district in Paris. He had travelled much, and had seen a little in every division of the world, except Australia. He had got a glimpse at many of its wonders, but none of them could approach his beloved Montmartre. Hadn't it a church equal to the cathedral of Burgos? quarries equal to those of Carrara, or Pentelicus? a basin — well, a basin hardly inferior to the basin of the Mediterranean? windmills livelier, noisier and far more picturesque than the windmills of Holland? a tower that leaned over nearly as much as the famous tower of Pisa? a bit of virgin forest — a remnant of the old Celtic times — not to be surpassed in age or wildness by anything of

the kind in America? and, finally, a mountain, a real
mountain, which nothing but the envious tongue of
jealousy could desecrate into a mound? Yes; you
might hack Ben into a thousand pieces before you
could make him confess that Montmartre was not one
of the mountain wonders of the world. In one of his
very excited moments, he even said that Mont Blanc
was only a pimple beside Montmartre. But from
this dangerous ground he soon retreated, and did
not care to approach it again. "Waiving for the present," he would say, "the unimportant and empty question of mere altitude, where else in the whole world
could you find such an astonishing collection of the
works both of Nature and Art combined, in any one
single point?"

"Nowhere else!" was the triumphant reply with
which he always closed the argument, for Ben would
never listen for an instant to any one disposed to
think his opinions regarding the excellent points of
Montmartre somewhat exaggerated.

He had now but one idea, one hope — to return to
Montmartre and end his days on the sacred ground
where they had begun — of course in company with
his Captain. Accordingly, on every occasion, favorable or not, Servadac's ears had been so dinned with
the changes that Ben would keep on eloquently

ringing on the peerless beauties accumulated in the Eighteenth Arrondissement of Paris, that he was of late beginning to entertain a serious horror even of the very name of Montmartre. Ben had a surmise of this, but, nevertheless, he was quite confident of being able to convert the Captain in the long run. At all events, he would never desert him. His time of military service had expired. He was now perfectly free. He had already served two terms, but without rising to any higher grade than that of simple private of the Third Cavalry. He was even thinking of quitting the service altogether, at the age of twenty-eight, when he was unexpectedly promoted to the rank of Captain Servadac's man. This gave him at last some interest in military matters. He went through two campaigns with his officer. He fought by his side on several occasions, and once even so bravely that his name had been sent in for the Cross of the Legion of Honor. But he refused this decoration, preferring the Captain's service. If his Captain had saved Ben's life in Japan, Ben had had the good fortune in Soudan to save his Captain's. These are things not easily forgotten.

You have now the chief reasons why Ben Zouf still devoted to the Captain's service a pair of arms steeped to the marrow in muscular vigor, an iron frame case-hardened to every climate, a physical strength great enough to have him nicknamed the "Rampart of Montmartre," and, in short, a courage to confront any extremity, and a devotion to shrink from no danger. If not an "original" poet, like his master, he was a walking cyclopedia of all the jokes, smart slang, comical stories, jests, quibbles, and "good 'uns" in general, that form the staple of camp conversation, but which, in general, are absolutely untranslatable into English. These he would let off by the hour to any one willing to listen to him, and with a native drollery that his master at times found irresistibly facetious.

The Captain fully understood the worth of his man, and thoroughly appreciated his excellent qualities. He would, it is true, occasionally give his prejudices a little dig; but for this he more than atoned by the pretty things he would say at moments when Ben was far from expecting them.

With a little instance of this kind we shall conclude the present chapter.

Ben had been one evening fully an hour riding his hobby furiously up and down the sides and along the summit of Montmartre, when he suddenly interrupted himself to investigate the effect his eloquence had produced on the Captain.

After a few seconds' silence, the latter observed :

"Ben Zouf, there's one thing more left for you to say about Montmartre."

"What's that, Captain?" asked Ben, timidly, taught by experience to be always on the lookout for a sly thrust.

"Paris is a great city, Ben Zouf!"

"The greatest city in the world, Captain, except Rome!"

"Do you know, Ben Zouf, that your Montmartre is really higher than the two highest mountains of Rome piled on each other?"

"Oh, Captain, you don't say so!" cried poor Ben, in an agony of joy, while a gleam of mingled pride and affection flashed from his brimming eyes.

From that day his "mountain" and his master's images had been engraved so deeply and inseparably on his heart, that the grateful creature could never think of one without immediately recalling the other.

CHAPTER III.

AN INTERRUPTION BOTH UNSEASONABLE AND UNREASONABLE.

A GOURBI is simply a kind of open framework hut, covered on the top and sides by a peculiar straw, called by the natives "driss." In architecture, it ranks somewhat higher than the Arab tent, but far lower than a Mexican adobe or an American log-house The Captain's *gourbi* was in fact no better than a mere hovel, which would never have been able to accommodate its guests but for having been backed up by an old military post-house, solidly built of stone, and now serving as sleeping place for Ben Zouf and the two horses. Sometime before this being occupied by a corps of engineers, it still contained a quantity of their tools, such as picks, spades, shovels, and other implements of the kind.

The Captain and his man, never hard to please, submitted to the irksomeness of their present quarters without a murmur, looking on it as merely temporary and bound to come to an end in a month or two.

"With a little philosophy and a good stomach, there is not much difficulty in getting along anywhere," the Captain would occasionally observe when contemplating longer than usual the sorry accommodations offered by his present abode. This reflection was a sovereign consoler. Philosophy being the only pocket-money a Gascon never runs out of, the Captain had always a good stock on hand. Nor did his stomach trouble him much. Ben said it was almost as good as his own, which, as everybody knew, was a regular ostrich's, capable at a pinch of extracting almost as much nourishment out of nails and gravel as out of roast beef and spring chickens.

Talking of food, we may as well here state that our friends had a month's supply of provisions, a tank full of good sweet water, and plenty of food for the horses. Besides, this western portion of the plain lying between Tenez and the mouth of the Sheliff is fully as rich as the best portion of the famous Metidja. Game is very abundant, and it is hardly necessary to say that as long as a staff officer does not forget his theodolite, he can carry his fowling-piece wherever he pleases.

In less than a quarter of an hour after his return, the Captain was dining with a furious appetite. Ben Zouf was a famous hand in the kitchen. No one could

ever complain of the insipidity of his dishes. He
salted, peppered, vinegared, mustarded, pickled, in
the high military style. None of your dainty tid-
bits for him or his master. They had stomachs of
the cast-iron kind, latest patent, warranted to stand
the hottest condiments, and proof against anything
short of *aqua fortis.*

Dinner over, and while Ben was still industriously
stowing away in what he called his abdominal cup-
board the remains of the repast — just to prevent
waste, as he said — the Captain, lighting a cigar,
went out and began to take a quiet stroll up and
down on the edge of the cliff. But he was soon
brought to a stand-still. Though he was never a
very close observer of cosmical phenomena, the unusually strange appearance of the sky that evening
struck him at once with some surprise.

No star was visible, but a lurid reddish light lay
all round him, of which he looked in vain for the
cause. To the west, beyond the bay of Mostaganem,
nothing could be seen except the thick, heavy cloud
masses, behind which the sun had set a few hours before. In front, directly north, the view was equally
limited, the heaving, phosphorescent sea being nowhere visible beyond a quarter of a mile. Nothing
at all could be seen east and south. But, over head,

through the dark misty atmosphere, a pale, noiseless, dusky kind of light seemed to be struggling, tinging the clouds faintly like a distant reflection of Vesuvius in eruption. What made this strange light? It was not the aurora borealis, for it revealed neither the clean-cut fringes so well known in the arctic regions nor the flashing corruscations so often witnessed in the temperate zone. Besides, the latitude, 36° N., was altogether too low to permit the present steady and persistent meteoric display to be attributed to an effect of the shimmering, restless northern lights. Even an experienced meteorologist, therefore, would have been decidedly puzzled if asked to account off-hand scientifically for the luculent phenomena penetrating the sombre clouds so mysteriously this last night of the year.

But the Captain was no meteorologist, experienced or otherwise. Since his school-days he had probably not looked twice into his *Course of Cosmography*. In any case, on this particular evening, he felt himself little disposed to indulge in physical investigations. He soon resumed his slow promenade, puffing his cigar, thinking probably over his "stanzas," or, still more probably, over his approaching meeting with Count Timascheff. If his thoughts dwelt on the latter subject, it must be acknowledged that they were by no means of a bitter nature. The rivals were far from hating each other. They fought, not to kill each other, but merely to simplify an entanglement in which two were one too many. Nothing, therefore, disturbed the Captain's thoughts regarding the Count. He looked on him as a highly honorable gentleman, and it is quite probable that the Count, in his turn, held the Captain in the greatest possible estimation.

About ten o'clock the Captain returned to the *gourbi,* whose single apartment contained a camp bed, a little work-table with adjustable arrangement, and a few boxes that discharged equally well the double debt of seats and bureaus. As already mentioned, it was in the old stone guard-house, next door, that Ben not only kept the horses but cooked the meals and also took his regular nap of twelve hours at a stretch, his bed being no better, as he said himself, than the softest side of a good oaken plank.

The Captain, unusually wakeful, took a seat at the table, and, mechanically seizing a compass in one hand and a blue pencil in the other, began to trace on a piece of drawing-paper some lines in zigzag, which, candor compels us to admit, by no means recalled the severe contour of a topographical sketch.

Ben Zouf, stretched in a corner, was waiting orders to retire, and meanwhile was calmly digesting his com-

THE GASCON TROUBADOR.

fortable and abundant supper. He was even beginning to drop off into a gentle doze, as he had often done before, when he found that his efforts in this direction were decidedly thwarted by his master's most singular and unaccountable proceedings.

He started up and looked at him. What was the matter? Never before had he seen him flourish the compass so wildly, dash down his pencil-marks so hurriedly, or blot them out so recklessly. Was he working against time in dotting off some important triangulations, or was he — yes, was he only — writing poetry? Ben had guessed right. The staff officer was now replaced by the Gascon troubadour. But the troubadour soon became the desperate soldier, fighting fiercely in the very thickest of the battle. He worked, he struggled, he gesticulated, he mouthed. The labor seemed terrible, but the success, so far, indifferent enough.

At last the rebellious words seemed somewhat willing to obey orders, and fell into line. The Captain's fingers moved like lightning, as he wrote:

> " Life without Love is but a clouded day,
>   A starless night—"

"Poetry, or I'm a Dutchman!" muttered Ben, hardly suppressing his voice from surprise. "Who'd have expected such a thing from the Captain? He turn poet! He! To be a good poet you must be good for nothing else. The Captain — a sketcher, certainly, and a marcher, and a rider, and a commander, and a fighter! — but a poet — bah!" and Ben shrugged his shoulders and shook his head in a manner anything but complimentary to the Captain's poetical talents. "Can it be that little English widow?" he went on, hardly caring whether he was heard or not. "What taste, my heaven, what taste! Those widows bewitch the men! Look at him now, running up and down there like a hen hunting up her lost chicken!"

Sure enough, the Captain was now furiously striding up and down, a prey to the full blast of poetic inspiration.

After a few minutes he suddenly stopped, and down went two more lines:

"His glorious presence makes the grave heart gay,
   The sad eye bright."

Then the Captain began marching up and down again.

"Writing poetry to a woman, especially to a widow," resumed Ben, sententiously, and with a tone of conviction founded on experience, "acts like a two-edged sword. It cuts both ways. It makes the woman vain and silly. It makes the man foolish, and, what is worse, exceedingly selfish. For a proof, look at the Captain! At heart the best-natured man in the world, yet for the last hour he never bestows a thought on a poor fellow dying to get a wink of sleep! Let us wake him up!" Here Ben was suddenly seized with a fit of mingled coughing, hemming, and sneezing, that was too well done to be quite natural.

"What the fury's the matter, Ben Zouf?" roared the Captain, quite startled.

"I don't really know, Captain," answered Ben, with a fearful yawn. "Only the nightmare, perhaps," he added, with a demure glance at his master.

"Hang your nightmare, you sleepy lubber! You have ruined the fine flow of my versification! Ben Zouf!" he added, in a tone of command.

"Present!" cried Ben, jumping up nimbly, and putting one hand to his cap and the other to the seam of his pantaloons.

"Attention! Strict attention till further orders! I'm approaching the end of my stanzas!"

Then, in the full tones of wrapt inspiration, he repeated as he wrote down the following lines:

> "Then waste not woefully, my sweetest saint,
>   Thy life's best years
> In ranging mem'ry's halls with bootless plaint
>   And endless tears.
> I swear—"

What the Captain swore will never be known to mortal man. The oath was never pronounced. Before another word could be uttered, a sudden shock struck both Captain and Man to the earth with tremendous violence

CHAPTER IV.

QUESTIONS HARD TO ANSWER.

WHY, at this very instant, to any one that happened to be in these regions of the Mediterranean on this particular night, was the horizon so suddenly and strangely modified that even the most experienced mariner could not have recognized the circular line where the earth and sky seem to meet?

Why, at this very moment, would he have seen the sea lift its waters to a height never before paralleled, not even deemed possible in the annals of science?

Why, at this very moment, would he have heard the solid earth rend and tear itself asunder with the crashing din of ten thousand pieces of artillery?

What could have produced that furious seething of the mighty waters, dashed wildly together in unknown depths? Or those wild screams of severed masses of air louder than a cyclone's shrieking blast?

Why flashed through space a sudden and extraordinary splendor, intenser than the rutilant fulgurations of the aurora borealis, lighting up the whole heavens instantaneously, and for a moment eclipsing every star of every magnitude?

Why, at this very moment, did a part of the Mediterranean present the appearance, for one instant, of a yawning chasm of black walls and bottomless depths, filled, in the next, with raging waters, fuming, hissing, and violently convulsed?

Why, at this very moment, did the moon suddenly seem to have grown of such enormous size as to appear to be ten times nearer the earth than she really is?

Or was it the moon at all, but rather some spheroid, vast, glittering, unknown to cosmographers, that had flared for a moment across the sky with dazzling radiance, and was then instantly swallowed up in a womb of pitch-black clouds?

What possible phenomenon could have caused the terrible cataclysm that convulsed with such violence at once earth, sea, sky, and space?

Who could answer these questions? Was any one on earth able to answer them? The suddenness and velocity of the catastrophe made a direct answer unlikely. But, what is more to our purpose, on the surface of the strange spheroid that had been just whisked off the earth like a lamb in an eagle's claws, was there any human being at all left alive to tell the tale of the marvellous journey on which it had just started?

THE GOURBI IN RUINS.

CHAPTER V.

WHAT'S THE MATTER WITH THE WORLD?

THE stupendous phenomenon alluded to in our last chapter, whatever else it might have done, did not seem to have produced much change in the portion of the Algerine coast bounded on the west by the Bay of Mostaganem, and on the north by the Mediterranean Sea. The fertile plain indeed may have looked unusually "hummocked," here and there, and the sea, no doubt, appeared to be unnaturally agitated, but neither the peculiar windings of the shore, nor the general arrangement of the overhanging cliffs, appeared to have undergone any decided change in their physical aspect. The guard-house was still standing, and, with the exception of a few slight cracks, apparently as safe and sound as ever. But the *gourbi* was as flat as a card-castle blown over by a child's breath, and its two former occupants were still lying senseless and motionless underneath the wreck. The lamp had been fortunately extinguished by some accident before it had time to set anything on fire.

In about two hours after receiving the stunning shock which had felled him so unceremoniously to the earth, Captain Hector recovered his consciousness. His senses came back only by very slow degrees, and the first words he uttered were:

"I swear —"

Then, quickly interrupting himself as the strangeness of his situation flashed upon him, he asked in an impatient tone:

"Halloo! what the fury is the matter?"

Finding that no reply came to this question, he tried to sit up, and having at last with some difficulty extricated his head from the straw and *débris* covering it, he tried to look around with eyes full of wonder.

"The *gourbi* down!" he exclaimed, in great amazement. "Some whirlwind then must have swept over us!"

He ran his fingers rapidly over his body. Nothing broken, nothing sprained, no blood, not even a scratch.

"But my Orderly!" he suddenly cried, looking around with great eagerness. "Is he all right, too? Ben Zouf!"

"Present!" cried Ben, poking his head through a hole in the straw.

"Have you any idea of what has befallen us, Ben Zouf?" asked the Captain.

"Seems to me, Captain," replied Ben, speaking slowly and deliberately, "as if we're near the end of our last campaign."

"Fudge, Ben Zouf. It's nothing but a whirlwind, a little whirlwind."

"Well, a whirlwind it is!" replied the Orderly, with the resignation of a philosopher. "Nothing broken, I hope, Captain?"

"Nothing whatever, Ben Zouf. Everything sound as a bell. Jump up!"

In an instant both were on their feet, clearing away the wreck and picking out their instruments, arms, and furniture from the rubbish. Very little real damage. they soon had the satisfaction of learning, had been done to anything.

"What time is it, Ben Zouf?" asked the Captain, trying to arrange his instruments in something like order.

"Eight o'clock, at least," replied Ben, glancing at the sun, now pretty high above the horizon.

"Eight?"

"Can't be a single second less, Captain."

"Impossible!"

"Impossible or not, Captain, it is full time to start."

"To start? What for?"

"The meeting."

" What meeting ? "

" With the Count."

" Oh, by Jove ! " cried the Captain, " I was near forgetting all about it ! "

He looked a few moments at his watch, and then exclaimed :

" What 's that you're saying about eight o'clock, Ben Zouf ? You're crazy. It 's hardly two o'clock, yet ! "

" Two in the morning, or two in the afternoon ? " asked Ben, with another glance at the sun.

Before answering, the Captain held the watch awhile to his ear.

" My watch is all right," he then observed. " It goes as well as ever."

" So does the sun," replied the Orderly.

" Certainly," said the Captain, now looking carefully at the sun, " to judge by its height above the horizon — Ah ! by all the wines that ever grew in Medoc ! — "

" What 's up, now, Captain ? "

" Could it be eight o'clock in the evening ? "

" In the evening ! "

" Yes ! Don't you see the sun is in the west, and going to set ? "

" Set ? Not at all, Captain. The sun is getting up, getting up as lively as a conscript at the first tap of the morning drum. Only look ! while we 're talking, he 's already got a little higher above the horizon."

"The sun rising in the west!" muttered the Captain to himself. "There's no denying it. Can I be really losing my senses?"

The fact was unquestionable. It admitted no dispute whatever. The bright king of day, reflected in the waters of the Bay, was absolutely climbing the very same western vault of heaven where from time immemorial he had always and invariably got through the second half of his diurnal journey.

Captain Hector was astounded. A phenomenon of this kind was never heard of before; it was utterly inexplicable. It actually reversed the very first and fundamental element of all astronomy, namely, the direction from west to east of the earth's daily movement on her axis.

It was enough to turn his brain. Could the impossible then be true? If there had only been a member of the Astronomical Bureau at hand, how eagerly the Captain would have questioned him! How intently would he have listened to the abstrusest calculations! But now, thrown as he was entirely on his own resources, after a few moments' reflection, he abruptly cut the matter short, observing:

"Well! after all, it's none of my business. Let the astronomers settle it among them! I must say, however, I shall be somewhat curious to learn from the papers how they will extricate themselves from the snarl. Come on, Ben Zouf!" he continued, turning to his Orderly; "whatever has taken place, even though the whole architecture of the heaven and earth has been turned topsy-turvy, one thing must be done. I must be the first man on the ground. The Count must never say I kept him waiting."

"Couldn't you manage to take a little breakfast before starting?" asked the Orderly.

"No time!" replied the Captain, already far ahead on the road. "Forward!"

Ben obeyed orders at once, though the Captain's answer gave him anything but satisfaction. The truth is, his master's whole manner made him somewhat uneasy. He had never seen the Captain in such a state before. He was panting like a man who had run himself out of breath. He could hardly speak four words in succession without stopping. Then his voice — usually a powerful baritone — was now so faint and squeaky that Ben had great trouble in catching his words. What was the matter with the Captain? Was he simply hungry? Or was it his approaching en counter with the Russian that rendered him nervous and timid? him, the daring pursuer of the redoubtable Si Hamed, with no let-up for two days and two nights? him, gazetted in four different languages for especial bravery at Samosaki? Or, happy thought, was it his own, Ben Zouf's, senses that had gone wrong? Had that unaccountable shock of last night injured his hearing? And, now that he came to think of it, was not his own voice also somewhat squeaky and feeble? Did he not now experience as much difficulty in catching his breath as on that memorable day when he came up with the Kabyles after a long chase up the slopes of the Jebel Amur? Could his lungs have been affected as well as his hearing?

Nothing whatever was wrong with either his ears or his lungs. The simple truth was — though neither the Captain nor his Orderly had as yet suspected it — the air had suddenly become much less dense than they had been accustomed to, and consequently both harder to breathe and less suitable for the transmission of sound.

The Captain seemed but little inclined to trouble himself with these questions just now. His whole desire was concentrated on being the first to be present on the field of battle. Closely followed by Ben Zouf, he made a bee-line for the little meadow under the cliffs, where he had agreed to meet his rival.

In the meantime, the weather was undergoing a remarkable change. The sun was no longer visible. Black, copper-colored, electric-looking clouds, lay so

low as almost to hide the horizon. Not a breath was
stirring. Everything, in short, announced an impend-
ing rain-storm of torrential proportions, or, at all events,
a frightful tempest. Still, no doubt for lack of sufficient condensation, the black looming clouds held up
bravely, and not a single heavy drop fell to announce
that the storm was close at hand.

The sea, on their right, as Ben soon remarked, foɪ
the first time seemed completely deserted. Mostaganem
Bay is generally pretty animated, at some parts of the
year particularly so, but this morning not a single sail
flecked the grayish clouds, not a single streak of smoke
betrayed the distant steamer. This, we have said, was
Ben's remark, but the Captain could not help noticing
something still more puzzling. Could it be an optical
illusion? The horizon was much nearer, even when
looked at seawardly. The cliff on which they moved
being about one hundred feet high, their horizon, according to a well known law in geometry, should be
at least twelve miles distant. The Captain's most careful observation would hardly allow it to be three miles
distant. The convexity was certainly more decided
than he had ever noticed it before. Could the earth's
diameter have suddenly contracted? What *was* the
matter with the world?

But a new surprise soon struck them as still more

astonishing. They had not been ten minutes on the road when they began to experience less difficulty in breathing. Their lungs gradually began to act with the easy play of those of a tired man after he has taken a little rest. But the Captain and his Man were anything but resting. Far from it. They were marching with greater rapidity than ever. This was the strange part of it. With all their speed, they were hardly conscious of increased muscular exertion. Trees, rocks, and bushes flew past them as if they had been in a railroad train. They were floating rather than walking. It had been always one of Ben Zouf's ineradicable principles never to start in the morning before breakfast. His fidelity to this rule sometimes brought him into trouble — but no trouble, as he said, was as bad as to undertake anything serious while fasting. To do so spoiled all his chances of success, besides rendering him heavy, dull, and sick all day. But this morning he was at the opposite extreme of sick and dull. His spirits were quite hilarious, and his body moved along as if he had wings to his feet.

Suddenly, a disagreeable barking attracted the travellers' attention, and at the same moment a jackal jumped out of a mastic jungle skirting their path on the left. The animal belonged to a species peculiar to this part of Africa chiefly remarkable for the black splashes that spot the sides and the black stripes that run along the forepart of the legs. At night, and forming part of a troop, it may be dangerous; but in the daytime and alone, it is no more formidable than an ordinary dog. Night or day Ben was never afraid of jackals, but he never liked them at any time — probably because Montmartre counted no such animal among its fauna.

The animal, hurriedly quitting the thicket, ran to the foot of a steep rock, where, turning round, it began to survey the travellers with an air of considerable uneasiness. For a moment only, for, at Ben's gesture of presenting a gun, the timid creature was so alarmed, that, to the profound stupefaction of the Captain and his Orderly, it made a spring and landed itself on the summit of the rock in one single bound.

"What a jumper!" cried Ben, in amazement. "That rock is thirty-six feet high if it is an inch!"

"Not a line lower!" observed the Captain, no less surprised. "Never before did I witness such an astounding bounce."

Sitting quietly on the top of the rock, the jackal appeared to regard the travellers with such a jeering glance that Ben, losing patience, stooped for a big stone that lay at his feet. What he picked up was certainly a stone, to judge from its look and touch, but, as far as weight was concerned, it might as well have been a piece of sponge.

"Hang the cuss!" muttered Ben. "I might as well fire a crust of bread at him as a stone like this! What's the matter with it anyway? It's big enough to be ten times as heavy!"

So saying, and having nothing better at hand, he flung the stone, but missed the jackal. That prudent animal, mistrusting such hostile demonstrations and unwilling to stand another shot, took to immediate flight and soon disappeared, bounding over the shrubs, rocks, and even the trees, in a series of jumps that would do honor to an india-rubber kangaroo filled with hydrogen gas.

But it was the stone's course that surprised Ben the most. He actually thought it was never going to stop. It went up in the air like an arrow, described a very long and flat parabola, and fell at last so far away that he could neither see the spot nor hear the sound.

"Name of the Prophet!" cried Ben, swearing like an Arab. "I never knew I was so strong! I could back myself heavy against a four-pounder!"

Quickening his pace a little, he was soon ahead of the Captain. Seeing a ditch crossing the path before him, ten or twelve feet wide and filled with water, he started off at a run to give himself the necessary momentum for clearing it at a jump.

He rose at once in the air like a kite, to the Captain's inexpressible astonishment, and, we must add, even consternation.

"Where are you going, Ben Zouf?" he exclaimed, almost unconsciously. "Do you want to break your neck, you madman?"

But Ben only kept on getting higher and higher, till he was at least at an altitude of forty feet. The startled Captain did not know what to think, but seeing the ditch before him, he also took a little run to jump it. His upward muscular effort must have been not quite so great as Ben's, for he rose only to a height of about thirty feet above the ground. But his forward impetus was considerably greater; for while he was still on the rise he shot past Ben Zouf, who was on the fall. Then in his turn obeying the laws of gravity, he began to approach the earth with accelerating velocity. But, to his great surprise as well as to his supreme satisfaction, he experienced no worse shock on coming in contact with the earth than if he had made an ordinary jump of no more than four or five feet.

"Circus, Captain!" cried Ben Zouf, with a roar of laughter. "The flying men can't hold a candle to us!"

Before the Captain would venture a reply, he laid his hand on Ben's shoulder for a few minutes in deep thought; then he said, gravely:

THE JUMP.

"Look at me straight in the eye, Ben Zouf! If I'm not awake, pinch me till I am! Pinch me, if need be, till the blood comes! If you and I are not dreaming, you and I are mad!"

"We must be dreaming, Captain," answered Ben, without a moment's hesitation. "At least I remember to have often dreamt of flying over Montmartre like a swallow. But somehow all that was different from all this. A dream is quite natural like, but these here doings are against all nature! Something strange is the matter somewhere, but what it is, I'm blest if I know!"

"It would puzzle Old Nick himself!" cried the Captain, completely nonplussed. "We're neither asleep nor dreaming, that's certain — and if we're mad! —"

But the Captain was not the man to puzzle himself too long in trying to sound the unfathomable. He soon started off again, gayly exclaiming:

"Happy thought! Reasoning does more harm than good! Only perplexes a fellow's brain! Here goes! Come what may, I shall never wonder again! *Nil ad-mirari!* as we used to say in school."

"What does that mean, Captain?"

"Be surprised at nothing!"

"Except as to how you and the Count will manage

to fight this morning," said Ben, who, being of a practical turn, never forgot the main business on hand.

A comparatively few minutes more brought them
to a little meadow, green, smooth, velvety, surrounded
by palms, carobs, sycamores, cactuses, aloes, and green
oaks, interspersed here and there by a few gigantic gum-
trees — all planted here about fifty years before, now
in full maturity, and completely screening the meadow
from all impertinent observations either by land or by
sea.   It was, in fact, the very arena in which the rivals
had agreed to settle their dispute by a hand-to-hand
conflict.

"First on the ground!" cried the Captain, throwing
a rapid glance over the meadow.

"Or the last!" observed the Orderly.

"The last?   Impossible!" answered the Captain,
pulling out his watch, which he had tried to set by
the sun before they had left the *gourbi*.

"Captain," asked Ben, "do you see that little
whitish spot in those clouds right over our heads?'

"I see it very distinctly," answered the Captain.
"What of it?"

"It's the sun!" said Ben, calmly.

"The sun overhead in January, thirty-six degrees
north of the equator!" cried Captain Hector.   "Do
you know what you are saying, Ben Zouf?"

"Begging pardon, Captain, that's the sun and nothing else. He marks twelve o'clock too, and nothing
shorter. He appears to be uncommonly lively to-day.
My cap against a plate of soup, he will set within three
hours!"

In spite of his recently formed resolution, Captain
Hector was once more astounded. He looked long
and steadily at the whitish spot in the clouds. Then
he took a careful survey of the four cardinal points.
At last he spoke:

"The laws of gravity changed! The cardinal points
changed! The length of the day cut down fifty per
cent.! My meeting with the Count indefinitely postponed! There's something wrong! What is it? My
head seems all right, and nothing unusual seems to be
the matter with Ben Zouf's! — Look around Ben Zouf!
Do you see anybody?"

"Nobody, Captain," answered Ben, very quietly.
"The Russian gentleman is gone!"

"Well, suppose he's gone, would not my friends
have waited for us? And, seeing no sign of our approach, wouldn't they have started for the *gourbi* to
know what had detained us?"

"They would most certainly, Captain."

"I conclude, then, that they have not come at all."

"Because, Captain —?"

"Because they have not been able to come. As to
the Count — but before saying anything, let us take all
the observations we can."

He ran across the meadow to the right, and climbing
a very high and steep rock, he looked carefully up and
down the coast for some sign of the *Dobryna*. The
Count, he thought, might have started for the place
of meeting by water, as he had done the previous even
ing.

The sea was completely without a sail. This fact,
unusual at any season of the year, might, however,
be explained by the state of the sea, now observed
by the Captain for the first time. Not a breath of
wind was stirring, and yet the waves were agitated
in an extraordinary manner. In fact, they were
boiling, bubbling, and seething, as if some tremendous fire was raging in the bottom of the ocean.
The *Dobryna*, he readily concluded, could have never
kept her moorings in such a perilous swell.

From his elevated position he could now convince
himself more positively than before that the horizon
had considerably contracted. From the summit of his
rock, about four hundred feet above the level of the
sea, he should be able in ordinary circumstances to
command a view oceanward extending at least twenty
or thirty miles. The horizon that he now saw could
not be at most more than two or three miles distant !

Again he asked himself, how could such things be? how could the volume of the earth have been contracted so considerably in a space of a few hours?

"It beats *Sturm's theorem*," he muttered, unconsciously using a phrase he had often employed in his school-days to express a state of great mental perplexity.

In the meantime, Ben, nimble as a monkey, had run up one of the gum-trees, and from this elevated point taken a careful survey of the land, eastwardly towards Tenez, westwardly towards Mostaganem Bay, and southwardly towards the Sheliff. He looked long and earnestly in each direction. His sight was keen, and he knew the country well. But as he descended the tree, his face wore a disappointed and even troubled look. The Captain on his return found him shaking his head as a sign that he could really say nothing or even guess nothing. "Tenez," he muttered, "was too far away to be noticed; of the Mostaganem country he could see nothing whatever; but the Sheliff puzzled him more than anything else. The river certainly was there — at least as far as water was concerned — but it appeared to be a river with only one bank. The bank on the other side had completely vanished. Of the bridge not a trace could be seen." Ben could not help adding that he felt a little as if he were bewitched.

"No bank on the other side!" cried the Captain,

hearing no more. "Nonsense, Ben Zouf! The most arrant nonsense! However," he added hastily, "nothing is nonsense any more! To the Sheliff!"

The point of the Sheliff which they now wished to reach could not be more than a few miles away; still, it was quite evident that, if they were to cross the river and reach Mostaganem before nightfall, they had no time whatever to lose. In spite of the thick clouds still enveloping the sky, they felt that the sun was already making for the horizon, and, another inexplicable puzzle, instead of describing the oblique arc required by the latitude of Algeria at this time of the year, he was actually descending vertically.

How to offer any plausible explanation for all these startling prodigies? The Captain's brain had become a regular whirligig between overpowering astonishment on the one side, and on the other swarms of theories, each one more perplexing than the last. What incomprehensible phenomenon had changed the rotation of the earth so that the east had become west? How had the Algerine coast been transported beyond the equator, far into the southern hemisphere, so as to be directly underneath the sun in January? What could explain the extraordinary modification of the earth's convexity except the supposition that the earth itself had suddenly shrunk to a size far from that corresponding with its ordinary dimensions? There seemed, however, to have been no very great change made in the immediate neighborhood. The shore to-day presented the same aspect as yesterday — the usual succession of cliffs, beach, and arid rocks red with iron rust. Far as the eye could range, it could detect no serious modification in the coast. It was just the same when the Captain cast a glance towards the mountains in the south-east — or at least what he persisted in calling the south-east, more from habit than conviction, for he could not deny that at least two of the cardinal points had been decidedly inverted. Six or eight miles off, the foot-hills of the Merjejah could be plainly distinguished; and the sierras in the back ground still showed their peculiar and well-known outline.

Suddenly, through an opening in the clouds, an oblique ray of the declining sun flashed across the landscape. Yes, there could be no more doubt about it. The orb of day had risen in the west and was now setting in the east.

"What the thunder will they think of all this at Mostaganem?" exclaimed the Captain, in a loud voice, though speaking to himself. "What will the Minister of War say when he learns by telegraph that his African colony is — not morally — that she can't be — but physically turned topsy-turvy?"

" The Minister of War is severe but just ! " ob
served Ben Zouf, not quite understanding the Cap·
tain's words. " If his African colony has done wrong,
let her be punished to learn to behave herself ! "

" That the cardinal points are completely at variance
with the military regulations ! "

" Court-martial the cardinal points, like so many
rebel Kabyles ! "

" That the sun strikes me with vertical rays, in mid-
winter ! "

" Strike an officer ! Take the sun out and shoot
him on the spot ! "

In high discipline, General Boum, in comparison to
Ben, was simply nowhere.

By this time they were already far on their way.
Profiting by their extraordinary lightness, and now
completely recovered from the choking sensation caused
by the sudden rarefaction of the air, they ran rather than
walked,— in fact, they bounded like hares, they sprang
like chamois. Nothing could divert them from their
bird's track, as the English have it, or, as the Ameri-
cans say, their bee-line. The ordinary paths, winding
along the cliffs and considerably lengthening the journey, they quitted altogether. Did they meet a line of
shrubbery ? they sailed over it ; a stream ? they jumped
it ; a clump of trees ? they cleared it ; a hill ? they

flew over it. Ben found himself wishing Montmartre
was around to try his hands or rather his feet on.
The Captain's only apprehension was that their vertical course, by taking them so much out of the horizontal, would considerably lengthen their journey. In
fact, they lit only now and then upon the ground; and
then it acted like a vast spring-board of an elasticity
almost boundless.

At last, a turn brought them within sight of the
Sheliff, and in a few minutes they were on the summit
of its right bank. There they had to stop. The
Captain rubbed his eyes in renewed amazement. Ben
was right. Not a trace of the bridge was to be seen
over which they had ridden twice yesterday. And for
a good reason too,— there was no left bank!

"Some terrible earthquake must have been making
a lake here," was all the Captain could exclaim after
a few moments' silence.

"Deluge number two!" quietly observed Ben.

What had become of the fertile plain over which
they had galloped yesterday towards Mostaganem?
Where was the river itself? Its right bank they were
still standing on, only it was no longer a bank, but
a shore, from which they looked out over a boundless
bay. Where was the left bank? Where, they asked
again, was the well-known muddy river that had been

murmuring yesterday with its sleepy motion over its bed of well-worn rounded rocks? Those blue waves, foaming, agitated, tumultuous, far extending, could not be the placid Sheliff. Could the river have been suddenly metamorphosed into an ocean?

The Captain's impatient desire to answer this question he soon gratified. Scrambling down the steep bank among tufts of rose-laurels and other native trees and shrubs, he hastily made his way to the brink, dipped his hand in the water and touched it to his tongue.

"Salt!" he cried. "The earthquake must have swallowed up all Western Algeria!"

"It's worse than a deluge then?" asked Ben Zouf.

"It's a cataclysm that has changed the whole world!" cried the Captain, in accents as expressive of extreme sorrow as of surprise. "No one can calculate its terrible effects. Oh, my friends, my dear comrades, what has become of you?"

Never before had Ben seen his master so profoundly moved. He was far from realizing the full extent of his emotion, but he had the good sense to perceive that the present was no time for light or jesting remarks. He restrained his tongue, therefore, and even tried to assume as grave a countenance as the Captain's. His sense of duty would no doubt have just as readily induced him to partake of his master's sentiments, had

THE UNKNOWN SEA.

he only known precisely what they were. As it was, he did his best to manifest his sympathy with the Captain's feelings.

The new shore of the Sheliff ran north and south in a line very slightly curved. It did not seem to have been affected at all by the earthquake, or whatever it was, that had so seriously changed the rest of the country. It still showed, as the Captain had mapped it out on his topographical sheets, the same groves of towering trees, the same peculiar and rather fantastical outlines, the same emerald carpet of its sheltered meadows. No change could be noticed except the great one — instead of being the right bank of a quiet river, it was now the shore of an unknown sea.

The Captain had not time to reflect on half the changes wrought in the physical aspect of everything all round him, when the night fell. The sun plunged plumb into the horizon as straight as a stone falling in air. Had they been on the equator on the 21st of March or the 21st of September, our travellers would not have felt the night approach more rapidly. No twilight now, no twilight in all probability next morning. Earth, sea, sky, were all instantly swallowed up in profound darkness.

CHAPTER VI.

THE NEW DOMAIN.

IN spite of all these overpowering surprises, the Captain kept wonderfully cool. Was this the effect of pure philosophy? Hardly. We are more disposed to attribute it to his indomitable curiosity. What *had* happened possessed little interest for him in comparison with his intense desire to know *why* it had happened. That this *why* he had not yet even begun to answer is true enough, but his efforts in the one direction certainly blunted his sensibilities in the other. Under the stimulating influence of this curiosity he felt himself gradually recovering from the effects of a stupor that at first had threatened to completely benumb his senses. He began to look at things squarely in the face, and, though almost as indifferent as Ben to consequences, he watched intently for every sign or hint that could cast even the least possible light on the cause of the extraordinary state of things surrounding him.

The sudden darkness bewildered him only for a few moments. Then he spoke:

"All further inquiries must be postponed till day-light — that is, if we ever have daylight again, for what has become of the sun, hang me if I know!"

"Captain," said Ben, touching his cap even in the darkness, "I'm waiting orders."

"We remain where we are to-night, Ben Zouf. To-morrow we shall return to the *gourbi*, after some further reconnoissance to the south and east. It is hardly necessary to observe, Ben Zouf, that in order to arrive at a just conclusion regarding the probable cause of this extraordinary state of things, our first step is to find out where we are ourselves; our second, to ascertain the exact state of things around us."

"All right, Captain. May I consider myself dis-missed?"

"Yes, for the night."

"To sleep or keep guard, Captain?"

"To sleep, if you can! Good-night!"

"All right, Captain!" answered Ben, with the regu-lar military salute, and, as unconcerned as the horses he had left at the *gourbi*, he groped about in the dark for the sheltered side of a rock, stretched himself out as comfortably as the nature of his stony couch would allow, and in a very few minutes was sleeping the sleep of the ignorant, which is always deeper and sometimes even happier than the sleep of the just.

But the Captain could not sleep. His brain was too busy hunting after answers for innumerable *whats*, *whys*, and *hows*. What, in the first place, had been the limit of this catastrophe? Had it been confined to a comparatively small portion of the African continent? Had Algiers, Mostaganem, and Oran been spared? Or had these cities, with their contents, been all swallowed up, like Lisbon, in 1755, with its fifty thousand inhabitants? Or had the Mediterranean, disturbed by some tremendous, but local explosion, merely overflowed that portion of the Algerine territory that lay immediately south of the Sheliff? This last theory certainly explained the sudden disappearance of the river, but it explained no more. The cause of the other great cosmical but undeniable facts it left in the dark as much as ever.

Another theory. Could the North African coast, together with the whole adjacent Mediterranean Sea, have been suddenly transported by the operation of some stupendous agency to the Torrid Zone? This would readily explain the new path described by the sun and the total absence of twilight. But how about a day six hours long replacing one of twelve? How about the sun rising in the west and setting in the east? Towards furnishing the slightest plausible reason for these extraordinary phenomena, such a theory was evidently not worth an instant's serious consideration.

One fact was unquestionable; two of the cardinal points had changed places — the east had become west and the west had become east. But what of the north and south? Had they too been inverted? A single glance at the stars would have enabled the Captain to answer this question with little difficulty. Though never strong on cosmography, he knew enough of astronomy to feel assured that, if the North star kept its place, the earth was still spinning on its old axis. And, on the contrary, if Polaris was replaced by some other star, the earth was certainly turning on a new axis, and — ha! — perhaps even in a direction different from that of its former rotation. This theory would undoubtedly explain several things besides the endless puzzle of west and east.

But, unfortunately, the clouds would give no glimpse of the sky. They were almost as black as ink. They looked watery enough and threatening enough to contain a deluge. A few moments' observation convinced the Captain that through such a screen as that he could see just as much of the sky with his eyes shut as with his eyes open.

From the moon, he was well aware he could receive no aid. This very day of the month she was "new," that is, close to the sun; when he had disappeared below the horizon, she of course had borne him company

But — could he believe his eyes? He had been an hour or two promenading up and down the shore, when suddenly, just above the western horizon, he suddenly caught sight of a strong light rising behind the clouds and struggling to break through them.

"The moon!" he quickly exclaimed. "Who knows! She might take the notion, too, and startle people by rising in the west? But — no! that can't be the moon! Her light could never be so intense — unless, in fact, she was coming so close to the earth as to endanger a collision!"

The light certainly was far stronger than ordinary moonlight. To whatever heavenly body it owed its existence, it was powerful enough to penetrate the screen of dark clouds, and diffuse a soft, steady light over the landscape almost as great as that of a dark day in winter.

"Can it be the sun?" the Captain asked himself. "No! An hour and a half ago he set in the east. But if neither sun nor moon, what can it be? Some tremendous bolide? Hang those clouds! Will they never open?"

After a few moments' reflection, he burst out again:

"What a confounded jackass I was at St. Cyr, not to study astronomy better! What opportunities I lost through idleness! In all probability this is quite a simple matter, though my brain is almost burst trying vainly to understand it!"

These angry regrets did him no good. The mysteries of a strange sky, though becoming every moment more and more wonderful in his eyes, continued to be as unfathomable as the grave. The stupendous light, evidently projected by some dazzling disc of enormous dimensions, went on inundating the upper regions of the clouds for at least an hour. Then, what was even more surprising, the enormous disc, instead of describing such an arc on the sky *as is usually done by celestial bodies, and then descending towards the opposite horizon,* seemed to retire slowly in a line perpendicular to the plane of the equator, gradually withdrawing as it retired that peculiar light so agreeable to the eye with which it had at first pleasantly flooded the atmosphere.

Then all was pitchy blackness again. The Captain was more in the dark than ever, physically as well as morally. The most elementary rules of mechanics were disregarded before his eyes. The celestial vault, instead of being, as it always had been, a majestic chronometer eternal in its laws and invariable in its movements, seemed now to be no better than a miserable Yankee clock with a disordered escapement. The lordly planets themselves treated the commonest rules of gravity with the utmost contempt. After this, who

could tell if even the sun would ever deign to show himself again in any quarter of the horizon !

As if in silent mockery of such reflections, up rose the
sun suddenly on the western horizon, his rising, like
his setting, announced by no twilight. The black
clouds were instantly whitened by the morning rays.
The day at once replaced the night, and the Captain,
consulting his watch, saw that it was exactly six
o'clock.

It was now time to wake Ben Zouf.

"Hillo!" cried the Captain, shaking him vigor-
ously. "Get up! Time to start!"

"What, Captain!" muttered Ben, jumping up, but
hardly able to open his eyes. "Seems to me I have
not had my regular allowance !"

"You've slept a whole night !"

"A whole night ! Oh, Captain !"

"Yes, a whole night, of six hours ! The kind of
nights we have now. You must get used to them."

"A whole night !" repeated Ben to himself, feeling
something to be wrong. "But it must be a whole
night, since there's the sun ! No matter ! It's all
right, Captain. Good-morning, Captain," he added,
in a few seconds, now fully alive to the whole situation.

"No time to lose now, Ben Zouf. Instead of going
any further on foot, let us return at once to the *gourbi.*

I wish to know how the horses are, and what they think of all this."

"They don't think at all, Captain. They know the world has gone wrong, because Ben Zouf gave them no supper last night nor breakfast this morning."

"Let Ben Zouf teach them better, then, as soon as possible," said the Captain, already starting. "When they're fed and groomed, saddle them, without delay, so that we may know as soon as possible how much is left of Algeria!"

"All right, Captain, and then — ?"

"Then, if we can't reach Mostaganem by the south, we must fall back on Tenez, in the east."

Their route back to the *gourbi* lay a little more to the right than yesterday's. Though more inland, it was quite as deserted as the sea-coast — a circumstance, however, which did not surprise them much, as the few agricultural laborers employed here lived mostly in villages on the other side of the Sheliff. Though moving pretty briskly, they did not fail to stop now and then to pick and eat some of the choice figs, dates, and oranges growing in the country all around them. For our travellers were very hungry, having eaten nothing for a day and a night, and the new government plantations had turned this portion of the territory into a vast and luxuriant orchard.

They soon reached the *gourbi*, and found things there in exactly the same state as they had been left in. Nobody had called in their absence — friend or foe. Nor was there the least sign of any human being to be seen around. This part of the country was evidently quite as deserted as the more western region which they had just traversed.

Preparations for departure were soon made. Ben flung a few eatables into his wallet; as for drinkables, there was plenty of sweet water to be always found in the beautiful little streams that came down from the mountains and flowed in murmurs across the plains.

Zephyr — the Captain's Arabian — and Galette (a souvenir of Montmartre), Ben's coal-black steed, were saddled in a second; in the next, the mounted cavaliers were galloping rapidly towards the Sheliff.

If yesterday's personal experience had led the riders to expect a corresponding activity on the part of their horses, we must say that such expectations were completely realized. Inasmuch as the muscular force of the animals surpassed that of the men, so much higher did the horses now rise in their wild bounds, and so much farther did they extend their tremendous .eaps.

Simple quadrupeds no longer, they fully realized the fabled hippogriffs of old, whose flying hoofs seldom

ZEPHYR AND GALETTE.

touched the plain. The Captain and his Orderly were, fortunately, superb riders; in no danger of falling off, they never dreamed of restraining the wild speed of their horses; on the contrary, they seemed to take a fierce desire in urging it to the utmost.

Twenty minutes brought them to the Sheliff, where, assuming a more moderate pace, the horses began to ascend the right bank of the river in a south-easterly direction. The other bank was still invisible. The only horizon visible south and east, as well as west, was a horizon of sea and sky. Such a state of things tended to but one conclusion — all that portion of the province of Oran lying in the neighborhood of Mostaganem had been swallowed up during the night of December the 31st.

Hardly any other conclusion seemed possible. The Captain knew the country perfectly. He had surveyed it and mapped it, and was quite familiar with all its permanent features. His chief desire now was: first, to take a hasty general glance at the whole territory in its present condition; secondly, to survey it over again, and to accompany the new map with a written report omitting no important detail. This map and this report he would then dispatch — to whom? and at what time? But all such questions he was obliged to leave unanswered for the present.

During the remaining hours of daylight the travellers rode about twenty miles along the shore. Night caught them at the point where the river had formerly made a light bend to the north, and, according to the Captain's calculations, almost exactly opposite the spot where its waters had been joined by those of the Mina, now swallowed up by the overwhelming sea. This day, like the previous one, was passed without meeting a single human soul.

Supper dispatched, horses picketed in the rich grass, and Ben's sleeping arrangements hastily improvised, our travellers were soon at rest, and the six hours of night passed quickly away without incident.

Early next morning — January 2d, according to our earthly calendar — the Captain and his Orderly resumed their tour of exploration. By sunset they had finished a journey of about forty-two miles, besides making some important discoveries. At a point about twelve miles above the old confluence of the Mina, they found that quite an important portion of the right bank had disappeared, carrying with it the village of Surkelmittou and its eight hundred inhabitants. The travellers stood appalled at the contemplation of such a calamity. Who could say that a similar fate had not likewise befallen Mostaganem, Orléansville, Mazagran, and other important places in this part of Algeria?

Doubling the little bay formed by the disappearance of a portion of the shore, the travellers soon found themselves again on the right bank. From here, if the Captain remembered aright, he should have been able to perceive, on the other side of the river, the town of Ammi Moussa, formerly Kamis, belonging to the Beni Ouraghs. But no trace of it could be discerned now, nor even of the Peak of Monkoura, which had risen behind it to a height of between three and four thousand feet.

Their camping-ground for the night was a sudden angle of the shore, which put an abrupt end to all further progress in this direction. The important village of Memoun Turray should have stood here, as well as the Captain recollected, but not the slightest vestige of it was now to be found.

"No chance of a supper or a bed at Orléansville, to-night," said the Captain, gazing over the dark sea with a troubled and disappointed look.

"Unless we hunt up a boat somewhere, Captain," said Ben, always ready with a suggestion.

"Why, things here are in a terrible state, Ben Zouf!" observed the Captain, dejectedly. "Do you know that we have had most extraordinary luck?"

"That's our sort generally, Captain," answered Ben, cheerfully, "and you'll say so particularly when we find ourselves safe and sound sauntering into Mostaganem!"

"Hm!" replied the Captain, with a dubious shake of the head. "If it's on a peninsula that we are — which is most likely — it will be at Tenez rather than Mostaganem that we shall learn something."

"Tenez or Mostaganem all the same," answered Ben, busying himself with the horses. "Everybody will be glad to see us. Good-night, Captain!"

A little after sunrise next morning, after a hasty breakfast, our explorers were again on the road.

The scenery all around had completely changed in character. No longer east and west, the shore now ran north and south. In fact, it was no longer shore at all, at least in the sense that the right bank of the Sheliff had been shore. A perpendicular crack or rupture had put a sudden end to the former plain. East, as well as south, no land appeared at the other side of the water. Ben galloped up a little hill on the left to make sure that this was really the case. No doubt at all about it. Not a speck of land in any direction. Of course nothing could be seen of Orléans-ville, which should have lain six or seven miles south east.

Nothing further remained to do but turn their faces northwards. Their new course was pursued with much difficulty. It lay through broken rocks, terrible earth-slides, cracks deep and straight like the crevasses of a glacier, trees partially uprooted and with branches half buried in the water — among others, some old olive-trees, whose gnarled, twisted, and fantastically shaped trunks seemed actually to have been chopped to pieces with an axe.

This obliged our cavaliers to move slowly. The creeks, cliffs, and rough headlands on the shore also compelled them to make considerable detours. The consequence was that they had made only about twenty-two miles when night overtook them at the foot of the Jebel Merjejah Mountains, which, before the late catastrophe, had formed the termination of the Lesser Atlas range in these quarters. Here the mountain chain had been suddenly snapped asunder, and cliffs now rose out of the sea, straight as a wall and high as the Rock of Gibraltar.

Next morning our travellers rode as far up into the mountain defiles as the horses could penetrate; then they alighted, and pursued their way on foot to the summit of the highest peak they could climb. From this elevated position they took the best survey they could, under the circumstances, of this particular portion of the Algerine coast.

A glance or two set their minds at rest at least on

one point. What they learned was not very satisfactory, but it was decisive.

The new coast which they had been following yester-day continued northward in a straight line all the way from the foot of the Merjejah Mountains to the Medi-terranean Sea, a distance of about twenty miles. The land on which they stood was no peninsula. It was an island. Tenez had disappeared. From their peak they could discern that water surrounded them on the south, the east, and the north. Look where they might, no trace of land appeared, except in the west, where, as they knew well, it came to a sudden termination near their. *gourbi.* There could be no longer any ques-tion about it : they were on an island, and cut off from the rest of the world by the salt sea.

The newly formed island resembled in shape an ir-regular quadrilateral. Its dimensions were nearly as follows : the line of the old bank of the Sheliff, running nearly east and west, was about seventy-five miles long ; a line of coast from the interruption of the bank to the Jebel Merjejah ran almost directly north and south for a distance of twenty-two miles; the line from the mountains to the Mediterranean extended a distance of about nineteen miles north-west by north; from this point the line ran along the sea-shore south by west for a distance of sixty miles, back to the mouth of the

Sheliff. The coast line of the island measured in all about one hundred and eighty miles.

"Well!" exclaimed the Captain, after he had carefully recorded in his note-book all these calculations — the result of previous knowledge, combined with new observations rendered easy by the excellent field-glasses provided for the staff — "Well! So far so good! Now we can tell the *what,* but who can tell the *why ?*"

" Why worry ourselves about it, Captain ?" answered Ben, philosophically; "the good Lord has allowed it. That 's why enough ! "

Descending the mountain to where they had left their horses grazing, they resumed their journey, and made such good use of the remaining daylight as to reach the Mediterranean coast before dark. This day's journey, like all the others, afforded no sight of a human being ; even of Montenotte, and a few other villages in the direction of Tenez, the ancient capital, not a vestige was visible.

Next day, January 5th, they made the last part of their journey, sixty miles along the Mediterranean. This part of the country, they found, had not been so much respected by the earthquake as the Captain's observations had led him to conclude. Four villages at least were missing : Callaat Chemah, at the mouth of the Chemah; Sidi-Mta-Achacha near Cape Khramis; Marabout and Pointe Basse, both on Teddert Bay.

All these had disappeared. The capes near which tney had stood, unable to resist the terrific shock, had been violently wrenched from the mainland, and in all probability swallowed in the waves. This day's journey moreover only confirmed, if confirmation were needed, their previous conclusions regarding the population of the island. There was not a single human being left on it besides themselves. Of goats, sheep, cows, and other half-domesticated animals, there was quite an abundance, flocks of them being visible in almost every direction.

The tour of exploration, counting from the moment they had left the *gourbi* until their return, had lasted five of the new days, or two and a half of the old — that is, a period of sixty hours altogether.

"It's all right, now, Captain!" said Ben, to his master, who, weary in body and troubled in mind, was getting ready to enjoy a good night's rest.

"How's that, Ben Zouf?" asked Captain Hector.

"You're Governor-General of Algeria!"

"Governor-General of nobody!"

"Excuse me, Captain. Don't I count for any-thing?"

"What do you count for, Ben Zouf?"

"The population, Captain; the intelligent and indus-trious population! Good-night, Governor-General."

"Good-night, Population!"

CHAPTER VII.

FRESH EXPERIENCES AND OBSERVATIONS.

IN a few minutes both Governor and Population were lying in a pair of tolerably comfortable beds hastily prepared by Ben in a room of the old station-house, the *gourbi* being still in a ruinous condition. The Population was not long in falling fast asleep, but official cares and very serious thoughts regarding the condition of his new domain kept the Governor awake for a long time. He pondered again and again over every item of the discoveries made in his exploring tour, but again and again he had to acknowledge that not a single one of them threw the least light on the cause of all the wonders just come to pass. The mysterious cause was as great a mystery as ever. He could not even say positively *what* had taken place. It is true that though, as said before, no great adept in cosmography, still, by dint of thinking, he found himself gradually recalling to his mind certain established physical laws once learned but long ago forgotten. Combining these laws with his recent discoveries, he went over his former reasoning again, point by point, in search of some clue to guide him out of this laby-rinth of perplexing uncertainty. But it was all in vain. A theory is useless which does not explain every diffi-culty. None of the Captain's could do anything of the kind. Their very explanation of one difficulty only left the others more unaccountable. They all ended somewhat like the following: Could a sudden change in the inclination of the earth's axis have given rise to the late startling phenomena? No. Certainly not. Such a change might account for the displace-ment of the sea, and, by a little stretching, it might even offer some explanation for the inversion of the cardinal points, but it did not afford the slightest ex-planation regarding the shortness of the days or the diminution of gravity.

It was so with all the Captain's other theories. He was at his wit's end. All the discoveries made so far told him absolutely nothing. But what about the dis-coveries yet to come? Who knows what to-morrow may bring forth? This question did not offer much consolation, but a drowning man will catch at straws. The Captain, though no drowning man, would catch at less, and even take comfort from less. Further thinking was evidently useless. Now to sleep. In two minutes after he had come to this resolution, the Governor, as well

as the Population, was fast wrapt in the arms of Mor-
pheus.

On waking next morning, the Captain found Ben
bustling about, preparing for breakfast. The Orderly
was evidently taking unusual pains to provide a princely
repast. The soup was nearly ready; the next item of
the programme was to boil a dozen of fresh eggs.

The cooking-stove was nicely heated; the copper
saucepan shone like a new coin. An unglazed Moorish
pitcher standing in the corner, its porous surface beaded
with condensed evaporations, furnished plenty of sweet,
cool water. The Captain, apparently absorbed in dress-
ing, quietly watched everything that was going on.

The saucepan, filled with water, was laid on the hot
hearth. While waiting till it commenced to boil, Ben
amused himself by tossing the eggs in the air and
catching them as they fell. They felt like so many
corks in his hands, and when, through awkwardness or
design, he let one drop on the floor, it no more broke
than if the shell had been papier-maché.

The saucepan had been no more than two minutes on
the hot iron when it began to smoke; in another minute
it was boiling over.

"Hey!" cried Ben, interrupting his egg-tossing;
"my fire is unusually brisk this morning."

"It is not your fire that's brisker this morning, Ben

Zouf," said the Captain, quietly. "It is not your fire that's brisker; it is your water that boils sooner."

Unhooking a thermometer from the wall, he plunged it into the bubbling liquid.

"There!" said the Captain; "your water is boiling at 148° instead of 212°!"

"What's the difference, Captain, so it boils at all?"

"A very great difference, Ben Zouf. Though boiling, it is very far from being as hot as ordinary boiling water. This you will soon find out for yourself, if you don't let those eggs remain at least a quarter of an hour in the saucepan!"

"A quarter of an hour! That would turn them into bullets, cast-steel bullets!"

"No, Ben Zouf; on the contrary, even a quarter of an hour's boiling in that water will hardly cook them well enough to give a relish to our bread."

The Captain was correct. After a quarter of an hour's cooking, the eggs were considered too "rare" to be pleasant.

From this new experience the staff-officer did not hesitate to draw the proper conclusion. In ordinary cases, water cannot boil without lifting an atmospheric column that presses with a force of fifteen pounds to the square inch; to do this, it must be hot enough to reach the temperature marked by 212° Fahrenheit. Here the

BOILING AT 148°.

water boiled at 148°, or about two-thirds of this temperature. What did that show? That the pressure of the atmosphere had been reduced one-third, and, consequently, the atmospheric column itself had been reduced one-third of its ordinary height.

This rarity of the atmosphere readily explained the shrill voices, the quicker breathing, the sense of smothering, which had been so surprising at first, but which had now become of such common occurrence as to be no longer noticeable. Identical phenomena would have taken place on mountain summits of great elevation. A glance at the barometer on the top of a mountain of about twice the height of Mont Blanc would have shown an equal depression of the mercurial column.

New theory. Could the territory have been lifted up to such an altitude by some tremendous upheaving power, existing long dormant underneath the earth's surface, and at last suddenly called into resistless activity? The answer was not long in coming. No. Impossible. Such a power might lift a mountain and even a mountain chain, but it could not lift the sea itself and all its waters that lay stretched out there before their eyes, vast, dread, unknown, and apparently illimitable in all directions. The new theory was therefore dismissed with as little ceremony as the others.

By this time breakfast was ready — soup, eggs, fritters, everything. Ben, always willing to accommodate himself to circumstances, mentally resolved to begin his future culinary preparations at least an hour in advance.

The Captain was hardly through when Ben was ready with his questions.

"Beg pardon, Captain!"

"All right, Ben Zouf; what is it?"

"I should like to know our next move, Captain."

"Our next move, Ben Zouf, is to be one of masterly inactivity."

"Yes, Captain."

"We shall quietly wait the logical **march of events,** Ben Zouf!"

"What kind of march, Captain?"

"When Mahomet can't go to the mountain, the mountain must come to Mahomet."

"Come in a boat?"

"Certainly, since we're on an island."

"You mean our friends at Mostaganem, Captain?"

"Of course. In all probability they are all safe and sound, this catastrophe having confined its ravages to a few points on the Algerine coast."

"That's what I think myself, Captain."

"The Governor-General of Algiers, by this **time re-**

alizing the full state of the case, I have no doubt has dispatched vessels in every direction along the shore. Of course, we are not forgotten. Keep a careful look-out seaward, therefore, Ben Zouf, and at the first sight of a sail, hoist a signal.''

'' But suppose no sail comes in sight, Captain ? ''

'' Then we shall make a boat ourselves, Ben Zouf, and try our luck at sea.''

'' All right, Captain ! Only, I never knew we were boat-builders and sailors ! ''

'' We can be whatever we please, Ben Zouf, if we only make up our minds to it ! '' answered the Captain, full of hope, energy, and resolution.

Ben said no more. Understanding what he was to do, he set about doing it at once. Selecting a rock that commanded a good view over the ocean, he took his post there, and searched every part of the horizon with one of the Captain's best telescopes. But nothing was visible except water and sky north and east, water and sky north and west.

Except when he fed the horses or attended to culinary affairs, this was his sole employment day after day. But day after day passed away quickly, no sail appeared, and Ben at last began to get somewhat tired of his fruitless watching.

'' Holy name of a bullet ! '' he would sometimes exclaim. "Our absence does not appear to trouble his excellency the Governor-General very seriously!"

The sun rose and set twelve times on our islanders without producing any change in the general aspect of things. The Captain, note-book in hand, travelled around in all directions, always on the lookout for something worth recording; but the last two days he did not find much to note down besides the date January 5th and January 6th, according to the old calendar. The new calendar he did not like, and would not reckon his time by. He preferred the other for many reasons, and by means of his excellent watch he had no difficulty in keeping his calculations right. Ben's wooden clock, hitherto a pretty fair timepiece, was now actually good for nothing, change of gravity having made its pendulum move too slowly. But the Captain's watch, as said before, a magnificent Frodsham chronometer, enabled him to record every hour on his note-book with perfect accuracy.

"Captain!" said Ben, one day, seeing the officer approach the rock where he had been watching so long and with such little purpose, "Captain, I've been thinking of something I read long ago, when a child at school in Montmartre."

"What is it, Ben Zouf?"

"That you're very like the shipwrecked Englishman

in the story-book — all alone on a desolate island, with nobody in the world to speak to except myself, your man Friday ! ''

" Oh, you 're Friday, are you ? ''

" Yes, Captain. Not exactly a Good Friday, and still not quite a Black Friday ! Ha ! ha ! ha ! '' and Ben laughed heartily at his little joke.

The Captain appeared to relish it also very highly, and, when they had both got through their laughing, the officer asked Ben to listen awhile to the result of the investigations to which he had devoted the last few days. He then read for Ben a pretty full and accurate report of the condition — physical, moral, animal, and vegetable — of the Island Gourbi ; so he now designated their present dominion. A short summary of this report will suffice for our readers.

Its area was about twelve hundred square miles. (That of Long Island is about fourteen hundred.) Oxen, cows, goats, sheep, etc., were tolerably abundant, but their exact number could not be given. Game was quite plentiful, "with no danger of its ever quitting the island," as Ben muttered, in an undertone. The cereals were well represented. In little more than three months later, wheat, Indian corn, rice, and other grain crops would be ripe for the sickle. There was abundance of food, therefore, for the Governor and the

Population of the island, and the two horses besides.
"And even in the contingency," concluded the Captain, "that other inhabitants should land on our island,
I have no reason to suppose — unless, indeed, they
landed in exceptionally great numbers — that we should
be at all likely to suffer from a dearth of provisions."

The Captain's explorations had been finished just in
time. The rainy season now set in. From the sixth to
the thirteenth of January it rained incessantly. Heavy
black clouds continually covered the sky, which no
amount of raining seemed to lighten. Several furious
storms also occurred — phenomena extremely rare at
this time of the year. This was not the only anomaly
that astonished the Captain. The temperature kept
rising steadily. January soon felt almost as hot as
July. Even then there was no pause. The mercury
rose higher and higher every day as regularly as if,
according to an expression the Captain used one day,
they were making a "bee-line direct for the sun!"

The light also grew more and more intense. In fact,
our travellers felt that, but for the thick screen of black
clouds that providentially covered the sky at this time,
the solar irradiation would be too dazzling to be toler-
able.

But if this screen was an advantage in one respect,
it was considered by the Captain to be highly objec-

tionable in another. It prevented him from ever obtaining such a glance at the sun, moon, or stars as
might enable him to form a just conception as to what
point of the universe the earth now occupied. Without
a suspicion of the real state of the case, he had serious
misgivings as to something dreadful having occurred.
One glance at the sky would be enough to give him an
inkling as to the nature of the cataclysm. But this
glance he could not get, though he watched and waited
patiently and hopefully every hour of the night from
sunset to sunrise.

Ben watched, too, just as patiently but not quite so
hopefully. Wrapped in an old water-proof, he mounted
guard every day on the top of his cliff, and, in spite of
rain, wind, or storm, remained manfully there all day,
contenting himself with a few hours' repose every night.
Nothing ever appeared on the lonely horizon. Besides,
what vessel could have ever made head against such
violent squalls, in such a furious sea? The waves rose
at times mountains high and the hurricane roared with
inconceivable fury. Even Ben had to acknowledge
that the sight of such phenomena drew him somewhat
out of his general indifference. But the Captain would
contemplate them with enthusiasm. They furnished a
vivid realization to the hazy notions regarding a former
state of things that he had studied in his school cos-

mography. Something like this, he thought, is actually taking place in the growing planets of to-day; something like this, he thought, took place in the early period of our own earth's history, when the waters, volatilized by the internal heat, were dispersed in space to an immense extent in all directions, and afterwards cooling, fell back to the surface in deluging torrents of incessant rain. Something like this, in all probability, is going on at present in Jupiter — a theory that would at once explain that planet's monstrous apparent, not real, size, and its comparatively slight power of attraction.

Indulgence in reflections of this kind did not prevent the Captain from noticing, on the 13th, that there was every sign of the deluge coming to a speedy end. The rain no longer fell in cascades; the clouds broke considerably during the day before the violent wind; and towards night they were driven flying all over the sky. The Captain waited for their disappearance with some impatience. Taking post near Ben Zouf, he watched the sun as it set, and the stars as they gradually took their places, one by one, on the azure vault. He felt himself thrilling with expectation. What was he on the point of discovering? Would that enormous disc, whose light had rendered it so perceptible the first night passed on the bank of the Sheliff, again make its appearance? Would anything be seen which might prove a clue to the nature and cause of the late strange experiences?

The wind had now swept away every vestige of cloud, and the sky was transcendently beautiful. Not even the faint haze of a summer night obscured the sweet quiver of the everlasting stars. There they blazed and glittered, spread out endlessly on the resplendent map. Never before had they gleamed so brilliantly in the Captain's eyes. They actually seemed nearer. He could distinguish without difficulty certain nebulæ that, he was certain, he had never been able to see before without the aid of a good telescope.

He had some trouble in finding the polar star, but he caught it at last. Yes; there it was, surely; but how strangely low on the sky! At the latitude of Mostaganem, it should be at least 36° above the horizon; now it was scarcely 10°. What was the meaning of this strange fact? Could the polar star have ceased to be the pivot of the earth's axis? What an absurd — but not at all — on the contrary, the conjecture was perfectly justifiable and perfectly correct. Right before his eyes it sank lower and lower, until within the space of an hour it almost coincided with the horizon. In a word, it described the same sort of circle in the sky that we see the stars of any of our Northern constella

tions describing during the long hours of a clear summer night.   Polaris was Polaris no more.

Next question — what star had replaced it?   Through
what new point in the sky would the prolonged axis
of the earth now pass?   For an answer to this kind of
question, nothing more was necessary than a short time
spent in careful examination.   The new Polaris should
be motionless, in the first place, and, in the second, it
should be the central point around which the other
constellations performed their diurnal revolutions.

These conditions, the Captain was not long in discovering, were completely fulfilled by a certain star
lying pretty low in the Northern horizon.   This star
he had no difficulty whatever in recognizing.   It was
Vega, the brilliant star of Lyra, famous for its bluish
light.   It was, in fact, the very same star that, in consequence of the *precession of the equinoxes*, is to be the
Earth's Polaris twelve thousand years from the present
day.   But as twelve thousand years could not possibly
have elapsed in the course of a few weeks, the new
discovery only threw the Captain into greater perplexity
than ever.

"Two facts," he found himself quietly muttering.
"two facts — both quite incredible, I admit, but both
quite incontestable — must have taken place within the
space of a few days.   1. The earth must be revolving

on a new axis, since Polaris is no longer the pivot of the old one. 2. Since Vega lies so low in the north, the Mediterranean must have been removed to some region between the tropics ! "

Lost in such conjectures, one more puzzling than another, his eyes wandered listlessly over the radiant sky, from the Great Bear, now one of the signs in the zodiac over head, to the strange constellations of the Southern hemisphere, many of which he had never seen before.

" The Moon ! " cried Ben Zouf, suddenly pointing to an orb just then lifting its bright disc above the western horizon.

Was it indeed the Moon, or only one of the inferior planets enlarged by increased proximity?

The Captain examined it long and carefully with his excellent telescope. " That cannot possibly be the Moon," he observed at last. " It is too far away. Not by thousands, but by millions of miles, the distance of that heavenly body is to be estimated. It certainly looks as large as the Moon, but where are the 'seas,' the 'gulfs,' the 'ring mountains,' the 'streaks,' the splendid irradiating centre of Tycho, and the other familiar features of our satellite which such a glass as this could easily discover? No ; that can't be the Moon — unless — who knows? — it is that side of her on which the eye of man has never before rested ! "

"Then it may be the Moon?" asked Ben, not liking to lose the credit of the discovery.

"No!" exclaimed the Captain, with decision. "It cannot possibly be the Moon on any account. The planet now before us has a moon of its own for a satellite!"

Even Ben had no difficulty in detecting the existence of a luminous point in the neighborhood of the new planet. It strongly reminded him of what he had seen long ago, when a boy, on the summit of Montmartre, on those lovely summer evenings when, for a sou, the telescope man allowed him a five minutes' peep at the planet Jupiter.

"It can't be the Moon!" the Captain went on, with increasing impatience. "What then can it be? Venus? Mercury? No! These planets have no satellites. Yet these are the only planets whose orbits lie within that of the earth! Neither the Moon. Nor Venus. Nor Mercury — Ben Zouf, I wish I had studied astronomy a little better!"

CHAPTER VIII.

SOME OF THE DANGERS OF QUITTING OUR ORBIT.

THE sudden appearance of the sun, dispersing every star, whether planet, satellite, or "ever-blazing orb," rendered all further observation impossible till the following night. Then the Captain expected to discover something also regarding the enormous disc whose mysterious light, witnessed on the Sheliff the first night of the catastrophe, still continually haunted his imagination. Not the slightest trace had he been able to discover of it ever since. It had completely disappeared, most probably because its erratic orbit had carried it too far away beyond his ken.

The weather was now magnificent. The wind, after having driven off every vestige of cloud and mist, blew like a sweet zephyr. The sun rose and set in the new horizons with perfect regularity, leaving the days and nights each mathematically six hours long — a proof that the new equator ran directly through the isle of Gourbi.

'The temperature, however, had increased so as to
begin to feel decidedly uncomfortable.   Looking at
the thermometer, the Captain found, to his surprise,
that the mercury stood at 90° in the shade, on the
fifteenth of January.

The *gourbi* still remained in its state of ruin, but the
principal room in the guard-house had been fitted up
very comfortably.   The stone walls, built thick and
strong expressly for these purposes, had sheltered its
inmates completely against the deluging rains, and
they now offered considerable protection against the
almost intolerable heat.   Except morning and evening, the Captain seldom exposed himself to the sun.
Not a single cloud tempered the burning rays.   Senegal
or Soudan, he judged, never had a more torrid climate.
A longer continuation of such a temperature, he sorely
dreaded, could hardly help burning every trace of vegetation completely off the island.

But on Ben the raging heat seemed to produce no
more effect than the torrential rain.   He never uttered
a syllable by way of complaint ; from the perspiration
alone, that flowed so abundantly from every pore of his
body as to leave his shape on the rock whenever he
went to his meals, could the Captain form an idea of
his invincible determination.   To advise or remon-
strance he paid equal disregard.   On his return he

quietly resumed his post without a word, and for the rest of the day swept the deserted ocean with his telescope as persistently and patiently as an amateur astronomer watches the transit of Venus. The Captain was lost in surprise and admiration.

"Not melted into a grease spot yet, Ben Zouf!" he exclaimed, one uncommonly hot afternoon that he found Ben sizzling on the burning rock. "Why, you must have been born at Gaboon!"

"No; at Montmartre, Captain. That's where I learned to bear this kind of thing!"

The Captain could make no reply. Ben's invincible determination to lose no opportunity of upholding the honor of his native mountain, through thick and thin, struck him actually speechless.

This ultra dog-day heat, in the meantime, had begun to tell decidedly on the productions of Gourbi Island, as the changed appearance of trees, shrubs, plants, and vegetation in general soon revealed. In comparatively few days the sap reaching the extreme ends of the branches, the buds burst, the flowers opened and bloomed, and the fruits appeared. It was the same way with the grain. You could almost see the ears growing on the wheat and Indian corn. Carpets of rich velvety grass overspread the valleys. It was all at once haymaking, harvest, and fruit time. The glories of summer and the riches of autumn, combining together, formed a season both beautifully picturesque and singular in the extreme. But in spite of his admiration the Captain felt uneasy. The tremendous heats should soon put a sudden end to this state of things.

But these new facts threw no additional light in the Captain's mind as to the cause that had brought them all about. It is true that, as often stated already, though no great adept in cosmography, he remembered enough of its principles to see very plainly that the axis of the earth must have been so changed as to form a right angle with the ecliptic, and that, consequently, things were now going on on earth pretty much as they are in Jupiter, where, the Zones being invariable, spring, summer, autumn, and winter are eternal !

This he could not help seeing. His consciousness told him its absolute and unimpeachable truth. But what did he gain by acknowledging it? The facts were so. The changes were undeniable. The phenomena were obvious.

"But, by all the wines of Gascony!" exclaimed the puzzled Captain, "what could have given rise to it all?"

He soon came to the conclusion, however, that for

THE WATCH-TOWER.

the present he could spend his time much better than in either wondering or thinking. The busy season was on him, and hands were woefully short. Ben and himself worked as hard and as long as the extreme heat permitted. The horses, too, were called into requisition, and between them all quite a supply of useful provisions was soon carefully and safely stowed away. Fortunately, however, very hard or long-continued work was scarcely necessary. They had still an abundant stock of stores untouched, and, the sea being now calm and beautiful, there was every reason to expect the early appearance of some ship. In fact, as the Captain said, some ship could not help coming soon into sight, this part of the Mediterranean being much frequented by vessels from nearly every part of the globe, not to speak of the French government steamers constantly engaged on the coast survey.

Notwithstanding the incontestability of this reasoning, for some cause or other no ship made its appearance. Ben watched as carefully as ever. Nothing in sight. He was melting like a piece of ice dropped on a hot sidewalk. Nothing in sight. He rigged up an old umbrella tent of canvas and grass on the summit of the cliff for the Captain's occasional accommodation, and from its shade he swept the dreary expanse of waters with his long ship-glass, morning, noon, and evening. The old story. Nothing in sight.

After the few days spent in stowing away provisions and taking stock, the Captain once more found that he had nothing better on hand than to tackle the problem that every day rendered only more and more perplexing. Upon his success he could not congratulate himself. It was, of course, incontestable that both the earth's rotation on her axis, as well as her revolution around the sun, had been considerably modified. Consequently, the duration of her year could be no longer the same as it had been before. But would it be longer or shorter? This question he could not answer. He had nothing to found an argument on.

One thing, however, was perfectly clear. The earth was approaching the sun. The unparalleled heat showed this in the first place, and, in the second, it was set beyond all doubt by the enlarged size of the sun's apparent diameter. It was at least double its ordinary dimensions. This was about the size, as he faintly remembered from his old astronomy class-book (what would he not have given for one now?) — this was about the size that the sun has been calculated to present to the inhabitants of Venus. But the distance of Venus from the sun is about two-thirds of that of the earth. What conclusion to draw from this? One

and one only. The visual angle increases strictly as
the distance diminishes. Consequently, the earth and
Venus must be now about the same distance from the
sun. And still more astoundingly consequently, in little
more than half a month the earth must have travelled
in a direct road to the sun a distance that could not
be less than at least twenty millions of miles! Would
this rate continue? Would the same line of journey
be persevered in? If these questions were to be answered affirmatively, only one result was possible. It
was inevitable. The earth, dragged to the sun's surface by the irresistible force of attraction, should be
instantaneously annihilated.

But *would* this rate continue? *Would* the same line
of journey be persevered in? The closest observation
alone could solve this terrible problem.

Even for the closest observation, it must be acknowledged, the Captain had every opportunity. Night
and day were equally favorable. In clearness of atmosphere and radiant effulgence of light the days were
simply superb, but never before had the nights revealed the starry splendor of the heavens so magnifi-
cently. There they lay, spangling the sky, planets,
constellations, nebulæ, flaming, gleaming, and glittering with a resplendence that was actually dazzling. Unfortunately, however, this richly illuminated manuscript

the Captain could comprehend little better than if it
had been a sealed book. Of the laws that guided the
stately march of the stars across the ebon plains of
night he knew about as much as he did of the laws
that had guided the pyramid builders. His regretful
remembrance of opportunities lost when he could have
made himself master of the great principles of astronomy availed him nothing now. He felt like a
man hopelessly trying to read a letter written in cy-
pher of which he had lost the key. He began to
lose courage and to yield a little to the gloom of
despair.

In this he was, no doubt, all wrong, and strangely
forgetful of his favorite motto. But a sense of opportunities neglected made him consider himself weaker
than he really was. Besides, like all half-informed men,
he overrated the advantages of a science of which he
had only a smattering. He labored under the impression that an astronomer's glance at the sky, like a
general's at the field of battle, would tell him instantly
all that he wanted to know. He little dreamed that
even a Sestini, in the presence of these eternal fires,
would be just as helpless as a child that tries to give
a reason for the rhythmic movements of the ocean
breakers. Under the present circumstances the most
advanced observatory, provided with the most im-

proved apparatus, could have told him very little more than he knew already. In fact, the most careful observation of the fixed stars, it need hardly be said, could have told him nothing at all. The most powerful of our telescopes never make them larger, never make them smaller, never change their relative positions in the slightest degree. We even know that, though our whole solar system is rushing towards a star in Hercules at the rate of 160 millions of miles a year, it would take thousands and thousands of centuries before the slightest appreciable distance in the relative positions of the fixed stars could be detected by the keenest eye.

The hopelessly insolvable problem of the fixed stars left the Captain in such a state of discouragement that for a few days he could not bear the idea of any serious calculations whatever. His burning curiosity, however, would give him no rest. What part of the solar space did the earth at present occupy? Where was it going? Foiled in one direction, he attacked this problem in another. The fixed stars told him nothing whatever on the subject; why not consult the planets, particularly Mercury and Venus, whose orbits lay between the earth and the sun? Mercury lay too near (30 millions of miles) the centre of the solar system to be of much consideration at present, but Venus's comparative prox imity to the earth, enables us to estimate with great approximation the intensity of her sunlight. It is about twice as great as that received by the earth in ordinary circumstances. Now, by means of his photometer, the Captain ascertained that the light received at the *gourbi* was almost exactly equal in intensity to that received by Venus. This was a new confirmation to a conclusion already ascertained by a different process — the earth and Venus must be now at the same distance from the sun.

Such a conclusion, a close inspection of the beautiful Venus herself did not tend to contradict. Never had Phosphorus, Lucifer, Hesperus, Vesper, Evening Star, Morning Star, Shepherd's Star, Star of Love — even the lovely Queen of Night herself could not boast a greater variety of pet names — never before had Venus presented to mortal eye such an enormous disc as that now gazed upon by Captain Hector. It was a regular moon with all her phases, easily visible to the naked eye. New, half, three-quarters, full, all her changes were readily distinguishable. The edge of her outline, no longer sharp and regular as it usually appears to terrestrial observers, was jagged and indented, showing her possession of an atmosphere, these irregular radiations being due altogether to the refraction of the solar rays. Certain other luminous specks, very visible and quite detached from the edge, were no doubt some of the mountains which Schroeter calculates to be thirty miles high — an enormous altitude, five times greater than that of the loftiest of our Himalayas.

These various considerations and reflections made the Captain pretty certain that Venus could not be much further off than five or six millions of miles. The thought alarmed him and disturbed him so much that he could not help imparting the fearful intelligence to Ben Zouf.

"Five or six millions, Captain!" was Ben's quiet reply. "But that's what I call a nice, safe, and respectable distance."

"Two hostile armies, I grant, Ben Zouf," said the Captain, "might find fighting somewhat inconvenient when so far apart; but for two planets such a distance is hardly a stone's throw."

"What's the difference, Captain?"

"No more difference, Ben Zouf, than that we shall probably run into Venus."

"Is there any air up there, Captain?"

"Most probably."

"And water, too?"

"Plenty of water."

"All right then. Ho for Venus!"

"But the shock, Ben Zouf! The two planets seem to

be moving at present in opposite directions, and, their masses being pretty nearly equal, the collision must be as destructive to one as to the other."

"Like two railroad trains," observed Ben, who seemed very far from realizing the terrible significance of the idea. "Exactly like two railroad trains. Won der which one will telescope."

"Yes, two trains, you simpleton!" exclaimed the Captain, out of all patience at Ben's coolness. "But two trains rushing at each other with a velocity actually too great for your comprehension! Whichever 'telescopes,' your Montmartre is gone up forever!"

Ben, touched to the quick, lost his coolness in an instant. Hastily springing to his feet, he gnashed his teeth, clinched his fingers, and for a moment became white as a sheet; but he mastered himself by a violent effort, and when he spoke, after a few seconds' silence, a slightly trepid voice alone betrayed his emotion.

"Captain!" he exclaimed, "here I am,— give your commands.—Whatever I can do to stop this meeting — look on as done."

"Nothing can be done, Ben Zouf. That 's the worst of it. No rudder, nor brakes, nor guiding reins for planets. They mind nothing but God, their maker. My only object in talking on the subject at all is to pre· pare you for the worst."

"I prefer to hope for the best," answered Ben, now completely recovered, while he quietly lay down and resumed his telescope. "God is good. Old Montmartre is not gone up yet!"

Next day, about the same hour, after a night entirely devoted to observation, the Captain returned, and resumed the conversation, or rather monologue, for hardly a single word could be extracted from Ben beyond what the strict laws of military discipline required.

"We're getting nearer and nearer to Venus, Ben Zouf. I don't see how we can possibly escape. We're approaching each other in a line that, as far as I can see, is perfectly straight. And even if we should only graze Venus, how are we to escape Mercury? He is now a little overhead, but I can easily see that he is rapidly wheeling right into line. I don't deny, however, that, danger apart, he is a magnificent sight. At school, when a boy, I hardly ever noticed him, partly because he was too near the sun, but principally because I never considered him an interesting subject. How often did the Professor remind me that Mercury should be particularly attractive, seeing he was the planet I must have been born under! In vain did he try to call my attention to his phases analogous to the moon's; to his intense brilliancy, produced by a sunlight seven times more powerful than our own; to the peculiarity of his

torrid and frigid zones, which, owing to the **great** inclination of his rotatory axis, are continually changing
places ; to his well defined equatorial lands ; to his mountains nearly twelve miles high ; to his well-earned claim
to the epithet 'Sparkler,' bestowed on him by the
ancients, etc., and so forth. I was the heedless scholar
on whom the good old gentleman's learning, science,
and eloquence were all equally wasted. Even when, for
politeness' sake, I pretended to take an interest in Mercury that I was far from feeling, I acted my part so
poorly as to come very near displeasing the kind, but
serious and methodical old Professor.''

Ben Zouf, looking on all this as little better than
Greek, made no reply whatever, contenting himself
with laying aside his spy-glass and listening to his
Captain with an air of respectful attention. After a
moment's pause to take breath, the latter resumed :

''How the old gentleman was delighted when, owing
to the fortunate coincidence of several favorable circumstances, he was lucky enough to obtain a good
look at Mercury ! How he scratched undecipherable
pencil-marks on bits of paper and despatched us to
the other professors with his compliments, inviting
them all to come at once and enjoy the entrancing
sight ! They never came, it is true ; but, no matter
for that ! next time he had forgotten all about the

slight and was scratching off his invitations as enthusiastically as before. But what would he say if he were here now, when Mercury is actually more clearly distinguishable than Venus ever was? What do you think he would say, Ben Zouf?" asked the Captain, suddenly, perhaps for information, perhaps because he was beginning to get a little tired of his monologue.

"Captain," replied Ben, pushed for an answer, "the gentleman would probably say, 'Ben Zouf, stick to your ship, and never mind Mercury.'"

The Captain, taking the hint, withdrew, after a few more desultory remarks, but he appeared again next day punctually at the same hour.

"Ben Zouf," said he, after the usual exchange of salutations, "my news this morning is partly good, but partly very bad. There is no danger to be apprehended from Mercury. Though at present approaching us rapidly, a careful examination of his course last night convinces me that he will have passed a certain point of his orbit long before we can reach it. Mercury, therefore, is all right!"

"*Vive Mercure!* Hurrah for Mercury!" exclaimed Ben, having nothing better to say.

"But as to Venus," resumed the Captain; "I am sorry to say she looks more threatening than ever.

Comparing her present light and apparent diameter with those of two days ago, she cannot be now more than two or three millions of miles off. You must have remarked yourself, last night, that she cast a shadow quite as strong as a full moon's. Judging from spots on her surface easily distinguished by my naked eye, I could ascertain that her rotation period is still the same as it has always been — about forty minutes less than the Earth's twenty-four hours. I could readily trace the lines of the clouds that lie so heavy here and there on her vaporous atmosphere. The seven bright misty specks, called 'seas' or 'oceans' by Bianchini, were plainly visible. I am even almost certain that my eye detected the outlines of the channels by which these 'oceans' intercommunicate. There's no help for it, Ben Zouf! We're hurrying headlong to certain destruction, as fast as ever the Earth can carry us!"

"Captain," was Ben's only reply, one hand to his cap and the other on the seam of his pantaloons, "I have the honor to make my report. No ship!"

"Report accepted, Ben Zouf," answered the Captain hastily, as he withdrew to resume his observations.

Next day, fully half an hour before the regular time, Ben saw his form toiling slowly and listlessly up the blazing slope of the cliff. He looked fagged out and sleepy, and, in all probability, had not slept a wink all night.

"Ben Zouf," said he, as he took the comfortable seat that Ben had fixed for him under the awning, "news from Venus is, if possible, worse now than ever. Put your head outside a little and look directly over us. Now a little to the west. You see something there like a very brilliant little cloud with sharp edges? Or rather something like a full moon in the eastern sky on summer evenings an hour or so before sunset. That's Venus! Grand sight, isn't it? Only we can't imitate Napoleon, who, seeing something like it before the battle of Austerlitz, took it as a signal from heaven, and called it at once his 'lucky star.' She will be anything but 'lucky' to us and our unfortunate *Terra Mater.* But which of our astronomers, even in their wildest speculations, ever dreamed of attributing the destruction of our planet to such a source?"

Ben Zouf not being able to answer this question, the Captain did not press it, but started off on another tack.

"What a terrible state our friends in Algeria must be in? But what do I say? What a state of awful consternation the whole world must be in? What crazy articles will appear in the newspapers? And the crazier they are, the more voraciously will they be swallowed! What

innumerable and contradictory telegrams must be exchanging from continent to continent? What crowds
must be in the churches? They all think the end of
the world is come! And they're right! It is come!
But little did I ever dream that it would ever come in
our own time! Never mind your ship, Ben Zouf! You
will never see a ship again! Has the Governor-General
nothing else to do but send ships after you and me?
Within less than two days, the two planets will have
collided with a force sufficient to melt each other to red
hot lava, or to knock each other into fragments numberless as the sands on the shore around us!"

The Captain was here so excited that he turned
hastily away without ever asking Ben what he thought
of the approaching and appalling catastrophe.

Next day he failed to come at all. He was either too
much discouraged, or too deeply engaged in his observations. Ben's regret at not seeing his Captain did not
prevent him from keeping as close a lookout as ever over
the widespread horizon.

The day following, fully an hour before the time, Ben
was delighted to see him springing up the incline with a
light and easy step. His uneasy, nervous expression, as
he entered, had all disappeared, and, though he still
looked as if in want of sleep, his face beamed with a
quiet smile.

"All right for the present, Ben Zouf!" he cried, cheerily. "Old *Terra Mater* has another chance!"

"How's that, Captain?" asked Ben, instantly jumping up and assuming the attitude of attention.

"The two orbits, fortunately, do not lie in the same plane. The angle they form, though small, is great enough to allow the planets to slip past each other without the least danger of harm. When we pass over Venus to-night, the two planets will be at least one hundred thousand miles apart."

"Only a hundred thousand miles apart!" drily observed Ben, in pretended disappointment; "two hostile armies might find some difficulty in fighting at such a distance, but for two plan—"

"Talk about what you understand, Ben Zouf!" interrupted the Captain, hastily; "or," he added, as he retired down the slope, "if you must wag your tongue, thank Heaven for having preserved us all from a terrible danger!"

"I thank Heaven fervently!" said Ben, lifting his cap and bowing his head; "but I never once despaired of old Montmartre!"

On January 25th, the Captain again put in an appearance.

"Nothing wrong this morning, Captain?" asked Ben.

"Nothing whatever," answered the Captain; "I merely wished to call your attention to the fact that, though we passed Venus very closely, we could discover no trace of a moon in her neighborhood. This puts an end forever to the speculations of Cassini, of Short, of Montaigne, of Limoges, of Montbarron, and others who seriously believed that Venus had a satellite."

"These gentlemen were no doubt all very great astronomers, Captain?"

"Yes, very great astronomers, Ben Zouf."

"Yet they could be as wrong as the most ignorant of us?"

"Very true, Ben Zouf. But I'm sorry they were wrong this time."

"Why so, Captain?"

"Because, if Venus had had a moon, we might have whisked it off as we swept past, and so we should now have two moons."

"Seems to me, Captain, at present we haven't even one moon. I have not seen the sign of one since the night of the accident."

"Right again, Ben Zouf. The accident, as you call it, took place nearly four weeks ago, and what has become of our moon in the meantime, I can't tell. That reminds me that I must go and make some careful observations on the subject."

"Beg pardon, Captain!"

"Well, Ben Zouf, what is it?"

"What do they call that building with the big round cap on its head, that I often saw on the other side of the Seine, from Montmartre?"

"You mean the Observatory?"

"That's it, Captain. And it's probably so called because the gentlemen inside the big cap are all the time making observations?"

"Precisely so."

"Wouldn't it be just as well for us, Captain, to let these gentlemen go on making their observations, and, if they have any explanation to give on the subject hereafter, to listen to it like philosophers?"

"Philosophers! Ben Zouf, do you know what it is to be a philosopher?"

"Of course I do, since I'm a soldier!"

"What is a philosopher?"

"A philosopher is one who gives himself no trouble when trouble does no good!"

The Captain walked away without uttering another word, and did not make a single observation the following night, either because he was too tired or because he thought there was something sensible in Ben's definition of philosophy.

Next day he was getting ready to start for the watch-cliff, when he saw Ben quietly moving in the direction of the guard-house.

"Well, Ben Zouf," he cried, as soon as the Orderly was within good hailing distance, "what's up now?"

"I'm come to make my report, Captain," answered Ben, still advancing, but with his hand to his cap.

"Ready to hear it, Ben Zouf."

"A ship in sight this morning."

"A what!!"

"A ship in sight, Captain. Nor' east by north."

Before Ben had quite finished his report, the Captain was half way to the cliff, and in such a state of excitement that he left his sword and cap lying on the table in the guard-house.

"I believe in my heart," said Ben, quietly, as he picked them up and started after him, "that nothing will ever turn my Captain into a philosopher!"

CHAPTER IX.

NOTES COMPARED.

THERE could be no doubt about it. A vessel was plainly in sight. Owing to the greatly increased convexity of the ocean curve, the keel was still out of view; but, judging from the comparative visibility of her masthead, she could not be more than six miles from the coast.

The telescope was glued to the Captain's eye for several minutes.

"The *Dobryna!*" at last he exclaimed, handing the glass to Ben Zouf, just coming up.

"The *Dobryna!*" cried Ben, much surprised. "Are you sure of that, Captain? There's no smoke visible."

"She's not using steam; she's only under canvas, Ben Zouf. Nothing is more certain than that we see Count Timascheff's steam yacht."

The Captain's state of excitement kept on increasing. A most extraordinary accident was about to set him face to face with his rival. The man he most desired to see at that moment was probably Count Timascheff. Not

that he bestowed an instant's consideration either on
their projected meeting, or on the motives that had
rendered it inevitable.   Circumstances had occurred in
the meantime of too wonderful a nature to allow him
to attach the slightest importance to such trifles.   His
desire to see the Count proceeded altogether from his
intense desire to have his burning curiosity gratified by
a long and serious talk on the one all-absorbing subject.
The *Dobryna*, during her long, twenty-seven days'
absence, must have visited not only the neighboring
shores of Algeria, but also those of Spain, France, and
Italy, and had, therefore, taken a hasty but comprehen-
sive survey of all that portion of the Mediterranean that
recent events had so strangely modified.   The Captain,
therefore, was about to learn what had been the nature
and extent of the catastrophe, and perhaps even the
probable causes of which it had been the result.   Besides,
the Count, an honorable and gracious gentleman, would
no doubt be delighted at the opportunity of being able
to restore the Captain and Ben Zouf to their native
country.

"Where can she land?" asked Ben Zouf.   "The
mouth of the Sheliff exists no longer."

"She'll not land at all," replied the Captain.   "She'll
just come to anchor in the first favorable spot, and the
Count will then send his gig ashore."

The *Dobryna* now advanced more slowly, for the wind was astern, and it would be dangerous to get too close to these rocky coasts. They were evidently very careful on board, most of the sails being reefed. Very few threatening clouds, however, flecked the sky, the weather was exceedingly fine, the breeze quite manageable, and, accordingly, the yacht made fair headway.

From her course it was evident that she intended to touch on the island.

"How greatly the Count must be puzzled," observed the Captain, "when he discovers an island where he had left a continent!"

"And seeing no harbor, Captain," suggested Ben Zouf, "he may hesitate about approaching us too closely, and even start off for somewhere else."

"That's a fact, Ben Zouf. Let us find them some good mooring ground, and then send them a signal!"

The *Dobryna*, now passing them, was evidently making for the former mouth of the Sheliff. Not a moment was to be lost. Zephyr and Galette were saddled, and the riders mounted in a few minutes; in less than a quarter of an hour afterwards, the Captain and his Orderly, both on foot, were carefully exploring the stretch of coast that lay south of the westernmost point of the island.

They were not long in discovering a little bay protected by high cliffs on all sides except one, where a narrow channel permitted a safe and easy approach from the sea. It was exactly what they wanted. A vessel of moderate tonnage could lie there in perfect security even from violent storms. The Captain, however, was much surprised to find in it the tracks of a very high tide, evident by the long lines of sea-weed clinging to the cliffs all around.

"What!" he exclaimed, "high tides in the Mediterranean? Who ever heard of such a thing? This must certainly have been an exceptional case, and is probably due to the neighborhood of the enormous disc that we caught a slight glimmer of in the beginning of the month. Now let us signal the *Dobryna.*"

So saying, he waved rapidly to and fro a white linen handkerchief which he had fastened to the end of a long pole. The signal was evidently understood, for the vessel, slightly changing her course, stood more to shore and began furling her sails, leaving nothing but her gib to catch the wind. Quietly turning the western point, she soon caught sight of the little channel, and, guided by the signals, steered boldly into it. In a few minutes she dropped anchor in the little bay; the gig, manned and lowered, instantly set off; the Captain left his post of observation as quickly as he could, but on reaching the landing-place he found

THE RIVALS.

the Count already on shore and looking around with the greatest curiosity.

Cap in hand, he advanced to greet him with the utmost eagerness.

"Count Timascheff," he exclaimed, "I'm beyond measure delighted to see you! But, first of all, tell me what in the world has been the matter!"

The Count, a cold, phlegmatic man, whose remarkable gravity presented a singular contrast with the unrestrained vivacity of the French officer, took off his hat, and, drawing back a step or two, bowed ceremoniously, and said, in the well known and not unpleasing Russian accent:

"Captain Servadac, first of all allow me to assure you that your presence here is an honor that I did not expect. I left you on a continent, and I find you on an island —"

"No fault of mine, Count, I assure you. I never left the spot!"

"I am aware of that, Captain Servadac; but I hope you will kindly excuse my non-appearance at our appointed place of meeting. As soon as I shall —"

"My dear Count," hastily interrupted the Captain, with a pleasant smile and in the heartiest of tones, "let us drop that subject for the present. We can resume it, when it is your pleasure, on some other occasion."

"As you choose, Captain Servadac," replied the Count, putting on his hat; "I shall always hold myself in readiness for your orders."

"And I for yours, my dear Count. Now let me repeat my question. What, in the name of all that is startling, has been the matter?"

"The very question I was going to put to you, Captain."

"What? You can't tell—"

"I can tell you absolutely nothing."

"You can't tell what is the nature of the cataclysm that has turned this part of the African continent into an island?"

"I have not the faintest idea."

"Nor how far its effects have extended?"

"No conception whatever."

"But you certainly can say if the north shore of this Mediterranean—"

"Is this the Mediterranean?" was the singular reply that interrupted the Captain's question.

"You should know that better than I, my dear Count, since you have been just sailing over it."

"Excuse me, Captain. ! have not been sailing over the Mediterranean."

"You don't mean to say, Count, that all this time you have landed nowhere?"

"Not for a single day, hour, or minute have we touched land since December the thirty-first!"

For a few seconds the Captain looked like a statue, so motionless was he and dumb from surprise.

"But, my dear Count," he at last observed, "you must surely have remarked that ever since that day the east has taken the place of the west?"

"Oh, yes; we have remarked that."

"And that the day is only six hours long?"

"Certainly."

"And that the force of gravity is considerably diminished?"

"And that too, Captain."

"And that we have lost our moon?"

"Undoubtedly."

"And that we just missed running into Venus?"

"Precisely so."

"And that, consequently, the Earth's movements, both of revolution and rotation, have undergone very considerable change?"

"Nothing is more certain, Captain Servadac."

"Excuse my profound astonishment, my dear Count. I ask these questions not with the idea of giving you any information; on the contrary, I had the greatest expectation of receiving much from you."

"I can tell you everything I know, Captain, in a very

few words. On the night in question the *Dobryna* was
moving along quietly towards the part of the coast intended for our place of meeting, when, all of a sudden
—without an instant's warning—we felt the vessel lifted
up, as it were, on the back of an enormous wave. Up
we rose—up, up, to an altitude altogether too great to be
even approximately calculated. The water was at once
around us, above us, below us, and on all sides of us.
Earth, sea, sky, land, light, darkness, seemed to us, for
a while, to be mingled together in inextricable confusion, while, to the few of us that retained consciousness,
the fearful noise was deafening in the extreme. Some
of the crew have probably lost their hearing forever.
From that moment to this we have been tossed about
completely at the mercy of wind and wave. To the
violence of the elements we could offer but little opposition, the first effect of the shock being the disablement
of our machinery. Indeed, it is still a mystery to me
how the vessel was not completely destroyed by the
furious storm that raged around us for several days.
It seemed to be unchained, at once, from all quarters of
the globe. The only way I should at all venture to account for our safety, is by supposing our vessel to have
occupied a spot somewhere near the centre of the vast
cyclone that enveloped us, and, therefore, to have been
comparatively little exposed to its destructive **effects.**

This is all I know on the subject. Your island is the first land we have caught the slightest glimpse of."

"In that case, my dear Count," observed the Captain, still completely mystified, "would it not be well, without losing an instant longer, to take to sea once more, explore the Mediterranean thoroughly, and make a complete investigation of the extent and nature of the disaster?"

"That is precisely my own opinion, Captain."

"Will you permit me to accompany you, Count Timascheff?"

"To the end of the world, Captain, if such a voyage would give you any pleasure."

"Many thanks, my dear Count; but, for the present, a voyage on the Mediterranean will answer every purpose."

"Perhaps," said the Count, shaking his head. "But suppose a voyage on the Mediterranean was the same thing as a voyage to the end of the world!"

To this singular remark of the Count's, Captain Hector made no reply, really not knowing either what to say or what to think.

The plan of action to be immediately pursued was, however, soon decided upon. They were, first, to examine, or rather discover, what was actually left of the African coast, and obtain at Algiers whatever news they could regarding the rest of the inhabited world; secondly,

in case the whole southern shore of the Mediterranean
had disappeared, they were to turn at once northwards,
and put themselves in communication with the coast
population of Europe.

The state of the *Dobryna's* machinery interfered a
little with the immediate execution of this plan. Her
engine required a general overhauling, the boiler in particular needing some new tubing and other repairs. In
spite of the Captain's impatience, therefore, the Count
was unwilling to put back to sea instantly. He had
great faith in steam, looking on canvas as slow and far
from safe. The little time lost at first, he observed,
could be easily made up for afterwards. The *Dobryna*
had been expressly prepared for a trip in the eastern
Mediterranean, and her coal and other stores were still
untouched. These could be utilized for a rapid run to
last as long as ever they held out, and then, of course,
they could be easily renewed at the first convenient stop-
ping-place.

The Captain submitted at once with the best grace
to this sensible reasoning, and found the few days
required for repairing the steamer pass by almost
unnoticed. He rode with the Count around the
island, pointed out its most remarkable changes,
showed him his various maps and sketches, and read
him the reports which he had prepared for the Min-

ister of War. In spite of his habitual phlegm, the Count showed himself intensely interested in everything. In the course of their rambles they passed by the little field in which they had agreed to meet in mortal combat; but though the Count readily recognized the spot, he never appeared to take the least notice of it. He compared weather notes with the Captain, and, by way of return for the report, read him portions of a *journal* that he had kept pretty regularly on the *Dobryna*. He visited his vessel comparatively seldom, evidently preferring to spend as much time as possible in the Captain's company on the Captain's island.

In taking their weather observations both gentlemen noticed and recorded a decided and steady fall in the thermometer, which, as may be remembered, had maintained an extraordinary height for several weeks before the *Dobryna's* arrival. What did this lower temperature mean? Was the arc of the earth's orbit changing its general course? Such a question as this would admit of no answer, however, for several days, perhaps for several weeks. The weather was still very fine; nothing more threatening could be discovered than an occasional accumulation of mist, which made itself readily felt by a slight depression of the barometric column.

The reader must not imagine that we have all this

time forgotten our friend Ben Zouf. On the contrary,
we have reserved the rest of this chapter to be devoted
to him exclusively. The Count, fully appreciating his
extraordinary coolness and clear-headedness, with traits
of which the Captain never lost an opportunity of entertaining him, took a warm interest in Ben, and person-
ally invited him several times to be his guest on board
the *Dobryna,* during her contemplated voyage. But
Ben, whom several long conversations which he had
contrived to carry on with the boatmen had made
unusually thoughtful and serious, felt himself compelled to respectfully decline the favor. Of course,
he acknowledged that it would be a great pleasure
to attend the Captain — but the horses? There was
no accommodation for such animals on board, the
yacht being built for a different purpose, and nothing
could induce him to separate himself from Zephyr and
Galette. Other considerations, too, urged him to remain on the island until his master's return. Somebody, he said, should be left in charge of the new domain, where, likely as not, strangers might land at any
moment. The flocks in the immediate neighborhood
of the *gourbi* could not be left altogether to themselves; they needed some care, as possibly, though
improbably, they might prove, in course of time, to be
the sole dependence of the islanders. Ben himself
incurred no possible danger by remaining behind,

and, for a while at least, he should not feel too lonely. They would soon find out the state of things in other parts of the world and would then lose no time in returning to the island, taking him on board and restoring him either to Algeria or France, his native country.

He was so earnest on the subject and spoke so thoughtfully, that he easily gained his point.

On the morning of January 31st, he carried the Captain's trunks and instruments down to the landing-place and arranged them carefully in the boat. When everything was ready, he bade the Count a warm and respectful good-by, and then, taking his officer's hand affectionately, he said, in a low, quiet voice:

"*Adieu, mon Capitaine!* Should you ever happen to be in the neighborhood of old Montmartre, don't forget to see how he has stood this terrible collapse!"

Then climbing the rocks hastily and jumping on Galette, he made straight for the watch-cliff where he had patiently passed so many weary days. Quickly climbing it, he could see the *Dobryna*, now a few miles off, steering eastwardly under a full head of steam. As long as she remained in sight, Ben stood firm as a rock at his post on the old watch-cliff. There the Captain, the Count, and the other passengers of the *Dobryna*, telescope in hand, could see the faithful creature waving his cap, until the rapidly rising ocean curve at last cut him completely out of view.

CHAPTER X.

THE CHASE AFTER A CONTINENT.

COUNT TIMASCHEFF had not exaggerated the *Dobryna's* capacity when he offered to take Captain Hector to the end of the world. Columbus, or even Magellan, never had such vessels when venturing their daring voyages over unknown Atlantic or Pacific waters. Built in the best shipyards of the Isle of Wight, the *Dobryna* was a model vessel, combining in the highest degree strength, speed, burden, and beauty of form. Just before the catastrophe she had laid in a supply of two hundred tons of coal, and provisions enough to last her while making a leisurely tour of the Mediterranean shores. Her short stay at the island of Gourbi had been sufficient to restore her machinery to perfect order. She had taken in no additional ballast there, very little being found necessary. In the new order of things she was much lighter now, it is true, than before. But so, likewise, was the water. Her loss of weight, therefore, being counterbalanced by the lightness of the water, she lay just as deep in the waves, and moved through them

PROCOPIUS.

almost quite as freely as she had generally done before the catastrophe.

On reaching deck, the Captain found himself in presence of a gentleman in naval uniform, whom the Count introduced as Lieutenant Procopius, the acting commander of the *Dobryna*.

Procopius was a thoughtful, scholarly-looking man, about thirty years old. Born on the Timascheff estates, of parents emancipated some time before Emperor Alexander's famous edict, and carefully raised by the Count's family, he belonged to his patron body and soul, as much through solid friendship as through undying gratitude. Of good natural capacity, he had first studied theoretical navigation thoroughly in the State school-ships; he had then tested and solidified his knowledge by several years' active employment in the merchant service. This gave him such ready and available experience, that he had no difficulty in receiving from the board of government examiners the honorable diploma of lieutenant of the first class. Since then he had taken the sole charge of the *Dobryna*, devoting himself altogether to the gratification of the Count's marine tastes; he carried him around the sunny islands of the Mediterranean in winter. and in summer they explored together the sounding shores of northern seas.

The *Dobryna* could hardly be in better hands. A

skilful and experienced commander was efficiently aided
by a devoted and intelligent crew.   Six in number, four
sailors, the engineer and the cook, and all sons of the
Count's tenants, the Captain soon found out that the
recent convulsions in the physical order of nature gave
them no concern whatsoever.   So long as their master
stood by them, they were perfectly ready to endure any
change and to face any danger.   But the Captain soon
found out likewise that the Count himself, in spite of his
natural coldness and assumed indifference, felt serious
secret alarm, and that even Lieutenant Procopius, though
he pretended to think lightly of the matter before the
men, was very far from being at his ease.

The Captain had not been more than a few hours on
board when, the western breeze having freshened into
a gale, he felt himself the prey of a sensation peculiar
if not absolutely unpleasant.   He had never experienced
sea-sickness in all his life — once, while crossing the
English Channel from Newhaven to Dieppe, he was
the only soul on board that was not afflicted — but
he now felt himself suffering from something pos-
sessing a close resemblance to that distressing malady.
Much surprised, he questioned Lieutenant Procopius on
the matter, and soon learned the cause.

In consequence of diminished terrestrial attraction,
the molecules of water being much lighter, and con-

sequently much more readily affected by the wind, enormous billows were the inevitable result. Arago, who, when measuring the height of the Atlantic waves in the fiercest storms, could never find one more than twenty-five feet high, would have opened his eyes in amazement at now seeing the *Dobryna* riding on billows reaching fifty, perhaps sixty feet in altitude. Being also much lighter through the diminution of gravitation, the heaving wave flung her up like a cork. She felt like a vessel sailing over a storm-tossed sea of mercury; or, as the Captain said it, shĕ went bobbing up and down like a chip of wood in a steep street gutter on a wet day. But, as the Lieutenant predicted, this jerky, chopping motion was only the beginning, and it soon came to an end. The billows formed themselves by degrees into vast undulations, slowly swelling, softly sinking, miles and miles in length. The only inconvenience the Captain at last felt was a slight decrease in the *Dobryna's* ordinary velocity — reminding him a little of his jumping journey to the Sheliff with Ben Zouf, the morning after the catastrophe, when their vertical course took them so much out of the horizontal as to considerably lengthen their road.

In a few hours, however, the *Dobryna* was at the eastern — the new western — extremity of the island, but without the slightest delay or hesitation she continued

to follow at about a mile's distance the line that had
lately marked the Algerine coast. All sight of land
being soon lost in every direction, the Captain was
curious to know how Procopius marked the ship's
course. He certainly could not guide himself by the
planets or the moon, since moon there was none,
and the relative positions of the planets had now become very difficult to understand. Nor could he mark
his position by taking his latitude and longitude by
sextants or other instruments for observing the sun —
latitude and longitude thus found being evidently useless for charts made before the new order of things
had been established. But the Lieutenant did not
need much time to show him how he could point out
on the chart the exact spot occupied by the ship at
any particular moment, or, if not the exact spot, a
spot approximately exact and near enough to the true
one to be trusted in a short voyage like the present.
Without the aid of sun, moon, or stars, he did it by
what is called dead reckoning; that is, by the log he
measured the distance of his courses, and by the compass he ascertained their direction. For, most fortunately, in the midst of all the trouble, the compass
had neither varied nor been disturbed in the slightest
degree. The vast cosmical phenomena that had upset
everything else seemed to have exercised no influence

whatever on the magnetic needle. It still pointed north and south, making, of course, due allowance for the usual variation from the true north to be expected in these points of the African coast.

The Captain had very little trouble in exchanging ideas with the Lieutenant. Procopius, like most Russians, could speak French perfectly, and was just as willing to give as to receive information. Regarding the cause, however, of the late phenomena, or even their precise nature, he could tell the Captain very little that the Captain did not know already. They had many discussions on the subject; the Count added the acumen of a clear and well cultured mind; there was a very fine scientific library on board which they often consulted ; but they soon came to the unanimous conclusion that now, at the end of the month, their positive knowledge regarding the exact nature of what had taken place was not a bit more extensive than it had been on the very first day.

A few mornings after leaving the island, the explorers were walking up and down deck, discussing, as usual, arguing, guessing, propounding different questions, offering different answers, the subjects of conversation being the regular stereotyped ones, *Where were they now? What had happened? What was going to happen?*

" We agree with you completely in one respect, Cap-

13

tain," said the Lieutenant, replying to an observation of Servadac's; "the Earth certainly has abandoned her old orbit, and the new one she seems to follow has approached the sun pretty closely."

"More closely than Venus's," said the Captain; "perhaps more closely than Mercury's."

"But not so closely, I hope," observed the Count, "as finally to run into the sun altogether."

"Where our inevitable fate would be an instantaneous reduction to ashes," said the Captain.

"Unless the reduction had occurred long before we ever got there," rejoined the Count.

"Gentlemen," said Procopius, quietly, "I think I can affirm, with every likelihood of certainty, that, at present, we are in no danger whatever of running into the sun. We are now describing a new orbit, it is true; but, like the old one, it takes us around him, not into him."

"I should like to hear some valid reasons for that assertion, Procopius," said Timascheff.

"Father," replied the Lieutenant, giving the Count the title usually addressed to their lords by the Russian peasants, "I can give you reasons; but as to their validity you and the Captain must decide for yourselves. We cannot be falling into the sun, simply because we are too slow about it. A fall into the sun becomes possible only by the destruction of our centrifugal force. If that was suddenly destroyed, the Earth, at her normal distance from the sun, would take only sixty-four and a half days to fall into him, as a short calculation can make quite clear.''

"No doubt about that," observed the Captain. "Pray, continue."

"Consequently," resumed the Lieutenant, "we cannot now be falling into the sun. We have followed our new orbit for more than a month, and now we have only just passed Venus's. That is, we have not yet reached even the third of the distance. And, latterly, instead of approaching him with accelerated velocity, as we should do in case of a fall direct, I think we are not even approaching him at all. On the contrary, I think that we are retreating from him. I think our perihelion point is past. Our temperature is certainly diminishing. The heat, at present, is no greater than it is usually in Algeria in midsummer, or elsewhere on the thirty-sixth parallel.''

"Your reasoning seems pretty sound," observed the Captain, slowly. "I at least have nothing to urge against it.''

"Nor have I," said the Count, "except that the second argument, founded on the diminution of the temperature, is much better than the first, based on the comparatively short distance traversed in a month.''

"Another conclusion, gentlemen," resumed Procopius, after waiting a few moments for some other remarks from his auditors, "another conclusion quite as evident to me, though possibly not to you, I would just now take the liberty of calling your attention to. It is, that one of the consequences of the tremendous and most mysterious cataclysm has been the sudden and unceremonious translation both of the African coast and the Mediterranean Sea to the lines of the equatorial zone."

"There, Lieutenant," smiled the Captain, "I'm afraid you're making only a brilliant induction. You must prove to us the actual existence of an African shore."

"And of a Mediterranean too," observed the Count, whose previous doubts on this subject were now rapidly assuming the consistence of certainties.

"To resolve these questions, gentlemen, is one of the chief objects of the present voyage," said the Lieutenant. "So far, I am sorry to say, we have seen very little indeed that can give the slightest support to my assertion, and I am really beginning to believe that your doubts, though monstrously unintelligible, have some appearance of being well founded. It is now two days since we have left the island; but, though continually on a careful lookout, I have not been able to see Tenez, anciently *Cartenna;* nor Cherchell, anciently the fine Roman city of *Cæsarea;* nor Kolea, first inhabited by the Spanish Moors; nor Sidi Ferruch, celebrated as the first landing-place of the French army when invading Algeria. These towns, Captain Servadac, the Count and myself have often visited, and we know them well. You can find them all carefully marked on this chart; but no sight of them elsewhere! I can't discover the slightest sign of the Sahel range, though one of its summits, Bou Zarea, rose more than thirteen hundred feet above the sea."

He stopped for awhile to look over the chart, which lay on a drawing-table screwed to the deck. As he looked, they saw him suddenly start and rub his eyes, evidently in the greatest astonishment. He looked again carefully and thoughtfully, ran back hastily to the wheel-house, exchanged a few words with the steersman, and returned to his companions much disquieted, if not alarmed.

"Do you know where we are now, gentlemen?" he asked, hurriedly. "Of course you don't. Neither should I, if I had not come at it by indubitable calculation. We are at this moment in 36° 47′ north by 3° 14′ east: that is to say, we are at this moment sailing over *Government Square*, the heart and head of the city of Algiers!"

"Algiers, therefore, as well as Tenez, Cherchell, Kolea, and Sidi Ferruch must have been swallowed in the waves!" cried the Count, in accents of mingled grief and profound surprise.

Captain Hector could not say a word. Of the correctness of Procopius's statement he did not entertain a doubt. His heart as well as his eyes told him it was too true. Withdrawing hastily from his companions, he leaned against the mast, and looked out gloomily over the cruel sea extending infinitely all around him. His heart almost ceased to beat.

How well he remembered the morning when the unparalleled panorama burst on him for the first time! How deeply its chief points were engraved on his memory! Cape Caxine, with its lighthouse two hundred feet high; the beautiful church of *Notre Dame of Africa*, crowning the summit of one of Bou Zarea's wooded spurs; the graceful mosque of Sidi Abderraman peeping from the greenery of the Marengo Gardens; Algiers itself, with its terraces of white houses resembling a gigantic staircase climbing a mountain of Carrara marble; its culminating point, the Kasba, the old fortress of the Deys, commanding the upper town; Fort Emperor frowning down on both upper and lower; Koubba easily recognized by the immense dome of its church; the Hamma Garden readily traced by its avenues of gigantic forest trees ascending the verdant slopes; the Square House, a fortress commanding the entrance to the

GAZING AT THE CRUEL SEA.

famous plain of Mitidja, whose southern boundary was the main ridge of the Atlas Mountains; finally, Cape Matifou, with its lighthouse, on the eastern end of the magnificent curve that forms the Bay of Algiers. All this panorama framed in the green background of lofty mountains, many of whose peaks were wreathed in eternal snow, flooded by the magic light of an eastern sun, and floating midway, as it were, between the azure sky above and the blue waters beneath, had photographed a picture of ravishing beauty on the tablets of his memory that he could never forget to his dying day.

And now it was all gone! Algiers, the lively city where he had spent so many happy days, where he had possessed so many dear friends and agreeable companions, swallowed up without a moment's warning, without a single wreck to tell its story.

He leaned over the vessel's side and tried to peer into the blue waves. The wind was now still, the surface mirror-like, and the water as clear as crystal. A sudden idea struck him.

"Over Algiers!" he exclaimed quickly. "Then some trace of it must be left! A great city cannot suddenly disappear like a cloud from a mountain peak! Every sign of its existence can't have vanished in a moment! Its high places can't be far beneath the surface! Of the Kasba, the old citadel of Algiers,

nearly four hundred feet above tide water, and of Fort
Emperor, the new citadel, of the solidest construction,
and fully two hundred feet higher, surely every sign
can't have been completely swallowed up, unless, indeed, the whole continent of Africa has disappeared in
the ocean depths!"

The Count and the Lieutenant now hastily approached him. To them the same idea had also
occurred.

"Where are the timbers of the numberless frame
buildings?" asked the Count. "Some of them should
still be floating around."

"Or the branches of the palms, the planes, the
yuccas, and other numberless trees lining the squares
and streets?" cried Procopius.

"Or the planks, logs, masts, and other wood of the
countless ships, that I myself saw here not quite two
months ago, not only anchored in the port, but sailing
in every direction around the splendid bay, which
could not be less than twelve miles wide between
Pescado Point on the west and Cape Matifou on the
east!" continued the Count, looking eagerly all
around.

"I can't believe in such a complete and overwhelming destruction!" cried the Captain, catching, like a
drowning man, even at a straw.

And it certainly was very strange and even quite unaccountable that such a city as Algiers should have so suddenly sunk in the waves without leaving behind some mark to bear record of the overwhelming catastrophe. But not the slightest sign of a wreck or waif of any kind floated on the quiet bosom of the deep — not a plank, not a branch, not a log, not even a buoy.

The Count looked at Procopius interrogatively and doubtfully. But the Lieutenant, confident in the correctness of his calculations, replied without hesitation:

"The Captain, as I am well aware, is, naturally enough, still incredulous. He sees nothing convincing on the surface of the sea. Let us try to convince him by ascertaining what is under it."

One of the sailors, detailed for the purpose, threw out the line. To the great surprise of the Captain and the Count, but to the unbounded astonishment of Procopius, the lead, after reaching a depth of only five fathoms, sank no farther.

"Something must have caught it!" cried the Lieutenant. "Haul up, and fling out again."

The order was obeyed.

"Four fathoms and a half!" sang out the reelsman.

"Haul up and fling out again!"

"Four fathoms and three-quarters!"

"Head her south-east by south," cried Procopius to the helmsman, "and keep her so for five minutes!"

"Ay, ay, sir!" cried the man at the wheel, changing the ship's course as directed.

"What is the lead now?"

"Five fathoms!"

"Haul up and fling out again!—What now?"

"Four fathoms and a half!"

In something like this way the operation of sounding went on for nearly two hours. It ended by convincing even Procopius that the bottom of the sea was singularly level, and that it lay at a uniform depth of no more than four or five fathoms below the surface! This was simply astounding. Everybody knows that Algiers is not built like Philadelphia, on a wide plateau almost perfectly smooth and level, but somewhat like Genoa, on the steep slope of a mountain, amphitheatre-like, street rising behind street in terraces, to a height of five or six hundred feet above the sea. What had become of this extreme difference of level? Could the ocean, after drowning the city, have not only filled up the streets with sand, as the streets of Pompeii had been filled with ashes, but also kept rolling in the sand, pile upon pile, until every irregularity of surface had disappeared, and the city, with its forts, palaces, churches, hills, and towers, was left enveloped in a shroud of sand, like an exhausted traveller covered up in a deep snow drift, or, rather like a submerged forest of Siberia lying hundreds of feet below the ice-bound surface?

But against the above theory of Procopius, stated at fuller length and in more precise language, both Count and Captain loudly protested.

"What an idea!" exclaimed the Captain. "It is simply impossible, because it is inconsistent. Where could such piles of sand have come from?"

"What an idea!" exclaimed the Count. "It is not only improbable, but inconceivable. How could the sea have risen to such a monstrous level?"

"Father," replied Procopius quietly, "after what we have already seen, nothing is inconceivable. That my theory is improbable, I certainly admit. But, before pronouncing it impossible, Captain, we must first learn what we can by actual experiment.— Panofka!" he cried to one of the men, "tallow the lead well, sink it, and haul up! — Now let us see what kind of sand lies on the sea bottom!"

In a few minutes they were all curiously examining the numberless particles of foreign matter sticking to the tallow attached to the sounding lead.

"Why, it's not sand at all!" exclaimed the Captain; "nor even gravel!"

"Nor ooze, nor shell, nor anything else that's usually

dredged from the bottom of the Mediterranean!" cried the Count.

"Really, it is nothing but metallic powder," cried Procopius, in a surprised and still more disappointed tone. "See! it glitters like gold, and decomposes the light like iridescent pearl shell!"

"Your calculations evidently can hardly be right, Lieutenant," observed the Captain. "We are much further from the coast-line than you imagine."

"Impossible, my dear Captain," said Procopius quietly. "In the first place, my calculations are made too carefully and check each other too frequently to admit serious error. In the second place, supposing we really were further from the coast, it is not a depth of four or five fathoms that we should find, but a depth of two or three hundred."

"How do you reconcile the appearance of this metallic dust with your late theories?" asked the Count.

"Father, I can't reconcile them," was the candid answer. "I must say that I am now more nonplussed than ever."

"Count," said the Captain, "instead of continuing a direct easterly course, suppose we change it for a southerly. This would soon turn every possible doubt regarding our distance from the coast into positive certainty."

"Quite correct, Captain. Your proposition is probably the best we can adopt under the circumstances. What do you think of it, Procopius?"

The Lieutenant approving the idea, the helmsman received the proper order; the *Dobryna*, changing her course, sailed for the next thirty-six hours in a southerly direction.

Observations were continually made, and soundings taken with the most scrupulous care. Everywhere the bottom was found to lie flat and at an average depth of four and a half fathoms. But soundings alone were deemed far from sufficient for a proper exploration. The bottom was carefully scraped by iron drags, and scoured by a dredge of the best pattern, made expressly by Ball of Dublin for a scientific examination of the depths of the Mediterranean. But it was all of no avail. The drags never met a bit of cut stone, a particle of metal, a morsel of broken branch, a stick of timber; nor did the dredge, which could have fished a penny from the ocean depths, ever bring up a single one of these minute shells which are found, millions to the cubic inch, covering the bottoms of other seas in layers countless yards in thickness. What had become of the ancient bottom of the Mediterranean? What strange substance was that which now covered its bed? To these most natural questions, even Procopius now acknowledged himself unable to give anything resembling a sensible reply.

The *Dobryna*, her course carefully marked every hour on the ship's chart, slowly and watchfully pursued her way towards the 36th parallel. She was now sailing over the Sahel, the lovely range of lofty hills that forms the north-western boundary of the fertile Mitidja. The Captain had passed a pleasant summer once in the very centre of this Sahel, and he could not now recall without emotion its charming walks along the old Roman or Arabian roads, shaded by the luxuriant and perfumed trees of the south, and every now and then suddenly leading into some open space whence the eye could wander over the distant Algiers, its sail-studded bay, or its hills spangled with villas of the daintiest Parisian style and koubbas whose white domes seemed to float on oceans of greenery!

They were soon over Douera, a few years ago nothing but a French fortified camp, a few weeks ago a flourishing and important settlement, the chief town of the Sahel district. In half an hour they were over Bou Farik, in 1830 a pestilential marsh, the habitation of wild boars and other savage beasts, lately a beautiful and healthy town, the centre of the Mitidja plain, and remarkable for its great fair held every Monday in the year. In less than an houi the Lieutenant an-

nounced that they were sailing over Blida, the beautiful little city situated, as the Captain well remembered,
at the south-western extremity of the Mitidja, the scene
of several sanguinary encounters with the Moors, and
protected by Fort Minieh rising nearly five hundred
feet above the River Kebir. The Captain well remembered having visited in its neighborhood the ruins
of the former city destroyed in 1825 by a terrible
earthquake which killed at the same time nearly four
thousand of its inhabitants.

Procopius began to get weary of this useless journey.
It had not the same interest for himself or the Count
as it possessed for the Captain. He showed no impatience, however, but steadily held the ship's head
still to the south-west.

On they sailed over the Gorge of the Chiffa, where
a road had been constructed more wonderful for engineering skill and daring than even the famous Via
Mala of Switzerland. They should now be in the
neighborhood of the mountains of the Mouzaia, with
their legendary grottoes, mineral springs, precipitous
slopes, but particularly remarkable for the famous
Tenia or Pass more than three thousand feet above
the sea, the scene of terrible battles in 1841 and '42
against Abdel Kader's bravest battalions.

Where was this bloody Pass now? Or the Dakla?

Or the Gontas? Or the Beni Salah? Or the Zakkar? Or the other lofty summits of the lesser Atlas? The sea, that had remorselessly engulfed them in its bottomless chasms, now rolled over them, smooth, calm, shining, like a mirror of molten silver.

Servadac had intended to pursue the investigation a few points farther south, as far, at least, as the 36th parallel, where the Upper Sheliff had burst its winding, tortuous way through the foot-hills of the Great Atlas. But the complete disappearance of the Peak of Mouzaia seemed to unnerve him. He gave one steady, piercing glance for at least five minutes along the whole southern horizon from east to west. Nothing, absolutely nothing, but the long black line which hardly separated the water from the sky.

His gesture of despair was instantly understood and acted upon by Procopius, who neither liked useless sailing in unknown seas nor marking his ship's course on a part of his chart intended to represent land.

"'Bout ship!" cried the Lieutenant.

On the sixth of February the *Dobryna* found herself once more sailing in the former waters of the Mediterranean, about a mile north of Cape Matifou. Her southern trip had proved a complete failure. So far they had not discovered the slightest sign to show that what had been a short time ago the Province of Algiers, still existed.

CHAPTER XI.

A DISCOVERY OF SOME KIND.

THIS southern trip had, however, established some facts beyond all possibility of doubt. First, the complete disappearance of the land. But, besides this, something far more astounding, far more incomprehensible. The bowels of the earth must have suddenly opened to swallow up an entire territory, and then as suddenly closed to lock it up forever in its vast profundities. Lofty mountains had vanished without leaving a vestige behind, and a new soil, formed of some mysterious and unknown surface, covered the shallow bottom of an unknown sea.

So much was unquestionable, but the *cause* of it all? This question as yet admitted of no satisfactory answer, but on its solution our travellers were still resolutely bent. The first step in this direction was evidently to find out how far the disaster had extended, and, with this idea steadily in view, the *Dobryna* once more resumed her eastern course.

As before, she still pursued, as closely as possible, the

line of the former African coast. The navigation being
now easy and the weather propitious, her time was good
and her prospect of early discovery as favorable as could
be expected.

But from Cape Matifou to the frontiers of Tunis she
saw absolutely nothing. Nothing of Dellis, lately a
flourishing Arab town, formerly a Carthaginian colony,
and afterwards a powerful Roman city named *Rusucur-
rus*. No Jurjura Mountains in the interior, looking
down on the country of the brave Kabyles from their
snowy summits more than seven thousand feet high.
No Bougie, so famous for its wax that it has given its
name to the best French candles, and overlooking a bay
that resembled a vast lake surrounded by perpendicular
mountain curtains of the most original and picturesque
contour. No Gouraia, with its slopes so dark and steep.
No Jijelli, the *Ilgilgili* of the Romans, built on a rocky
peninsula separated from the mainland by a low and
narrow isthmus. No Cape Bougiarone, the most northern point of the Algerian coast, the spur of a mountain
mass thirty-five hundred feet high. No Collo, the *Kol-
lops magnus* of Ptolemy, clinging to the eastern slope of
the lofty Jebel Gaufi. No Stora, the ancient port of
Constantine. No Philippeville, the modern port. No
Iron Cape, with its bare and ferruginous peaks. No
dark crest of the Edour Mountains, terminating in the

Cape de Garda, so well known in the Roman times for its quarries of white marble veined with blue. No Lion Rock, a freak of nature which, according to Procopius, who furnished all these and many more details, bore a most extraordinary resemblance to the animal after which it was named. No Bona, one of the loveliest cities on the Mediterranean shores, formerly *Hippo*, a Roman colony, the birthplace of St. Augustine, and till lately presenting ruins of antiquity magnificent enough to surpass the grandest flights of modern civilization. No Cape de Rosa, where the finest coral was found. No La Calle, lately the liveliest coral market on the African coast. But now no coral greeted our travellers' eager gaze. Again and again the dredge was sunk. But all in vain. It still brought up nothing but the same strange, mysterious metallic dust.

Here the Count called his friends together for a new consultation. They were now at the frontiers of Tunis. After quitting the Province of Algiers, they had followed the line of the Province of Constantina for three hundred miles without meeting the slightest sign of encouragement to continue their easterly course any further. What was to be done next? Continue their present direction or attempt another southern trip? The Captain advocated the latter; the Lieutenant the former; a sort of compromise between the two pleased the Count better than either.

"Let us push on in an easterly direction as far at least as Cape Bon," said he ; "the sea there being very narrow between the African continent and the island of Sicily, we shall be likely to meet some peculiarities worth noticing. We can then turn southwardly, following the new line of the coast as far as the Gulf of Cabes, where something has been attempted towards admitting the waters of the Mediterranean into the Sahara. There, and more especially in the vast depression of land, occupied at present, as you see on this chart, by the Shotts, or salt lakes, Kebir, Grarnis, Faroun, and others, we shall be most likely to find the great crack to which the disappearance of a considerable portion of Africa is probably due. Beyond that point the Tripolitan coast may have resisted the fearful shock with sufficient firmness to set an effectual limit to the further spread of the disaster."

The Count had here alluded to a project started about this time to let the waters of the Mediterranean flow into a portion of the Sahara Desert, which was expected in consequence to become a vast inland sea. This great project, if successfully executed, should prove one of incalculable advantage regarding the amelioration of climate, productions, and inhabitableness, not only to Soudan itself, and all Northern Africa, but also to France and even to the world at large.

The Sahara, as was said, being nothing but the bed of an ancient sea, whose waters, cut off from the Mediterranean by a sudden upheaval of land and thus rendered incapable of being renewed, had been all evaporated by the fiery action of a Lybian sun. To turn it once more into a sea, therefore, nothing more was necessary than to cut through the narrow isthmus forming the obstruction and thereby restore the communication. To show the feasibility of the project, and probably also to excite more confidence among the shareholders, Lesseps, the famous originator and successful engineer of the Suez Canal, a kindred work, had employed a few hundred men under Captain Roudaire to do the preliminary work of cutting a narrow channel through the rocky peninsula that separated Lake Melghigh from the Gulf of Cabes. It was at this channel that the Count expected to find the vast scene of destruction come to a final end. Beyond it, in all probability, the firmer coast of Tripoli could still be seen emerging from the waters and extending south-east towards the Gulf of Sidra.

The Count's proposal was hailed with universal approval.

"Beyond that point," said Procopius, referring to the town of Cabes, where the channel commenced, "it would be useless to extend further researches. If

we should still find nothing there but the sea extending indefinitely towards the south, we shall have to
turn northwards and seek on European shores the solution of a problem that as long as we continue in
African regions appears to be impossible.''

The *Dobryna*, accordingly quitting the Algerian,
sailed along the Tunisian coast, at the distance of a
mile or two as well as could be understood from the
chart. Missing Capes Negro and Serat on her way,
she was not long in arriving at the site of Bizerta.
But it was in vain that our travellers look around for
some vestige of this charming little city, built in quite
the oriental style, with its pretty neighboring lake and
numerous mosques shaded by wide, spready palms. ''A
flat and shallow bottom with metallic dust for sand,''
was still the report made by the leadsman.

Turning the site of Cape Blanco, the most northern
point in the African continent, the vessel entered, on the
seventh of February, the Bay of Tunis, or at least what
was so till lately. For of this splendid bay nothing now
was to be seen. Tunis itself, built like so many other
Mediterranean towns in the style of an amphitheatre, its
fortress the Kasba, its port and arsenal Goletta, the
lofty peaks of Bou Kournein, even Cape Bon at the
other extremity of this bay, formerly the Gulf of Carthage, had all disappeared, all apparently absorbed, like

the rest of the continent, in the black jaws of the mighty caverns that lay beneath the rolling sea.

Instead, however, of immediately turning south, the *Dobryna* pursued for a while an eastern course in the direction of Cape Bon, to make certain investigations alluded to already by Count Timascheff. Both he and Procopius, to whom every peculiarity of the Mediterranean region was perfectly familiar, was well aware that in these latitudes the Mediterranean, generally very deep, became suddenly shallow, a ridge, like a submerged mountain chain, extending all the way under the waves from Cape Bon in Africa to Cape Boeo, the extreme western point of Sicily. In fact, both these amateur explorers had very little doubt that, in ancient times, Europe had been united to Africa at this particular point as well as at the Straits of Gibraltar, a thousand miles further west, where the two continents are still only about fifteen miles apart. This ridge, as they had often ascertained, lay under the surface at a depth of only fifty or sixty feet, whereas, at a short distance on each side, a sudden depression sank the bottom to a depth of more than five hundred feet. To ascertain if the great inequalities of level due to this steep submarine crest crossing the Lybian Strait still existed, was now the object of the *Dobryna's* proceedings. Procopius superintended them; the Count and the Captain, of course,

equally interested, watched every detail of the sound·
ing.

"Fling!" cried Procopius to the helmsman.

"Ay, ay, sir!"

A few minutes elapsed.

"Haul in!"

"Ay, ay, sir!"

"How many fathoms?"

"Five!"

"The bottom?"

"Flat!"

To the helmsman, "Turn her head directly north, **and**
keep her so for fifteen minutes!"

"Ay, ay, sir!"

After a quarter of an hour —

"Let go the sounding-line!"

"Ay, ay, sir!"

"Haul in! — How many fathoms?"

"Five and a quarter!"

"Any sand or shell?"

"None! Same as before — metallic dust!"

"Turn her head round, and steer directly **east for** ten
minutes!"

Again the same operation was attended with exactly
the same results. Everywhere five fathoms! Everywhere a flat and level bottom! Everywhere the same

unknown metallic dust! No sand, or sponge, or coral, or hydrophytes of any kind — no sea-weed even, which had been here till now so remarkably superabundant. The submerged crest existed no more. The cataclysm must have reduced the whole bed of the Mediterranean to the same uniform and ubiquitous level.

Further explorations of this kind being now evidently useless, the *Dobryna* wheeled round and, as had been agreed upon, headed directly south.

Another of the astonishing peculiarities of this most perplexing voyage, was the complete and total absence of anything like a sail on this most strange and dreary sea. How eagerly our travellers' eyes swept the horizon in search of a vessel! Even an unpretending fishing-boat might be able to give them some important point of the information they were dying to know. But nothing could be seen. Look whichever way they might and as long as ever they would, absolutely nothing. The *Dobryna* was apparently the only vessel that gave any signs of life in this Sahara of water. The isolation was growing every day more appalling, more dispiriting, more crushing. Was their little yacht the only vessel freighted with life that sailed on the waters of the terrestrial globe? Was she, indeed, a new Noah's ark, holding the sole human survivors of a catastrophe than which even the mighty Deluge was not more terrible?

On February 9 they had crossed the 37th parallel, and were sailing in the direction of Queen Dido's fortress city, *Byrsa*, now not more completely destroyed than old Carthage of which it had been so long the citadel, or than new Carthage razed to its foundations by Hassan the Sassanide towards the end of the eighth century.

That very evening, just as the sun was fast approaching the eastern horizon, Captain Hector, leaning on the taffrail, absorbed in disquieting reflections, and peering out over the dreary expanse of sea stretching darkly before him far into the unknown south as if into infinity, suddenly imagined that he had beheld the twinkling of a light. Fearing it was only imagination, he looked again with fixed and ardent gaze in the same direction. Yes! there it was again! a light beyond all doubt! But, to make assurance doubly sure, he called up a sailor and, pointing ahead, asked him if he saw anything. Yes: the sailor saw a light distinctly.

"Tell the Count and the Lieutenant to please come on deck immediately!"

The sailor disappeared; and in a few seconds the three gentlemen, telescope in hand, were eagerly discussing the nature of the light.

"Land?" asked Servadac, eagerly.

"Or a light-ship?" suggested the Count.

Both looked at Procopius, who, however, made no reply.

"Another hour will tell us all about it," said the Captain.

"Afraid not," said Procopius, still with eye to glass.

"Why not, Procopius?" asked the Count, much surprised. "Are you not going to head her for the light?"

"That light, Father, could not be reached before dark," answered the Lieutenant. "I should prefer lying around here till morning. We cannot be very far now from the site of the ruins of Carthage. We have not been here before, and I must say that, as a careful sailor, I should prefer not to approach too closely during the night-time."

"As you please, Lieutenant," said the Count. "Captain, we must smother our impatience as well as we can till morning."

The *Dobryna*, taking in sail and cutting off steam, slackened her pace so as to make no more than a few miles slowly during the whole night.

Even a whole night of six hours is not very long; but this particular one was a whole century to the Captain. He never quitted the deck, and would hardly take his eyes a moment off the light for fear he should never find it again if once lost. But there it remained, glimmer-

ing steadily all night through the darkness, like the
lantern of a lighthouse of the second rank seen at about
fifteen miles' distance.

"And always in the same spot," observed Procopius
to the Captain, who had made the comparison.

"It must be land then!" cried Servadac. "No ship
could be so motionless!"

"Unless a light-ship, Captain," quietly persisted the
Count.

Morning came at last, and the light instantly disappeared before the rays of the rising sun. But, in its
place, at a distance of five or six miles, suddenly arose
the black speck of an islet in the midst of this deserted
sea.

"No light-ship!" exclaimed the Count, after a careful glance with his telescope. "More probably the
peak of a submerged mountain!"

In a quarter of an hour they were near enough to
examine it at their ease.

It was a kind of rocky hill, bare, sterile, steep, flat,
rising out of the waves to a height of forty or fifty feet.
No reef forbade approach to the shore — a proof, as
Procopius remarked, that the summit had sunk gradually and slowly under the influence of some inexplicable phenomenon until, finally reaching some solid foundation, it had sunk no farther.

"That's a very remarkable-looking building on its summit!" cried the Captain, whose sharp eyes enabled him to catch distant outlines with great readiness. "Where there's a house there is an inhabitant!"

"There *was* at least!" said the Count, sententiously, and with a slight shrug of the shoulders.

"That's a problem of easy solution," said Procopius, touching off the little cannon always standing on deck, ready for signalling. A muttering as of distant thundering was re-echoed from the rocky islet by way of reply. But this was all. No living being, animal or human, moved over its cheerless surface.

By this time they were near enough, however, to see very distinctly the building, somewhat reminding them of a Christian votive chapel, that crowned the summit of the rock. It was, of course, to be at once entered and thoroughly explored. In a few minutes the vessel's yawl, rowed by four seamen, landed Count, Captain, and Lieutenant at the base of the rock just under the chapel. Jumping ashore and climbing an ascent of some ruined steps, they were not long reaching the summit. Here they were abruptly stopped for a while by a wall incrusted, inlaid, and covered with the wrecks of old ornaments, such as vases, pillars, statues, inscriptions, and pedestals, all tossed about or lying upon each other in the utmost disorder.

Turning to the left and following the wall for a short distance, our travellers reached an open doorway, which they immediately entered. Here they found themselves on the esplanade that surrounded the temple. Standing in the centre, on a platform reached by ruined steps of a circular shape, was an octagonal building surmounted by a dome, from whose summit a glittering cross reflected the bright rays of the morning sun. An open doorway gave access to the temple's interior, which they entered respectfully, hat in hand. The walls all around were sculptured and ornamented in the Moorish-Gothic style that is so much sought after of late in many European countries. But in the middle point of the only apartment of the building, right under the dome, stood an altar-like tomb quite impressive in its simplicity. Behind the tomb the building had been considerably injured by the shock, and among the brick and mortar rubbish might be seen portions of a white marble statue broken into numberless fragments. Above the tomb hung an enormous silver lamp whose reservoir still contained several gallons of oil; a long wick, rising in the centre, still burned with a steady flame — evidently the light that had caught their attention the previous evening.

THE CHAPEL.

The building was completely deserted; no sign of its inhabitants could be found; its guardians had probably escaped in time to avoid destruction. A few cormorants alone, which had taken refuge within its walls, disturbed by the approach of visitors, flew out hurriedly, and made their way towards the south, filling the air with discordant cries. On a corner of the tomb lay an old French missal; it was open at the page devoted to the festival of the twenty-fifth of August.

A sudden revelation flashed like lightning through the Captain. The locality of the islet, the isolated tomb in the midst of the sea, the page which the last reader of the missal had been perusing — all told him at what particular spot himself and his companions now found themselves, and that it could be no other!

"Saint Louis's tomb, gentlemen!" he cried. "It was on this very spot that our martyr king died in 1270, surrounded by a plague-stricken army!"

"And this is the chapel that was built in 1842 in the midst of the ruins of Byrsa, on the site of the ancient temple of Æsculapius!" exclaimed Procopius, rapidly taking a note for the benefit of his chart.

"Nothing can be truer!" exclaimed the Count. "It is well known that the Bey of Tunis generously presented the French government with the hill of Byrsa, a spot particularly dear to France as the consecrated scene of the glorious death of one of her greatest and most beloved monarchs.''

And so indeed it was. Here had one of the noblest mortals that ever sat on a king's throne breathed his last sigh six hundred years before! And here, after six hundred years of grateful memory, had pious French hands been guarding his lonely tomb!

The Captain bowed before it with unspeakable emotion. His companions imitated him with heartfelt sympathy and profound respect.

This lamp, life's emblem, now burning over a saint's tomb, was perhaps the only light-house that illuminated the endless waters of the Mediterranean! This lamp, again life's emblem, was soon to be extinguished forever!

Nothing more could be discovered on the rocky summit of Byrsa's acropolis.

Our explorers, soon on board, faced the *Dobryna's* head to the south, and quickly lost sight of Saint Louis's tomb, the only point on the Tunisian coast spared by the late terrible and still most mysterious catastrophe.

THE TOMB.

CHAPTER XII.

IT was towards the south that the startled cormorants, quitting the sainted king's lonely tomb, had winged their rapid flight. Was this a sign of land lying at no great distance in that direction? Somewhat buoyed by such a hope, the *Dobryna's* crew felt the time pass quickly as they glided over the peninsula of Dakhal that had till lately separated the Bay of Tunis from the Gulf of Hamamet. The sea being smooth and the wind steadily blowing from the north-west, in two days they reached the thirty-fourth parallel, the latitude of the Gulf of Cabes.

It was here, as may be remembered, that they had expected to see the preliminary operations of Lesseps' and Roudaire's famous undertaking, by which the waters of the Mediterranean were to be allowed to fill up the great depressions of the *Tritonis Palus* of the ancients, and thus form a vast internal sea. But no sign of channel or peninsula, of lighter or ship of any kind, was yet to be seen. The liquid plains of dark azure still extended endlessly to the east and endlessly to the west.

But how was it towards the south? Did not those blackish-gray clouds, maintaining their shapes so steadfastly on the southern horizon, look somewhat like land?

"No land can be there!" cried Procopius, pointing to his chart, "at least no land of that character. The coast of Tripoli, the only land in that direction, is so low and flat that it cannot be seen at any such distance. Besides, it is at least sixty miles farther south!"

But in less than five minutes after he had spoken these words, the man at the mast-head sang out "Land!" and the cry of "Land ahead!" was repeated a few seconds afterwards by the watch on the foredeck.

There could be no doubt at all about the matter. A long ridge of high mountains, strongly indented, soon appeared in sight. Extending east and west as far as the eye could see, they enclosed the northern half of the Gulf of Cabes, and completely hid from view the isle of Jerba its southern boundary.

"This puts an end, at least for the present, to the Sahara project," said Procopius, carefully marking down the newly discovered land in his chart.

"Wonder on wonder!" cried Captain Hector. "So far the Mediterranean has taken the place of a continent; now we find a continent to take the place of the Mediterranean!"

"It was about here, however, that we expected to find some trace of land," observed Count Timascheff. "And our expectations are realized, though the great crack is certainly somewhat farther to the south than we had calculated. What's to be done now? That range of mountains is too unbroken to admit a passage; and that coast is too steep to admit of much nearer approach. We must evidently sail either east or west. Which shall it be?"

"West, my dear Count, by all means!" cried the French officer, eagerly. "I should like to ascertain, in the first place, if there is anything left of our Algerian colony on the south of the Sheliff, and, in the second place, we could call at Gourbi for Ben Zouf, and then push on as far as Gibraltar, where we should most probably learn what has taken place in Europe!"

"Captain Servadac," answered the Count, with most gracious politeness, "the yacht is entirely at your service. Procopius, take the Captain's orders."

"Before you decide finally, Captain," said Procopius, "I should take it as a favor if you, and the Count also, would listen to an observation I have to make on the subject."

"Certainly, my dear Lieutenant," replied the Captain.

"Speak, Procopius," answered the Count.

"The wind," continued Procopius, "has been blowing steadily from the north-west for some days. It is now veering to the west and decidedly freshening up. With steam at high pressure we could of course make some headway against it, but not much, and even that with considerable difficulty. We should not be able to reach Gibraltar in less than two or three weeks at soonest; whereas, by taking advantage of the present favorable breeze, we may succeed in reaching Egypt in five or six days. At Alexandria or elsewhere we might readily obtain all the intelligence they could give us at Gibraltar."

"What do you think of the Lieutenant's amendment, Captain?" asked Timascheff.

"I think it excellent, my dear Count," replied the Captain, without a moment's hesitation. "Whatever natural desire I may have to learn something about the Province of Oran and to see Ben Zouf, I am still more desirous to pursue what is certainly the best plan for gratifying the general curiosity at the earliest possible moment."

The *Dobryna's* head was accordingly turned east, and for the following two days, under wind and steam, she followed the line of the new coast, at a distance of at least three or four miles from its dangerous precincts.

For some time past the explorers had been too busily occupied with terrestrial to devote themselves much to celestial observations, but now, having comparatively little else to do, they began to interchange ideas as to the present position of the earth in the regions of solar space.

"What is the thermometer this morning?" asked the Captain of Procopius as the three gentlemen met on deck after breakfast. They were rather warmly clad and found brisk motion backwards and forwards not unpleasant.

" 59° Fahrenheit."

(Procopius really said " 15° Centigrade," but here, as on many other occasions, we modify the exact language a little to save the English reader somewhat troublesome calculations.)

"Tumbling rapidly!" observed the Captain. "Within the last few weeks it must have sunk thirty or forty degrees."

" That 's exactly what we have to expect," observed the Count, " if Procopius is right regarding our increasing remoteness from the sun."

" On that subject I have very little doubt left," said the Lieutenant. "In the beginning of this month we were at the same distance from the sun that we had been at in the beginning of the last, though in the middle of January we had been much nearer. This shows that we went around him. That is, we did our perihelion, and we are now fairly started for our aphelion. It is all made evident not only by the gradual change of temperature but also by the gradual diminution of the sun's disc. Look at him now, gentlemen. I have examined his diameter very carefully with my instruments, and have ascertained that he presents precisely the same appearance to us now that he would if we were inhabitants of the planet Mars. The conclusion is irresistible. We quitted the Earth's old orbit in the first place; we then cut Venus's and Mercury's; we doubled the Sun; we cut Mercury's and Venus's again; we have just past the Earth's; and we are now approaching Mars, whose orbit, I have no doubt, we shall soon cut, as we have cut the others. Our own new orbit, therefore, if an ellipse, is very much flattened and, of course, very much prolonged. But it may not be an ellipse at all. It may be an open hyperbolic curve, in which case we could never return to the Sun again. If an ellipse, of course we may return, but it would be only after first enduring a degree of cold never experienced in the regions of eternal ice."

The correctness of these remarks of Procopius no body thought of disputing. Their general truth was almost self-evident. Besides, his companions, and even himself, soon found themselves again too deeply engaged in earthly investigations to trouble themselves much with heavenly.

In fact, their late change of direction, as they were not long in ascertaining, had given their voyage an aspect altogether new and startling. At first, they had seen no land whatever; now, they saw too much of it. Away, far away to the west it had appeared to extend itself indefinitely; and now it looked as if it was never coming to an end in the east. And it was land too of such a terrible, forbidding character that they were afraid to approach it. Even the closest observation could not detect an opening to get through, or a curving projection to take refuge behind, in case the wind blew them against this terrible coast. Straight as a wall, smooth as a block of ice, of a height varying from two to three hundred feet, at its dark base the long waves were ever dashing furiously, and continually whirling their foam and spray half-way up its dripping sides. Nowhere up or down in this terrible face could be detected a single fracture or cavity or projection of any kind to rest the foot, or be grasped by the hand of the daring climber. The summit bristled with a forest of crystallized needles, arrows, pikes, obelisks, and pyramids of all shapes and sizes, reflecting the sunlight in dazzling refulgence from their countless mirrors.

"Glassy," was the epithet by which the Captain de-scribed this appalling coast. "Spick and span new," was Procopius's expression. "Metallic," was the term employed by the Count. All three were right. It pre-sented much of the polish, the glitter, and the hardness of glass. It looked as new and fresh as if it had been just turned out of the machine-shop. No winds, or rains, or discoloring suns had as yet dimmed the polished steel of its glistening blocks, shafts, and pillars. No electric discharge or furious atmospheric disturbances of any kind had as yet broken up the sharpness of its out-lines, marred the purity of its shapes, blurred the clear-ness and variety of its figures. Its metallic lustre flashed with golden iridisations strongly recalling the peculiar gleam of pyrites.

"An idea!" exclaimed the Count, suddenly. "Does not yonder crystal coast seem to be formed of some one particular kind of metal upheaved from the bowels of the earth, like the other Plutonic rocks? And does not its lustre remind you of the metallic dust, the only débris so far found at the bottom of our new ocean?"

"Another idea!" exclaimed the Captain, "not con-tradicting yours, Count, but rather supporting it. The hardest rocks I have ever seen were streaked with little channels made by the water trickling over the surface. Here not the slightest rill, not even the faintest line can be detected. Consequently, yonder rocky coast is either glass or metal."

"Another idea, gentlemen," said Procopius, "though it has probably struck you both already. I have never before seen coast or cliff or mountain, however steep or rugged or bare, where some little plant had not taken refuge, where some little seed had not found safety and shelter. But here a speck of verdure is as rare as a cottage-porch; not even a bird can be seen flying among those desolate peaks. Nothing lives there, or moves there, or grows there; no animal or vegetable characteristic being found there, it must be exclusively mineral."

Nothing could be truer than such remarks; that about the birds was particularly striking. Latterly the yacht had become a special object of attraction for gulls, albatrosses, rock-pigeons, curlews, fish-hawks, and other sea-birds. Man, or even the gun, had no terror for them. Night and day they kept flying about the vessel, or rested perching on the yards. Whenever a basket of broken meat was flung for them on deck, they pounced wildly on the food, fighting for it furiously, and swallowing it as ravenously as if they had not tasted a morsel for a week. Was this a sign that habitable land was still far away? Did it show that the interior of the inhospitable region in sight was as bare of food and water as its exterior?

Along this most strange and uninviting coast, but always at a safe distance, the *Dobryna* sailed for several days without noticing any important modification of its most prominent features.　At times indeed it would show a crest straight, even, and as well defined as the ridge of a house, to change, however, in less than a mile to the normal outline of prismatic scales and needles in all their bewildering entanglement.　But at the foot of these precipitous cliffs never could be seen a bank of sand, a bed of shingle, nor even a group of the rocks often found in shallow waters.　Here and there narrow openings showed themselves; but they were cracks rather than entrances, no wider above than below, and impenetrable to any boat, for either water or exploration.　Here and there too the line of the coast would retreat a little so as to allow the formation of shallow semicircular bays entirely open in the north, and therefore capable of affording little or no refuge in case of a storm.

One day, after a run of about two hundred and fifty miles, the *Dobryna* found that her eastern course was brought to a sudden termination.　The line of the coast, giving a sharp turn to the left, directly barred her further passage.　Procopius, who had carefully marked in his chart every feature of the new continent, said that the new line lay between the 14th and 15th meridians, that it ran directly north and south, and that, if it continued far enough, it would cut Malta, Sicily, and Naples.

The question, What was to be done now? was easily answered. No alternative was left but to do the only thing that could be done, namely, follow the new coast-line as far as it went. If it reached Malta, Sicily, and Naples, all further eastern exploration was clearly impossible. The Mediterranean would be then cut in two, and Egypt could never be reached from its western half.

With the crystal coast still on their right, changed indeed in its direction but totally unchanged in character, our explorers, leaving Africa and approaching Europe, found themselves in a few days nearing the latitude and longitude of Malta. Would it be visible? Would the old island possessed in succession by Phenicians, Carthaginians, Sicilians, Romans, Vandals, Greeks, Mahometans, Knights of St. John, British — would that famous old island be spared by the terrible cataclysm that had spared nothing else?

Malta had shared the common lot. On the fourteenth of February, Ball's dredge, plunged into the Mediterranean over the site of Valetta, brought up nothing but the same metallic dust whose appearance was by this time so well known, but of whose precise nature our travellers were still as ignorant as ever.

" More than Africa then has felt the ravages of this

mysterious phenomenon," observed the Count at the close of a general conversation.

"We can really set no limit to its disasters," said Procopius. "But what is to be done now, Father? Having ascertained that Malta no longer exists, what course shall we now pursue?"

"Follow this coast as long as it runs northwards!" exclaimed the Captain. "To Sicily, to Italy, to France! Anywhere to get information! Anywhere to learn —"

"That we are probably the only survivors of the whole human race," observed the Count in grave tones. completing the Captain's unfinished sentence.

A north course being evidently the best to pursue. Malta's site was soon left behind. If the coast extended as far as Sicily, the only way left for the Count to reach Russia would be through the Straits of Messina. These would allow a passage to the Ionian Sea, the Archipelago, the Dardanelles, the Sea of Marmora, the Bosphorus, and so by the Black Sea to Sebastopol or Odessa. On the contrary, should the Straits be closed, Italy could be visited; the Apennines, and particularly the mighty Alps, could hardly have been swallowed up by the mysterious catastrophe.

But no later than the next day it was found that a northern course was more easily decided on than followed. The wind, which for some time had been blowing gently from the south-west, gradually veered round to west — a decidedly dangerous point, for if it freshened it threatened to dash the *Dobryna* to pieces against the crystal coast. The worst fears of her passengers were soon realized. The wind not only freshened but turned to a point still more dangerous, the north-west. Increasing gradually in violence, in less than an hour it was blowing a tremendous gale. The billows were soon running mountains high. The *Dobryna* struggled on as well as she could through the seething waters, the waves breaking over her in cataracts and washing her decks from stem to stern. A vessel of only two hundred tons burden, her sails useless, her screw almost powerless, being as often out of the water as in it, her progress was of necessity very slow. Procopius even dreaded that she was gradually but surely approaching the fatal shore.

This shore was only six miles to lee. Before such a storm such a distance meant hardly half an hour's respite from certain death. What was to be done? Run for shelter into some friendly harbor? The savage coast presented none! Of the two next and now only alternatives, which one? Turn round and run before the wind — or steer right in its eye? This question, our three explorers, maintaining their post on deck as well

as they could amidst the roaring storm and the drench·
ing waters, were not long in answering.   To turn round
and try to run before the wind, besides exposing them
to the instant danger of subjecting the vessel's broad-
side to the combined action of furious wind and wave,
would be certain to send the *Dobryna* back in a short
time to the blind corner formed by the meeting of the
two coasts.   Once there, certain destruction would be
simply inevitable.   Facing the wind not only avoided
this danger altogether, and offered the strongest possible resistance to the more obvious and immediate
peril, but would perhaps enable the *Dobryna* to hold
her own — nay, if her splendid machinery only held
out, she might even make some headway and so perhaps finally find some place of refuge.

So said, so done.   The *Dobryna's* stem boldly faced
the north-west, and her whirling, screaming, rattling
screw did all it could to bite into the liquid masses.
Her sailors, courageous and devoted, obeyed orders
with coolness and intelligence.   Not a single one hesitated an instant to execute the most dangerous man-
œuvre.   The Captain said the word, the Master was
present, God watched overhead ; now or never was
the moment to laugh at death !

But in spite of panting steam and stubborn machinery, in spite of intelligent and watchful seaman·

ship, in spite of devotion and obedience almost sublime, the *Dobryna*, though making some headway,
was also making leeway. The terrible coast was per-
ceptibly coming nearer. It could now be hardly four
miles distant. Not a muscle could be relaxed, not a
minute lost. The steam, full head, threatened to burst
the boiler. The *Dobryna* plunged through the gigantic
waves like a train through a tunnel, or like a bather
through a curling breaker. But from the summit of the
next billow, her crew could plainly see that she still
made leeway.

Tightly holding on to whatever was staunch enough
on deck, the sailors kept as close as possible to Procopius, calmly waiting orders.

"Nothing more can be done," said the Lieutenant,
gloomily, but in tones of resignation. "Our destruction is now only a matter of time."

"Is that so, Procopius?" asked the Count, quietly.
"Have you done everything that a seaman could do?"

"Everything, as far as I know, Father," answered the
Lieutenant; "but it is all to no purpose; in another
hour we shall be dashed to pieces on yonder shore."

"In another hour," said the Count, in a voice loud
enough to be heard by all around him, "we may be in
perfect safety. Procopius, never despair of the good-
ness of God!"

"Unless the wind changes, Father," replied Proco
pius, shaking his head despondently, "or unless this
coast opens to give us a passage, I don't see —"

"Procopius!" interrupted the Count, sternly. "We
are now in the hands of our Creator, the all-wise, the all-
good. Let us be resigned to His holy will!"

Taking off his hat, he crossed himself, and bowed for
a few moments in silent prayer. Servadac, Procopius,
and the sailors, filled with the pious emotion of sublime
resignation, quietly imitated his example.

But though Procopius had given up everything for
lost, he was by no means the man to sit idle with
folded hands, meekly awaiting his fate. All the crew, he
thought, could not possibly escape the fury of the waves,
but a few might. Why not make some provision for
their maintenance? The *Dobryna* would be sure to go
under, but might not a raft survive? Every available
moment, therefore, of this most valuable time was
instantly devoted to the construction of a raft. Half a
dozen stout spars, laid across half a dozen others, were
securely lashed together by means of strong ropes, and
rendered buoyant by a lot of empty casks carefully fastened beneath them. On this raft were secured several
water-tight boxes of provisions, some barrels of fresh
water, a compass, the vessel's yawl, oars, Procopius's
charts in water-proof cases, and such other indispensable

articles as could be hastily got together. In short, every means having been first taken that a good seaman should take to avoid shipwreck, everything was now done that a good seaman should do in case shipwreck was inevitable.

Every order now executed, there was a lull of active exertion. But no lull in the wind. It blew as fierce as ever from the north-west. No hope from the wind. From the shore? Still less. It was coming nearer and nearer, its precipitous cliffs were rising higher and higher; by an optical delusion they even seemed to lean out over the *Dobryna*, as if they were going to crush her long before she should be dashed to pieces against their base!

She still made some headway. Puffing, panting, screaming, struggling, as if madly fighting for her life, she bravely tore on through the hell of waters. But the leeway was as decided as ever. She was now but a few cables' lengths from those black and glassy steeps. The fearful dash of the pounding breakers could be heard in spite of the deafening din. All was lost.

"Good-by, Count Timascheff!" said Servadac, extending his hand to the Count, who stood beside him on the quarter-deck.

"Good-by, dear friend!" replied the Count, cordially pressing the proffered hand. "Good-by, till we meet in heaven!"

An enormous wave lifted the *Dobryna* on its gigantic shoulders, as if to hurl her with more deadly effect against the rocks now close at hand.

The Count and the Captain bowed their heads in silent submission to inevitable fate.

Suddenly a ringing voice was heard, loud and clear, coming from the forecastle:

"Look alive there, all hands! Hoist the main jib! Up with the storm jib! Helm amidship!."

It was Procopius giving orders through the speaking-trumpet!

"Ay, ay, sir!" cried the crew with one voice, electrified at the sudden but confident commands, and instantly hurrying to execute them.

Procopius ran back and seized the wheel himself.

"Now then!" he cried loud enough to be heard through the rush of the tempest, "see that the sheets are all clear!"

A sudden roar from the sailors drowned his voice. But it was no shriek of terror nor wail of despair; on the contrary, it was the wild cheer of unexpected triumph. They had suddenly caught glimpse of an opening in the perpendicular wall, dark, straight, narrow, but wide enough for a refuge if not for a passage!

AN OPENING IN THE CRYSTAL COAST.

Into this notch, amidst the dash of the foaming breakers, the hissing of the blinding spray, the roar of the
raging blast, and the cheers of the entranced sailors,
the *Dobryna*, impelled by furious steam, wind, and wave,
but still obedient to every motion of Procopius's able
hand, now desperately plunged, and instantly disappeared.

CHAPTER XIII.

THE ROCK FORTRESS AND ITS INMATES

WELL! I take your bishop, Major," said General Murphy. He had been two days thinking over this move, but he made it at last.

"Take it, General, take it by all means," answered Major Oliphant. "Now, what's the best reply?"

But the best reply, whatever it might be, was not made that morning. In fact, the whole day, February the seventeenth, passed, and left it still unmade. And, in all probability, the next day would be quite as unfruitful in its results.

This was all strictly in order. One move every three days was the average rate of these solid chess-players. They had been four months getting through twenty moves. Moreover, in all that time not a single pawn had been captured on either side, these devoted disciples of Philidor believing with their illustrious master that the management of the pawn, "the soul of chess," alone constituted the superior player. In this, however, they only followed up strictly the invariable rules that every British officer invariably practised, or thought he practised, on every conceivable occasion: "Look before you leap," and "Put no trust in chance."

In many respects General Murphy and Major Oliphant might be considered model officers in her Majesty's service. Both of middle age, both tall, both florid, with a tendency to stoutness, both mutton-chop-whiskered in the true British pattern, both always in uniform, both more supercilious in air than in nature, they hummed and hawed when they spoke, and considered it their bounden duty to petrify every stranger with the stony English stare. English they were everywhere, and English alone they wanted to be. Not to be English, in their eyes, was a blunder as well as a crime. In Murphy's estimation indeed it was the seven deadly sins rolled into one. Though born in Ireland and a scion of that Norman-Irish blood that has produced many of the most eminent men of modern times, he was far more English than the English themselves. He often alluded to "our illustrious ancestors, sir," Cedric and Offa, Aelfred and Eadwine, "Old-English" not "Anglo-Saxons," and never designated the battle of Hastings by any other name than the "disastrous affair at Senlac." But, notwithstanding these little peculiarities, rather amusing than otherwise, both these gentlemen, with all their affected iciness and want of emotion, were most excellent officers and thoroughly reliable soldiers. Judged by the standard of correct taste, "England" might be considered as of a little too frequent occurrence in their vocabulary; but the noble word "duty" often occurred there too, and with such excellent effect as almost to completely redeem the transgression.

The awful catastrophe that had so profoundly affected a portion of our earth they had met with a stolid courage, an imperturbable calmness quite characteristic. One memorable morning they had found themselves suddenly isolated in mid-ocean, with nothing left of their splendid fortress but a rocky islet, and nothing left of their splendid garrison but ten privates and a corporal.

"General," said Major Oliphant, touching his hat with the customary morning salute, "this — aw — well, this is — aw — peculiar."

"Very!" replied General Murphy, promptly returning the salute — though naturally slow and cautious he prided himself on his readiness of speech and promptness of action —"Yes! I should say very peculiar!"

"But — aw — England, you know, is all right!"

"O yes!   England is all right!"

"And — aw — one of her ships will be here soon!"

"Yes! an English vessel may arrive at any moment!"

"Till then we — aw — remain at our post?"

"Yes! Strictly at our post!"

"England expects us, you know, in such cases —"

"To stick to our posts at all hazards!"

The gallant gentlemen pronounced these words with the grand air of undaunted resolution, though they knew very well that "sticking to the post" was the only possible course left for them. For, in the first place, they had no place to escape to; in the second, even if they had, there was no means of getting there, the only thing left in the shape of a vessel being a small boat that by the merest accident had been drawn up ashore for repairs. Whether they would have acted with the same heroism in all circumstances is more than we can say; but one thing is quite certain. Every one of these brave Britishers, soldiers as well as officers, displayed the most ungrumbling patience and stubborn confidence in waiting for a sight of the English vessel that was to come and take them back to their native country.

The soldiers indeed did not appear to think that there was anything worth grumbling about. They had provisions enough left to last thirteen healthy stomachs — English stomachs too — for ten years at least. Mess beef, salt pork, wheaten flour, canned vegetables, dried meats, biscuits, etc., by the shipload, were still in the cellars entirely uninjured and in no danger of injury

As to Bass's Pale Ale, London Dock Port, Hennessy's Brandy, Holland Gin, and other liquors indispensable to British palates, the stores previously laid in as a five years' supply for the whole garrison had also completely escaped destruction, not a single bottle or barrel being lost.

The new order of things in the physical world, the transformation of west to east, the diminution of gravity, the shortening of the days and nights, the deviation of the rotation axis, the change of orbit, etc.— these startling phenomena had, of course, been all carefully noticed by both officers and men, but they had not appeared to give them much concern. The General and the Major, on recovering from the shock and ascertaining its immediate extent, had coolly replaced the scattered pieces on the board and quietly resumed their interminable game. One circumstance, indeed, had seemed at first as rather likely to disturb their equanimity— the strange lightness of the chessmen. They could hardly be made to stand, as if of cork instead of boxwood, the kings and queens being especially unsteady after such a revolution. But with some patience, precaution, and practice, in a few days the players had succeeded in reconstructing their little nations and once more securing them a pretty solid basis.

The private soldiers were not chess-players, and there-

"GENERAL AND MAJOR," BEGAN PIM.

fore felt no inconvenience from the lightness of the pieces, nor, I might add, from any other instance of that particular physical modification. Indeed, but for my strong love of truth, I might say no particular physical modification whatever appeared to give them the slightest concern. But in saying this I should be wrong. One item in the new order of things puzzled them considerably for awhile, and how they settled the question finally may be perhaps worth relating.

The third morning after the catastrophe, just as General Murphy seized a piece, preparatory to making his well-considered move, he stopped to listen to the light tramp of men marching outside, and soon heard a gentle tap on the door of the apartment.

"Come in!" said the General, putting back his piece.

The door opened and in marched the nine privates headed by Corporal Pim, their spokesman.

After a few steps, the Corporal ordered a halt, and, with hand to cap, awaited orders.

"Well, Pim," said the General, "what is it now?"

"General and Major, gentlemen," began Pim in a grand oratorical style but with a rather tremulous voice, "the men's minds is hexercised summat by this 'ere hextraordinary catastrophe, and, before mounting guard to-day, they thought they would come to 'eadquarters to get hencouraged a bit."

" Proceed, Pim," said the General encouragingly.

"General and Major, gentlemen," resumed the Corporal in more confident tones, "the men 'ave deputed me to make two hobservations, one hobservation to General Murphy regarding the pay, and another hobservation to our Major Holiphant regarding the grub."

"Permission to make the first observation is granted," said the General in a dignified but courteous tone.

"Has to our pay, General," resumed the Corporal, now quite at his ease, "the days being now only 'alf as long as they used to be before this 'ere haccident, the men wishes to know if the pay is to be cut down in a simular proportion."

"A sensible question indeed, Pim," answered the General slowly and thoughtfully, "hum — haw — yes, though it takes me rather by surprise, I must acknowledge it to be a very sensible question indeed. However, it admits of only one answer — hum — haw —" with a glance at the Major —"yes, of but one answer. A soldier's pay being calculated by the day, and the day being the period of time lasting from midnight to midnight, irrespective of the number of hours actually elapsing in the interim, the pay will remain as it was. England is still rich enough to pay her soldiers what she has stipulated to pay them."

"Hurrah!" said the ten soldiers with one voice but in a subdued tone, and touching hand to cap.

"Left oblique!" said the Corporal to his men; they obeyed the order and now stood all facing the Major.

"Proceed with your second observation, Pim," said Oliphant, imitating the dignity and urbanity of his superior officer.

"The second hobservation, Major Holiphant, has already remarked," resumed the Corporal as fluently as if repeating his little speech by rote, "refers to our grub. The days being now only six hours long, the men is hanxious to know if we are to heat only twice instead of four times a day?"

"A sensible question indeed, Pim," replied the Major, still paying his superior officer the most delicate of all compliments — imitation, —"hum — haw — yes, though it takes me a little by surprise, I must acknowledge it to be an exceedingly sensible question. However, — hum — haw —" exchanging a few nods with the General, "yes, it admits of but one answer. Military regulations being established in conformity with the ordinary — haw — phenomena of nature, extraordinary phenomena can never be taken into account. You and your men therefore, Corporal, will continue to take your four meals a day as usual. But, as military regulations as well as hygienic principles require these meals to be taken by daylight and at proper inter-

vals, you and your men must be ready for them after
the lapse of every hour and a half. England is rich
enough to feed her soldiers four times a day, and her
soldiers must be ready to take their meals four times
a day, whether the days are long or short!"

"Hurrah!" cried the ten voices as before, only this
time in a tone somewhat more elevated, as expressive
of a higher shade of satisfaction.

"Habout face! march!" said the Corporal, and in
an instant the officers were once more free to resume
their interrupted game.

This is the only instance we can find of any expression of curiosity on the part of these well-drilled Englishmen, as to the immediate results of the late tremendous and most astounding cataclysm.

The two officers, however, when not engaged at chess,
that is at dinner-time or when taking a smoke every
morning on the esplanade after breakfast, would occasionally ask each other why that English vessel was so
very slow in coming in sight? England, they were perfectly willing to acknowledge, had plenty of other
troubles to occupy her at this time. Not to mention
her other great projects, she had lately dispatched quite
a number of her vessels to Australia where, not to be
outdone by France's great Saharian enterprise, she had
determined to establish a vast inland sea of similar char-

acter in a colony exclusively her own. This might excuse her tardiness for a few weeks. Her Indian troubles, her complications with Turkey, her misunderstandings with Russia would perhaps readily explain the delay of a few weeks longer. But when seven weeks, of seven days each, each day being of the good old-fashioned English kind, twenty-four hours long, had elapsed without a single vessel, English or foreign, ever showing itself within sight of the island fortress, the two officers caught each other occasionally glancing at the sea with a shade of something very like uneasiness stealing over their faces.

"Hum — haw — yes," the General would then observe, "this *is* peculiar."

"Hum — haw — yes," the Major would invariably reply, "it is *very* peculiar."

Beyond safe and uncompromising expressions of this kind they never went. If any ugly doubts of England's omniscience and omnipotence began to crawl slowly into their minds, they quietly kept such doubts to themselves. No look, gesture, word or action of theirs ever contributed to give the men the slightest discouragement. Everything went on as usual. Every military regulation was strictly insisted on and invariably complied with. Orders were issued every morning, dress parade was held every evening, and guard was mounted **day** and night by these thirteen men with the strict regularity and attention to detail that had been necessary when a garrison of nearly three thousand soldiers was present. In short, the phenomenon might convulse the face of the world as much as it pleased by its mysterious nature and the stupendous scale of its operations, but it expended its forces in vain on the bull-dog tenacity of British discipline.

Not by any means that these indomitable soldiers had very hard times of it. Every day they got stouter and fatter. Their duties, more nominal than real, were a diversion rather than a toil. Out of Pim's nine men eight unanimously declared that such a life was "hawful jolly," and even the ninth, a constitutional grumbler who set up for a wit, restricted himself to saying that if this 'ere kind of thing lasted six months longer it would become "decidedly slow." As to their 3000 companions who had so suddenly disappeared, they regretted them of course, but they did not often speak of them. Indeed they even seemed to take considerable comfort from a stupid joke made by the grumbler the very morning after the catastrophe. Some one was saying it was a pity so many men were lost.

"Lost!" cried the grumbler. "Who says they're lost? Are n't they all to be found in the Report?"

With this consolation they appeared to be well satis-

fied and in a few days more completely reconciled to
the new state of things. The only emotion to which
they ever gave expression was curiosity, and—once satisfied on the pay and food questions — even their curiosity
they made apparent, not by questioning and talking, but
by always and ever looking out over the dreary sea. As
soon as his duty, whether of eating, sleeping or mounting guard, was over, each soldier invariably climbed the
steep face of the Rock to some favorite crevice, and
there he spent much of the day and even of the night in
watching with stolid gaze the dismal expanse of ocean.
At first, they had determined to look at nothing but an
English ship; then they found themselves anxious to
catch sight of any kind of a ship; at last, they felt that
even the sight of a porpoise's black back would be
a grand relief to the terrible monotony. But, though
their Rock had been one of the best known and most
frequented fortresses on earth, nothing whatever came
into sight in the east, or the west, or the north.

But on the south something was to be seen on which
they often rested their weary eyes and which they fain
would visit if allowed by the military regulations. It
was a black speck, barely visible over the waters and
twelve or thirteen miles distant. They knew very well
that it was the upper portion of a mountain fortress
that had somewhat resembled their own. The same

cataclysm had attacked both, and reduced them to mere
rocky islets hardly any longer habitable.

But, even if habitable, was it any longer inhabited?
Was it a mere deserted and abandoned rock, or was it
the refuge of some survivors of the terrible catastrophe?
This is the question the soldiers often asked themselves,
but always in vain. It was exceedingly tantalizing, but
they carefully suppressed all curious inquiries.

One morning, however, things took such a turn as
made it seem that their curiosity on the subject would
be gratified soon and satisfactorily. Instead of retiring, as usual, after the morning cigar, to their sitting-
room to resume the famous game of chess, General
Murphy and Major Oliphant, in full uniform, were
seen directing their footsteps to the creek where the
little boat was moored. They were followed by the
General's man Kirke (the Major's had disappeared
with the others), staggering under a pair of oars, some
cushions, two guns, a telescope, and a basket of provisions. Depositing his burden in the boat and ar-
ranging it as well as he could, Kirke jumped ashore
and held the chain whilst the two officers, stepping
in, took their seats and began handling the oars.
Then, throwing in the chain, he gave the boat a vigorous push that sent her several yards from the shore.
In a few minutes, to the unbounded surprise of the

little garrison thus so unceremoniously left in charge of Corporal Pim, the two officers, still in complete uniform, and now free from the land, turned the head of the boat towards the black speck on the southern horizon, and began to ply the oars with such vigor and effect that in an hour they had almost completely disappeared.

Thirty-six hours afterwards they returned, as quietly and as mysteriously as they had departed. Their faces looked a little flushed from the long row, but their scarlet uniforms were still without speck or stain. Leaving the boat and its contents in Kirke's charge, they quietly returned the respectful salutations of the men and, without exchanging a syllable even with Corporal Pim one way or another regarding the object of their voyage, proceeded quietly to their quarters.

What had brought them to the rock? A sentiment of humanity? A prompting of interest? The spur of curiosity? Nobody could tell. What had they seen?—a question as unanswerable as the former. On such a subject they were as silent as the grave. Even Pim knew nothing and could tell the men nothing except that the "Guv'nors" seemed pretty well pleased with the result of their trip, and had prepared a Report on the subject, signed and sealed with all the formalities and addressed to:

ADMIRAL FAIRFAX,

First Lord of the Admiralty,

United Kingdom of Great Britain and Ireland.

This they had given him in charge with strict orders to deliver it to the first English ship that came in sight.

But no ship, English or otherwise, had come in sight by the seventeenth of February, the day on the morning of which, as mentioned in the beginning of this chapter, General Murphy took the Major's bishop, and the rest of which had passed without any corresponding reply on the part of the Major.

Next morning at breakfast, after the usual salutations, the General asked the Major if he remembered what day it was?

"Don't I?" was the immediate answer. "It is the grandest day on the calendar!"

"Yes!" chimed in the General; "it's a day to make every Englishman's heart throb more proudly in his bosom."

"A day to be celebrated with — haw — salvoes — yes, salvoes of artillery from one end of the world to the other!" cried the Major with as much enthusiasm as he could show.

"I don't see," observed the General, "why the —

hum — haw — peculiar condition of our affairs on the
Rock should prevent us from celebrating the — hum —
haw — never-to-be-forgotten birthday of our glorious
sovereign with all the usual honors.''

"On the contrary!" replied the Major.

"Her Majesty's government has not placed itself —
hum — haw — in communication with us," said the
General, "but is her Majesty — hum — haw — to be held
accountable for that?"

"Certainly not!" replied the Major, "— hum — haw
— most assuredly not!"

"Bring tumblers, Kirke, and open a bottle of the
oldest Port! — Fill to the brim, Major Oliphant!"

"Most happy, General."

The gentlemen stood up ceremoniously, glass in hand.

"The health and happiness of her illustrious Majesty,
Queen Victoria the First, with all the honors!" said the
General, solemnly and impressively.

"Hip, hip, hurrah!" answered the Major, emptying
his tumbler.

"Fill again, Major! — With all the honors!"

"Hip, hip, hurrah!"

"Once more, Major! — With all the honors!"

"Hip, hip, hurrah!"

The loyal ceremony thus religiously completed with
"all the honors" (three tumblers of old Port each swal-

lowed at a gulp), the gentlemen took their seats and
filled their glasses once more.   The General then rang
the bell and summoned Corporal Pim.

The Corporal appeared in a short time, hastily wiping
his lips with the back of his hand while trying to make
the salute.

"Corporal Pim," said General Murphy, grandly and
even majestically, "you and your men are no doubt
well aware that to-day is February the eighteenth, reckoning according to the good old English calendar, and
therefore the birthday of Her Most Glorious Majesty."

The Corporal took off his hat, gave a hiccup, but did
his best to look grave and loyal, and bowed his head for
the five seconds required by military regulations.

"Corporal Pim!" resumed the General still more
grandly and impressively, "we shall fire, as usual, the
twenty-one guns prescribed for the regular celebration
of this — hum — haw — most glorious and ever-to-be
remembered anniversary."

"They shall be — (hiccup) — shall be fired, General!"

"Corporal Pim! let such precautions be taken that as
few arms or legs as possible may be shot off.   At the
present time, Corporal Pim, we want all the able-bodied
men we have, and a proper regard for the benefit of the
service suggests that the number of mutilations — hum —
haw -— be reduced to the lowest minimum attainable."

"They shall be cautioned, General, (hiccup) — shall be carefully cautioned," answered the Corporal, very willing to promise but too mindful of former experiences to promise much.

"Corporal Pim! — hum — haw — that is all!"

"All right, Gen — (hiccup) eral!"

Of all the innumerable pieces of ordnance that had till lately supplied this great Rock-fortress, there now remained but one, an old-fashioned muzzle-loader, with a caliber nearly a foot in diameter. From such an enor-mous cannon as this salutes were seldom or never fired, but it was now either this or no salute at all.

Pim, having cautioned his men as to the necessity for extra care in special regard to the General's request, ordered the twenty-one cartridges to be brought to the embrasure where the cannon stood with its muzzle projecting through a port-hole.

General Murphy and Major Oliphant, in full uniform with cocked hat and feathers, superintended operations with very particular interest, for their faces were much redder and their eyes more sparkling than usual.

The cannon was loaded in strict accordance with the rules of *The Artillery-man's Manual*, which Pim stopped every minute with great gravity to read, and the joyful salvoes commenced. After every shot the Corporal also tried to insist that the fuse should be completely extin-

guished, so as to render a premature discharge impossible and thus save the gunners their normal number of
legs, arms and fingers.   His exertions were not very successful.   The gunners, instead of extinguishing the fuse,
lit it at each end, and several times discharged the piece
before orders were given.   Strange to say, however, in
spite of a relaxation of discipline due to an over-allow-
ance of brandy in honor of the day, no untoward accident whatever occurred worse than one gunner losing
his thumb and another the small joint of his little finger.
With these exceptions everything passed off well.

Neither the men nor the officers were, however, at all
satisfied with the proceedings.   The big cannon, though
charged with its ordinary tremendous cartridge vigor-
ously rammed home, did not make half noise enough.
The air, not much more than half as dense as it had
been seven weeks ago, was not able to rush together
with the grand detonating effects of old.   No more of
those ear-splitting reverberations, rolled back from the
rocky projections, which had transformed the short simple cannon report into rattling peals of living thunder.
No more of these majestic rumblings, repercussions, and
undulations propagated by the elasticity of the air, and
extending themselves miles and miles in all directions.
The cannoniers listened for them in vain, and, not hearing them, began to be ashamed of themselves.   On

former occasions of this glorious nature, whenever they had not succeeded in rendering deaf for the rest of their days at least a half dozen of incautious civilians who had come too near the cannon, they considered the celebration a failure. But now they were all obliged to make the humiliating confession that the noise was not loud enough to deafen a twelve-month old baby.

"A miserable pop-gun!" muttered General Murphy every now and then, unable to control his fast increasing disgust.

"A wretched penny pistol!" was Major Oliphant's invariable reply.

"On any other occasion I should not care a pin!" cried the General at last, out of all patience.

"It certainly compromises the dignity of our Royal anniversary," observed the Major.

Twenty shots had been fired, but, just as the sponger was cleaning out the piece, preparatory for the twenty-first, a luminous idea suddenly struck the General.

"Put a shell in this time," said he to the rammer; "I wish to ascertain the range of this piece."

"The General desires to make an experiment," cried the Major to Corporal Pim. "You understand, don't you?"

"All right, Major," said the Corporal; "shperiment shall be made!"

He gave the necessary orders, and in a few minutes one of the men returned, dragging a truck which contained one of the shells that, though weighing at least two hundred pounds, the old cannon had often sent a distance of two or three miles. By following this shell with the telescope, as the General rather loudly and emphatically explained, they could easily measure the line it took to fall into the sea, and from that readily calculate what would be the cannon's range in the new order of things. Himself and the Major stood near the gun, one at each side, glass in hand, ready to observe.

The piece was loaded, pointed at an angle of forty-two degrees, the most favorable angle for distance, and fired.

The two officers jumped at least a foot in astonishment.

"By Saint George!" cried the startled General.

"By the great Saint George!" echoed the Major, surprised to the last degree.

The two officers looked at each other in momentary dismay, eyes staring, mouths wide open, arms stiffly extended, and fingers nervously clinching the useless telescopes.

Owing to the diminution of gravity, a phenomenon over which they had not expended much thought, the

FIRING THE GREAT GUN.

projectile had vanished like a flash. It could not have fallen in the sea; therefore it must have disappeared beyond the horizon or perhaps left the earth altogether!

"That horizon is at least twelve miles off!" cried the General, gradually recovering his breath.

"Twelve miles at the very least!" gasped the Major.

"Hark!" cried the General suddenly. "What's that? Can it be an echo?"

All listened intently.

Yes! Three separate reports were heard coming successively from the very quarter in which the shell had disappeared! The sounds, though extremely faint, were too distinct to be a mere echo.

"A ship!" cried the General.

"A ship, undoubtedly!" cried the Major.

"An English ship!" cried the General.

"Of course an English ship!" echoed the Major.

All eyes were now fixed on one point of the horizon with breathless interest.

After the lapse of some minutes, two little specks showed themselves, and were immediately pronounced to be mast-heads.

"I told you so," said the General; "England is hastening to relieve us!"

"England must have heard the sound of our cannon!" cried the Major rather hastily.

"Which I 'ope our shell has n't struck that 'ere wessel!" murmured Pim to himself with some misgiving.

In less than half an hour her whole keel was visible; a long line of black smoke showed her to be a steamer; she was evidently making for the island, though the little flag fluttering from her gaff was still too far off to be distinctly seen.

"Run up the colors to salute our vessel!" cried the General in great excitement.

"Up with the colors to salute the English ship!' repeated the Major to Corporal Pim, who had the order instantly executed amidst loud cheers and great hat-wavings.

But suddenly the two officers simultaneously dropped their glasses, and would have fallen in a fit if Pim had not held them. They had at last caught distinct sight of the little flag fluttering from the gaff — an oblique blue cross on a white ground.

"The Russian flag!" they both exclaimed in accents of blank dismay, while they mechanically clutched on to Pim for support.

They looked at each other for at least five minutes in perfect silence. Mingled disappointment and surprise had struck the gallant Englishmen speechless.

CHAPTER XIV.

A STARTLING DISCOVERY.

THE yacht, soon near enough to allow her name to be easily read — *Dobryna*, made for a little roadstead in the south part of the islet. This was formed by a curving line of rocks extending far enough out to sea to afford some protection against the northwest wind, which was still blowing, but with considerably reduced violence. The anchor thrown out and the boat lowered, in a few minutes the Count and the Captain stepped ashore and found themselves in the majestic presence of General Murphy and Major Oliphant in full uniform and stiff as turkeycocks.

"Heaven be thanked! gentlemen," cried Servadac, hurrying up with his French impetuosity and eagerly stretching out his hands, "that we are at last arrived at a Christian country. You too have escaped the terrible disaster, and we are most happy to congratulate you."

He still held out his hands in the highest good-

humor, but no expected cordial squeeze was returned
by the English officers.   They stood there before him
as cold and reserved as a pair of cast-iron statues.

He was not, however, easily disconcerted, and, being
already aware that English stiffness oftener proceeds
from conscious awkwardness than from silly affecta-
tion, he endeavored to set these shy officers at their
ease by assuming a heartiness of manner that he was
very far from feeling.

He resumed the initiative, therefore, still speaking
French, not only for his own convenience, but also
because to be addressed in French an English gentleman always considers a delicate compliment.

"By this time, no doubt, you have heard from
France, Russia, England, Europe in general?   Are
you in communication with your own people?   Have
you been — ?"

"May I ask whom I have the honor of addressing?"
interrupted General Murphy in perfect French, but
drawing himself up with a proud air that added at
least another inch to his height.   The Major, also,
grandly twirling his moustache, surveyed the strangers
with an interrogative air.

"Ah!" cried Servadac with a shrug of the shoulders
which he did not attempt to conceal; "excuse my
forgetfulness!   We have not yet had an introduction."

THE INTRODUCTION.

Then taking off his cap and presenting his companion, he bowed and said:

"Count Wassili Timascheff!"

"Sir John Temple Oliphant, Major of Her Majesty's Hundred and Ninety-ninth of the Line!" said Murphy, presenting his companion with equal ceremony.

The two gentlemen saluted each other with a stiff bow.

"Staff Captain Servadac!" said the Count in his turn.

"Sir Hugh Fitzgerald Murphy, Brigadier-General, in command of the Garrison," replied Major Oliphant in a stately tone.

The Captain and the General bowed still more stiffly.

The laws of etiquette being now strictly complied with, conversation was rendered possible.

"This way, gentlemen," said Murphy, with a courteous motion of his hand to his guests, showing them the way to the sitting-room. This was a kind of casemate hewn in the rock, with the light admitted through port-holes. But it was sumptuously and even elegantly furnished: bright tapestry concealed the dark and dingy walls; sporting pictures, and statues — among others a beautiful bust of Her Most Gracious Majesty — gave it a gay and sprightly look; soft carpets and plenty of chairs made it cosy and comfortable; a decanter and

some empty glasses stood on a sideboard, and the whole
room was pervaded with the odor of rich old port.

All took seats, but an awkward silence prevailed for
several seconds. The Englishmen assumed a listening
air, but did not say a word. The Captain, chafing
under all this ceremony, seemed decidedly indisposed
to resume the conversation. The Count, finding the
initiative thus to devolve on himself, judged it best
to suppose everything said before the introduction to
be forgotten, and therefore began at the beginning.

"Gentlemen," said he, "you are no doubt aware
that a cataclysm, the cause and the full extent of which
are still alike unknown to us, took place on the night of
the 31st of December and the 1st of January. Judging
by what remains of the territory that you previously
occupied, you must yourselves have had severe experience of its effects."

The English officers signified their acquiescence with
this proposition by a nod of their heads so mechanical
and simultaneous that a pair of automatons could not
have done it better.

"My companion and friend, Captain Servadac,"
continued the Count, "has suffered considerably from
the visitation. He was engaged at the time in performing his duties as staff-officer on the coast of
Algeria —"

" You mean Algiers, Count, don't you?" interrupted Murphy, with his eyes on the ceiling. " Of course you do. Well, on the coast of Algiers —"

" Excuse me, General," said the Count, with a slight twinkle in his eye. " I don't mean Algiers just now; I mean Algeria."

" Algeria? Algeria?" said Murphy, closing his eyes and twirling his thumbs as if in close self-communion. " Oliphant, what is Algeria?"

The General, like most Englishmen, was rather weak in geography, and in a case of this kind unhesitatingly relied on the Major's superior information.

" Algeria is a Turkish country on the north coast of Africa," answered the Major in reply to his chief. " It was formerly notorious as a den of pirates, but for the last twenty or thirty years — hum — haw — it has been the penal colony of some European power, Spanish or French — I forget which — but it's really of no conse-quence — Spanish most probably."

" Excuse me for undertaking to correct you a little, Major Oliphant," quickly and somewhat excitedly ob-served Servadac. " Algeria is not Spanish. Never was Spanish. It is French of the French!"

Not a gesture from the automatons by way of reply, except the resumption of their listening air.

" My companion and friend," continued the Count

in a tone as cold as ice, "was stationed near the mouth of the Sheliff on the terrible night in question. In the morning he discovered that one part of the African continent had been suddenly turned into an island, but that the rest seemed to have completely disappeared from the face of the earth."

"Ah!" said Murphy, slightly lifting his eyebrows.

"Oh!" said Oliphant, tapping his finger-nails together.

And then a general pause ensued.

"Indeed!" observed Murphy, just to say something.

"Is it possible!" added Oliphant, helping out his superior.

The guests rigidly preserving a freezing silence, Murphy was compelled to give his tongue a little more play.

"Count Timascheff," said he, "may I ask — aw — aw — how you yourself spent the night in question?"

"At sea, General Murphy, in my yacht," replied the Count, "and I must really consider the escape of myself and my crew as simply miraculous."

"Quite miraculous," repeated Oliphant, to show how interested he was in his guest's narrative.

"Chance threw us on the Algerian coast," continued the Count, "where I was fortunate enough to

GENERAL MURPHY OBSERVES.

find in the new island my friend Captain Servadac and his Orderly Ben Zouf."

" Ben ——? " asked Murphy, to show that he was listening.

" Zouf! " cried Servadac impatiently, pronouncing the word as if it had been " ouf! " the expression used by angry Frenchmen when they want to let off steam.

"The Captain being as impatient as myself," continued the Count, "to find out how things really stood, we embarked together on the *Dobryna*, and, sailing eastwardly, endeavored to find out what remained of the Algerian colony. Not the slightest trace of it could be found ! "

The two Englishmen looked at each other with an expression that seemed to say "What else could you expect from a colony founded by these fickle Frenchmen?" So, at least, the Captain interpreted the glance, and he was jumping up to give an angry reply when a sudden accession of his native politeness fortunately restrained him.

" Gentlemen," calmly continued the Count, "the disaster, I am sorry to say, has been immense. Along the whole of the eastern portion of the Mediterranean we have not been able to find a single trace of the old countries — neither Algeria — nor Tunis — except one little point, a rock emerging from the sea, near the ruins of Carthage, and containing the tomb of Saint Louis.''

''Saint Louis? Saint Louis?'' asked Murphy, who was no stronger in hagiology than in geography. ''Oliphant, who was Saint Louis?''

''Saint Louis — hum — haw —'' answered the Major, a little more diffidently this time; ''Saint Louis is a seaport town in the United States famous for cotton and corn and Indians. But — haw — the Saint Louis spoken of by the Count — hum — was some martyr of that name in the old times — hum — haw — yes, in the old times.''

''You're right, Major Oliphant,'' observed Servadac. more impatiently than even before; ''Saint Louis *was* a martyr; but he was more, he was a king of France; he was still more, he was the best and greatest king that ever sat on a throne in any age and in any country!''

The automatons showed their appreciation of this volunteered information by a stiff formal bow, and the Count, rather disliking to be interrupted so often, hastened to conclude his narrative in as few words as possible.

He told how the yacht had sailed as far south as the latitude of the Gulf of Cabes; that no sign could be found of the Saharian Sea, the new French enterprise (''no wonder!'' said the Englishmen's mutual glance);

that a new coast of a most strange and startling formation had suddenly sprung up north of Tripoli, which,
having run eastwardly as far as a point between the
14th and 15th meridians, suddenly formed a right angle
with itself and followed a course directly north till it
reached the Island of Malta.

"Which island, I am sorry to say," interrupted Captain Hector in a tone expressive of anything but sorrow,
"together with its cities, its forts, arsenals, dock-yards,
soldiers, officers, and even its governor, has gone down
to keep company with Algeria at the bottom of the
sea!"

A shadow instantly fell on the automatic faces, but
only to vanish in a moment.

"The sudden disappearance of our Island of Malta,"
said Murphy, quietly, "is — hum — haw — rather incredible, Captain Servadac."

"Why so, General?" asked the Captain, firing up.

"Are you aware," asked Oliphant, "that — hum —
Malta is an English possession?"

"I am just as well aware of that fact as I am that an
Englishman is not a Fejee Islander," answered the Captain rather pertly, and by no means trying to conceal his
irritation. "Nevertheless, down she went like a lump
of lead!"

"Gentlemen," said Murphy, not knowing what to

make of this astounding information, and at last showing some real interest in his guests' story, "you must
have made some mistake in your bearings."

"Some mistake, you know," chimed in Oliphant.

"This confounding of east and west," continued
Murphy, "is calculated to puzzle —"

"I know it would puzzle me," candidly observed the
Major, "and I don't really see how serious error can be
possibly avoided —"

"No, gentlemen," interrupted the Count calmly.
"No error whatever has been committed. You cannot
help submitting to indisputable evidence. England has
had her share in the general disaster. Not only has
Malta disappeared, but a new continent has closed up
the eastern half of the Mediterranean. Only for a narrow break in the coast which we hit on almost providentially at an instant of the greatest danger, we should
have never been able to reach you. We are also very
much concerned to add that every trace of the Ionian
Islands has disappeared except what remains of your
Corfu."

"Our Corfu!" repeated Murphy, evidently not understanding what the Count meant by the expression.
In his trouble, as usual, he mechanically looked at Oliphant for assistance.

"Count," asked the Major, "did you really say *our
Corfu?*"

"Of course he did!" answered the Captain quickly. "Your Corfu — Corfu — what else could he say but your Cor-fu?"

(The Captain maliciously intensified the French pronunciation *Cor-fou*, amusing himself with the pun.)

The two Englishmen were this time really too much astonished to speak; Murphy simply had no idea of what the strangers meant; Oliphant kept silent for fear of making some blunder.

"Have you heard from England lately, General Murphy," asked the Count, determined to come to an understanding, "either by English vessel or submarine cable?"

"No, Count Timascheff, we have not," answered Murphy; "no vessel has arrived and the cable is broken."

"Then why not put yourself in communication with England by means of the Italian wires?"

"Italian? Italian? You mean the Spanish wires, don't you?"

"Well, Italian or Spanish, what's the difference," asked Servadac, "so you have received news from London?"

"We have received no news whatever for seven weeks," answered Murphy. "But no matter for that! It's a mere question of time!'

"A pure question of time!" echoed the Major. "It can't be anything else — that is —"

"Unless there's no London to hear from!" interrupted Servadac, but with much gravity.

"No London!!" cried both officers, with one breath.

"No London, of course, if there's no England!"

"No England!!"

The two Englishmen jumped from their seats as lively as if a spring had shot them up.

"Before England is destroyed," said Murphy slowly, "France must dis —"

"France is solider than England!" interrupted Servadac. "She must be solider since she is part of the solid Continent!"

"France solider than England!!"

"Certainly! England is only an island, and part of her were always low enough to be easily swallowed up by an angry sea!"

"Captain Servadac!" cried Murphy, hardly able to speak with anger. "You forget —"

"Captain Servadac!" interrupted Oliphant, red with passion. "You don't seem to be aware —"

"Gentlemen!" cried the Count, who, not being concerned in this bickering about nationalities, looked on it all as something very ridiculous, "gentlemen, with a little more coolness and patience —"

But the Captain would not let him finish. He was by this time so exasperated that he was perfectly willing, by fighting the two Englishmen then and there, to settle everything by the sword. But his French politeness shrunk from challenging a man in his own house, and he made a proposition.

"Gentlemen," he observed with studied calmness, "I think our little discussion would admit of easier settlement out of doors. You are here in your own house, you know. Suppose we adjourn to the fresh air."

So saying, he stepped out of the room and was immediately followed by his three companions as far as a little platform in the upper part of the island. This the Captain evidently considered a kind of neutral territory, for once there he stopped, and when all were once more together, he took off his cap and addressed the English officers with the most winning politeness.

"Gentlemen," said he, "however impoverished France may be since she has lost Algeria, she is still strong enough to reply to every attack, come from what quarter it may. Now I, a French officer, claim the same right to represent my country on this island as that on which you claim to represent England!"

"Eh!" exclaimed Murphy.

"What's that?" cried Oliphant.

"And since we are here on neutral ground —" continued the Captain.

"Neutral ground!" exclaimed Murphy.

"You're on English ground!" cried Oliphant.

"English ground!" repeated Servadac in great surprise.

"Certainly English ground," said Murphy, who began to suspect that the Gascon Captain was making some mistake, "or British ground rather, and protected by the British flag," he added, pointing to the royal standard of Great Britain and Ireland floating from a flagstaff on the summit of a high rock.

"That flag amounts to nothing!" cried Servadac, but in less assured tones; "you have simply run it up there since the catastrophe."

"Pardon me, Captain, it was there long before."

"Possibly, General, since you say so, but only as a flag of protection, not one of possession!"

"A flag of protection!" exclaimed the two officers, opening their eyes.

"Certainly," cried the Captain; "is not this rocky islet the sole remnant of what was once the territory of a Republic under English protection?"

"A Republic!" gasped Murphy.

"Under English protection!" re-echoed Oliphant.

THE FLAG OF THE ROCK.

"And for my part," continued the Captain in excited tones, "I never could understand on what ground you based your claim to protect the Republic of the Ionian Islands!"

"The Ionian Islands!" cried both officers simultaneously with the little breath that surprise had left them.

The Englishmen should certainly know where they were, and their surprise was too genuine not to impart to the Captain some little misgiving. Had he committed a blunder? If the *Dobryna* had not landed on the Ionian Islands, where could she have landed? He began to feel somewhat disconcerted, and even the habitually cool, clear-headed Timascheff appeared decidedly puzzled.

A short pause set the whole party more at their ease, and then Murphy addressed the Captain in calm and measured accents:

"Captain Servadac, you are certainly laboring under some misconception for which I cannot possibly account. Allow me to put an end to it. You stand this moment on a soil that is as English as England herself. It has been her property since 1704 by right of conquest, by right of possession, and by right of treaty. In 1727, 1779, and 1782, united France and Spain contested these rights, but without success. We are, therefore, now as much on English soil as if we were standing in the centre of Trafalgar Square, London.''

"Are we not in Corfu?" asked the Captain.

"Are we not in the Ionian Islands?" asked the Count.

"No, gentlemen," replied Murphy. "You are in Gibraltar.''

"Gibraltar!!" burst from the lips of the Count and the Captain, unable to believe their ears.

"Gibraltar! Impossible!" cried the Count. "We sailed to one end of the Mediterranean; how can we be now at the other?"

"Gibraltar! Impossible!" cried the Captain. "We sailed always east, and how can we be now in the west?"

"Nevertheless, Gibraltar it is," observed Oliphant in cutting tones — his blunder regarding Algeria was now fully avenged —"and I cannot understand how sailors of your experience — Hello, Pim, what's the matter now?"

Pim's sudden appearance on the scene cut short the Major's observation. No wonder. The Corporal was in a pitiable state. His clothes were torn, his eyes blackened, and his ears bleeding. He gave the military salute, however, with great gravity, and made the most praiseworthy efforts to "brace up and have some style about him," while he told his story.

"The men's had a (hiccup) a haltercation, Major and General," said the Corporal in English, of course, but rather thickly, "a halter- (hiccup) cation with them 'ere Rooshian fellers. I tried to stop the row, but this (hiccup) is the way I got served out. My own fellers, I must say (hiccup) tore my uniform, but a Rooshian 'it me on the 'ead with a hoar."

"Hit you on the head with an oar!" exclaimed Murphy to whom Oliphant looked for an expression of opinion. "Such conduct is monstrous! How was it all, Pim? I require to know it before ordering the fellow to be put in irons."

"It was all along of that 'ere last shot of ours, General," answered the Corporal. "It seems, when the shell burst, one of the fragments knocked the pipe out of the beggar's mouth, and another (hiccup) fetched him on the nose and drew the blood. Has well as our men could hunderstand his lingo, the Rooshian did not much mind the hinjury done his nose. But the loss of his pipe he could not abear, allowing it was our duty to give him one hinstead. Our fellers only laughed and jeered, but the (hiccup) beggar, seeing Private Brown smoking, he goes right up to him, snatches the pipe out of his mouth and (hiccup) claps it into his hown!"

"He shall be knouted for this!" said Timascheff, mortified at his serf's want of discipline.

"Not at all, Count!" cried Servadac quickly. "He did perfectly right! What business had these crazy Englishmen to fire a shot that broke his pipe?"

"Crazy Englishmen!" cried Murphy, reddening at the insult and involuntarily searching for his sword.

"Crazy Englishmen!" cried Oliphant, his eyes flashing with rage. "No gentleman should ever use such an expression!"

"Unless it is at once withdrawn," said Murphy, "our interview is ended."

"Yes, friend Servadac," hastily observed the Count, doing his best to keep cool; "such an expression can't be defended. Withdraw it."

"Count," said Servadac calmly, "I shall withdraw it with pleasure and even apologize for it, if you promise not to knout Panofka."

"Such a condition, Captain Servadac," interrupted Murphy, "proposed in our presence is only doubling the insult. We meant no harm to yourselves or your men. This being our Most Gracious Majesty's birthday, we were firing a salute —"

"Firing a salute with a hundred-pound shell!" interrupted Servadac. "Gentlemen, this is really asking a little too much of our credulity!"

"That such a proceeding was not in conformity with strict military regulations, I don't deny," said Murphy, somewhat in confusion, "but on Her Majesty's birth-day, you know, we — hum — haw — had taken, as usual, a few glasses of extra good Port —"

"And your men, no doubt, a few glasses of extra good brandy!" interrupted Servadac, once more in good-humor. "I see it all now! Come, Count! No need of further explanation! I have the honor, gentlemen, to bid you a very good-morning!"

"Yes," said the Count, "it's now all quite clear. Good-morning, gentlemen," he added with a most ceremonious bow, "till we meet again."

In a minute the two friends were at the little wharf, where they saw the Russian sailors resting on their oars, but far enough from shore to be in perfect safety from the heavy fists of the angry Englishmen. The Count and the Captain, however, made their way through the threatening crowd without any diffi-culty; the boat approached and picked them up without opposition; and two hours afterwards, the *Dobryna* could see no more of the remains of the great fortress than a small black speck rapidly dis-appearing in the southern horizon.

CHAPTER XV.

ONE SOLUTION OF THE RIDDLE.

THE Captain and the Count soon forgot the momentary irritation into which they had been thrown by
the inhospitable conduct of the English officers.   Under
other circumstances they might have amused themselves
over it, and even highly enjoyed the mystifications
under which both parties had been laboring while endeavoring to interchange their experiences.   Even
Procopius, with all his gravity and matter-of-fact ways,
burst out every now and then into a hearty fit of laughter while listening to the Captain's account of the interview with the haughty Englishmen who had been taking
too much wine.

But the astounding geographical fact they had just
learned soon put an end at once and forever to all ideas
of merriment.   Procopius, hardly able to trust his ears,
made both Count and Captain repeat several times the
exact words of the English officers, as well as they could
be recalled.   This statement he wrote out carefully, and
then corrected and amended the transcript according to

the suggestions of his listeners, until he was perfectly satisfied that he had learned all that could be learned from the English officers at Gibraltar.

Now what had this interview taught them that admitted of no possible dispute whatever? Procopius wrote down the whole case, and read it aloud for his listeners to comment upon.

"Starting from the west point of the Isle of Gourbi," so ran the paper, "that is to say, from thirty minutes east longitude (Greenwich), the *Dobryna* had met no stop in her eastern course until she arrived at 15° 30′ east; her direct eastern course, therefore, amounted to fifteen degrees. The strait, running also east, which had given them passage through the unknown continent and through which they had been driven with great velocity, could not be less than three degrees and a half in length. The distance from the east end of this strait to Gibraltar might be reckoned at about four degrees. Finally, the distance from Gibraltar to the west point of Gourbi is about seven degrees. The summary of this eastern course can be seen in the following table :

	DEG.	MIN.
From west point of Gourbi to New Strait	15	0
" west point of New Strait to east point of do. .	3	30
" east point of New Strait to Gibraltar . . .	4	30
" Gibraltar to west point of Gourbi	7	00
Total length of eastern course,	30	00

"That is to say, the distance travelled by the *Dobryna* from her point of departure back to the same point, on the same parallel, always following an easterly course, or, what is precisely the same thing, sailing round the entire circumference of the earth, was now no more than 30 degrees !

"First conclusion.—*The other* 330 *degrees of the terrestrial globe are absolutely and unaccountably missing.*

"Before the catastrophe if, starting from Malta, we desired to reach Gibraltar by following an exclusively eastern course, we should first sail through the eastern half of the Mediterranean, then the Suez Canal, then the Red Sea, the Indian Ocean, the Straits of Sunda, the Pacific, and finally the Atlantic Ocean. Whereas at present the face of nature is so changed that, instead of a voyage of enormous length, a new strait, less than two hundred miles long, had brought the *Dobryna* to within less than two hundred and twenty-five miles distance from Gibraltar !

"Second conclusion.—*Our terrestrial globe at present can hardly be two thousand miles in circumference.*

"This is, no doubt, a most astounding conclusion," said Procopius, commenting on his paper, "but it is logically inevitable. The diameter of the world on which we are at present is not quite five hundred miles in length, that is, sixteen times shorter than it was before the catastrophe. Our very existence is not more certain than that we have sailed completely around the world — or what remains of it ! "

"Any other conclusion appears to me impossible," observed the Count. "It certainly explains most of the strange phenomena so far observed. Thus, on a globe thus reduced in volume the force of gravity must be considerably diminished. And I can readily comprehend why the rotation of its axis has been so accelerated that the interval of time elapsing between two sunrises is no more than twelve hours long. As to the new orbit which we are undoubtedly describing around the sun — let us see — how do you explain that, Procopius ? I think you can do it."

"Father, and friend Servadac," said Procopius in the solemn tones of conviction, "there are no two ways of explaining our change of orbit. There is but one. A fragment has been blown off the surface of the Earth by some internal convulsion and has carried along with it a portion of the atmosphere. This fragment is now traversing the solar spaces in an orbit which is no longer the terrestrial. This fragment is our present and only home ! "

The three men remained looking at each other for a few minutes in perfect silence, as if thunder-stricken by the revelation. It was certainly a plausible theory. As the Count had said, taking all the facts of the case into consideration, any other conclusion seemed impossible. There was scarcely a phenomenon that it left unexplained. But, on the other hand, what a monstrous supposition! How repugnant to reason, to common sense, to the simplest natural law! And, if true, what would be the consequence? The mind instinctively shrank from dwelling on this question, though it could not help recurring to it again and again. Where was the enormous block going? What path was it following? What was the eccentricity of its orbit? How far from the sun would this new celestial body have to travel? How long would it take to make a complete revolution around the centre of attraction? Would it keep on moving, like certain comets, for myriad millions of miles through boundless space? Would it ever return to the source of heat and life? Finally, did the plane of its orbit coincide with that of the Earth's near enough to give rise to the hope that some day or other it might once more be reunited with the globe from which it had been so suddenly and so violently separated?

These difficult questions, running hastily through the Captain's mind, perplexed him enough to make him look on Procopius's theory with considerable disfavor, if not to reject it altogether.

"Lieutenant," he cried at last, "I can't accept your explanation!"

"No? Why not?" asked Procopius.

"Let us understand each other," said the Captain. "Do you mean to say that a fragment of the Earth, comprising that portion of its surface lying between Gibraltar and Malta, is a new asteroid, our present place of abode, and now travelling in solar space?"

"Yes, that is exactly what I mean to say."

"I need not remind you, Lieutenant," said the Captain, "that accounting for some or even many phenomena is not enough to validate a theory. To be unobjectionable, it must account for *all*. One I will allude to, but will not press just now. How does your theory account for our present rotation from east to west? If we were a mere detached fragment of the Earth, should we not be still rotating, like the parent planet, from west to east? I will not, however, press this question; I have another of far greater importance, and which, I think, attacks your theory in its most vital part. How does your theory explain the phenomenon of a crystal coast surrounding the sea? A fragment suddenly detached from the Earth should certainly show the granite and limestone

foundation of the earth's surface, and not a crystal
formation of so singular a character that we can't
form an idea of its real nature!"

"Yes, Procopius," said the Count, "that's a serious
blow aimed at your extraordinary theory. Not that
I consider your theory impossible or inconsistent with
any physical law. We can easily conceive a fragment
of surface to be suddenly detached from the Earth,
that it carries off with it a portion of the atmosphere
and of the Mediterranean waters, and even that its
motions both of revolution and rotation are no longer
identical with those of the Earth. All this we might
readily admit for the sake of argument; but, as the
Captain asks, how does your theory explain the appearance of this precipitous wall, bare, glassy, bleak,
columnar, more like the Giant's Causeway on an extensive scale than the green, beautiful, and picturesque
shores that fringe almost every portion of the Mediterranean?"

"I see the full force of the objections, Father," answered Procopius, "and at present I must acknowledge
that I cannot make the proper reply. Time, however,
I am sure, will effectually solve the difficulty. A theory
that explains many things otherwise totally inexplicable
is not to be lightly abandoned merely because it cannot
explain all."

" What do you think could have been the cause of the disruption ? " asked the Count.

"If I were permitted to guess at something of which I really know nothing," answered Procopius, "I should say that the sudden expansion of some of the inconceivably powerful forces at work in the Earth's centre was great enough to cause an explosion in a weak part of the Earth's crust. The natural result followed. The enormous block was detached, and whirled into space —"

" Like a ball out of a gun," said the Count.

" Like a cork out of a champagne-bottle," said the Captain.

" Such comparisons, gentlemen," said Procopius, smiling, " may not exactly dignify the treatment of our question, but they certainly illustrate it, and are therefore quite appropriate. We must not, however, forget that all we can say on such a subject is, and must be for many days to come, a mere guess. In our complex problem the unknown quantities still to be discovered are at present beyond number."

" What may be the cause after all is of little importance comparatively with the fact itself," said the Captain in a tone of forced resignation. " It's of little difference to me, for instance, whether I am on the whole Earth or only a part of it, provided France is there too ! "

"France, yes, and Russia !" added the Count.

"And of course Russia also !" said the Captain, hastily correcting his inadvertence.

"Gentlemen," said Procopius quietly, "I do not see the slightest reason for supposing that either France or Russia is to be found on our new spheroid. Remember how very small it is. Even of the presence of England I have the strongest doubts. For seven weeks there has not been the slightest communication between Gibraltar and the mother country, either by land or sea, by letter or telegraph — a pretty good proof that no such communication is possible !"

"If we have neither France nor Russia, nor England with us," asked the Captain, in an incredulous tone, "at what points do you think our spheroid must end?"

"That question admits of a mathematical answer," replied Procopius, "and presents no difficulty, certain data once admitted. Your Island Gourbi must occupy the equator, seeing that its days and nights are constantly equal. This equator being about 2000 miles long, the polar circumference must, of course, be also 2000 miles long, and the distance between the two poles should consequently be 1000 miles. Our north pole should therefore be about 500 miles north of the Isle of Gourbi, and the south pole should be at the same distance to the south. These points, marked on my chart, put our north pole on the shores of Provence, and our south pole in the Sahara on the twenty-eighth parallel.''

To all this neither the Captain nor the Count could offer any tenable objection. Still they were by no means convinced that Procopius was right. They neither accepted nor rejected his theory. Time alone could prove its validity. And with this settlement of the question they were for the present quite willing to abide.

In the meantime, the *Dobryna*, enjoying magnificent weather and a favorable wind, was rapidly making her way northwards. We say *northwards*, and mean it literally, because southern Spain had completely disappeared. Nothing but water could be seen in those points assigned by the chart to Malaga, Almeria, Cape de Gata, Cartagena, and Cape de Palos. It was not until the *Dobryna*, crossing the 37th parallel, had reached the latitude of Seville, that she once more encountered the same kind of crystal cliffs with which her eastern journey had already rendered her so familiar.

This coast, however, did not, like the other shores of the same nature, run exactly north and south, nor exactly east and west. It ran north-east as far as the parallel of Madrid, and then, turning suddenly to the south-east at a sharp angle, never stopped until it entered the site of the Mediterranean, disappearing in the direction of Formentera, the smallest and most southern of the Balearic Islands.

It was while cruising around in these waters, searching for some traces of Cape St. Martin, that our explorers made a most noteworthy discovery.

On the morning of February 21st, a sailor's voice was heard crying out :

" A bottle in sight on the starboard bow ! "

The Count and his companions had not yet finished breakfast, but the sailor's cry brought them quickly to the forecastle. The signalled object was seen plainly enough; lying only a little to the right of the ship's course, it was soon fished up and hauled on board.

It was no bottle at all, but a leather case, in shape somewhat like a closed-up telescope. The cover had been carefully sealed to keep the water out, and the wax bore the impression, still quite legible, of P. R.

Removing immediately to the cabin, they broke the seal, took off the cover, and drew out a written paper still quite dry and in no respect injured by the water. It was a simple ruled sheet, evidently torn out of a memorandum-book, and the words, followed by interrogation and exclamation points, all written in a large reversed hand, were as follows :

A WAIF.

Gallia ? ? ?
Ab sole, au 15 Fév., dist. 59,000,000 l.!
Chemin parcouru de janv. à fév., 82,000,000 l.!
Va bene! All right! Parfait!!!
(*Gallia ? ? ?*
From the sun, on February 15, *distant* 59 *million leagues!*
Distance travelled from January to February, 82 *million leagues :*
It goes well! All right! Perfect !!!)

"Now, gentlemen, what in the world is the meaning of all this?" asked the Count, when they had all carefully examined the paper, back and front, up, down, and sideways.

"It means one thing anyway," answered the Captain; "the writer, whoever he was, must have been alive on the fifteenth of February, that is, not quite a week ago."

"That would appear so at least," said the Count cautiously. "But mark the strangeness of the document. It is not signed. Nothing shows where it came from. It hardly gives a clue even to the nationality of the writer. It contains words in Latin, Italian, English, French—the last being certainly more numerous than all the others put together."

"There does not seem to be any attempt at mystification about it," said the Captain. "The case probably belongs to some astronomer who made his observations on board some ship or other."

"Hardly on board ship, Captain," said Procopius. "In such circumstances, it is a bottle rather than a case that he would have used to keep his paper dry. I rather think your astronomer must have been left all alone on some solitary island spared by the general catastrophe, and that, wishing to make known the result of his observations, he put his paper in a case, which no doubt he could have spared much more easily than a bottle."

"Well, on land or on water," said the Count, "it is of very little moment where you put your astronomer. The important matter is to decipher his document. Let us begin at the beginning. What is this *Gallia?*"

"No planet I ever heard of," said the Captain, "bears such a name."

"Captain, before going any further," observed Procopius, "may I ask you a question?"

"A thousand, if you like, my dear Lieutenant?"

"Don't you think that this paper, Captain, seems to conform with our theory of a fragment of the Earth having been whirled into space?"

"Well—rather—yes, I don't deny that it really does somewhat conform with your theory," answered Servadac, "though our objection regarding the material of the asteroid exists quite as strongly as ever."

"In such a case then," said Procopius, "the astronomer must have given the name *Gallia* (Gaul) to the new asteroid."

"Then the astronomer must be a Frenchman," said the Captain quickly.

"Not at all unlikely," continued Procupius. "Now then, notice, if you please, gentlemen, that, of the eighteen words contained in this document, eleven are French, three Latin, two Italian or Spanish, and two English. This seems to show that the astronomer, not knowing into whose hands his paper would fall, was desirous to increase its chances of being understood by employing words of four or five different languages."

"Suppose we admit that Gallia is the name of our new asteroid gravitating in space," said the Count; "let us continue our examination of the paper. *From the sun, distance on February* 15, *fifty-nine millions of leagues.* What is the meaning of that?"

"Such really was the distance, about 144 million miles, separating us from the sun at that date," replied Procopius, referring to his note-book; "we were then cutting the orbit of Mars."

"Good!" said the Count. "So far the document agrees with our own observations. Now then — *Distance travelled from January to February, eighty-two millions of leagues.* How's that?"

"That must refer," said Captain Hector, "to the distance Gallia must have gone in her new orbit."

"Precisely," said Procopius. "Now let us remember the law of Kepler that says a planet must describe equal angles in equal times. By virtue of this law, its velocity must diminish while performing the perihelion. On the fifteenth of January our thermometer stood at its highest point — a proof that we were then nearest to the sun, that is, performing our perihelion. What we read in this paper, therefore, is not at all improbable. Gallia might easily be moving at that time at a velocity of about 11 thousand leagues per hour, or 82 million leagues, or 200 million miles in a month."

"Such a velocity is neither impossible nor improbable," said Servadac; "but it throws no light whatever on other questions of far greater importance, namely, how far Gallia will be from the sun at her aphelion, and if she is ever to return."

"On these questions, Captain," said Procopius, "the paper so far certainly throws no light whatever. But, by means of careful observations made at several points of her orbit, we may ourselves succeed in determining her elements —"

"No doubt of it!" quickly observed the Count; "if Gallia *is* an asteroid, she must, like all moving bodies, obey the laws of motion, and, like all planets, she must submit to the influence of the sun. The instant such a block separates itself from the Earth, that very instant it is grappled by the invisible hands of attraction, and its orbit rendered unchangeable at once and forever."

"That is to say, Count Timascheff," observed Procopius, "unless some other asteroid comes near enough to disturb such orbit by its interference. We must remember that, Gallia being a mere pin's head in comparison with other members of the solar system, the major planets are likely to exercise an irresistible influence over her."

"Yes, it is pretty clear," observed the Captain, "that she may meet with very troublesome encounters on her road, and may even jump her track altogether.— But here we are all talking as if we really and truly believed ourselves to be all Gallians! Who knows but that the Gallia spoken of in the document is some new asteroid of the kind regularly discovered once a week?"

"No, Captain," said Procopius, "the asteroids of which you speak, about 160 to 170 by last accounts, are all found in a small zone lying between Mars and Jupiter. Consequently, they never approached the sun so closely as Gallia has done at her perihelion."

22

"We should soon settle the question," said the Count, "if we only had proper instruments to take an observation with —"

"But until we get them," said the Captain, "we must console ourselves with the last advices of our sanguine astronomer; '*It goes well! All right! Perfect!*'"

CHAPTER XVI.

A RELIC OF PROVENCE.

WHILST the explorers thus pursued a conversation in which, almost unconsciously, the word *Gallia* was fast assuming a geographical value in their eyes, the *Dobryna*, doubling the enormous promontory that had opposed her northern route, was now sailing as nearly as possible in the direction of the eastern end of the Pyrenees. Following the new coast-line as closely as could be done with safety and sailing almost directly north, she soon found herself near the site of Barcelona. But that important city had disappeared like all the rest. Dark waves rolled over its streets and broke themselves in fleecy foam on the new cliffs that had sprung up so suddenly to the west. Here the coast took a new turn to the north-east, following a line almost exactly straight as far as the site of Cape Creux.

But neither of Cape Creux, the most easterly point of Spain, nor of the Pyrenees, nor of Port-Vendres with the famous lighthouse, nor of the mouth of the

Tech, could the slightest trace now be seen.   The
explorers were now actually in French waters, and
the Captain's feelings may be imagined when he saw
a new continent take the place of his native land.
A lofty barrier, absolutely impenetrable and unscala-
ble, rose between him and the French coast.   A mountain wall, more than a thousand feet high, never presenting the slightest hold by which it might be climbed,
as bare, bleak, glassy, and "new" as it had been at
the other side of the Mediterranean, this crystal coast
now followed pretty closely the line once pursued by
the picturesque shores of Roussillon and Languedoc.

Than the plain close to which they were now
sailing, France could show none richer.   Even Lom-
bardy could not surpass it.   The warmest and at the
same time the best-watered soil in France, it seemed
to be the native land of the orange, the palm, and
the date trees; the home of perpetual orchards, gardens and vineyards.   But it had all disappeared.   It
was the same further north.   No sign of Cape Leucate,
whose chalky perpendicular cliffs two hundred feet
high so often reminded the sailor of the southern
shores of England.   No sign of the spires of Nar-
bonne, of the mountain-chain of La Clape five or
six hundred feet high, nor of the extinct volcano
of Saint Loup, nor of the little fort Brescon erected

on a lonely basalt rock, nor of Cette, built on the flanks of Mount Setius and till lately the second port of the Mediterranean. Nor of Frontignan, with its beautiful hotel de ville; nor of Aigues Mortes, the historical city of Saint Louis. The Camargue, the delta of the Rhone, gone! The stone-strewed plain of Crau, gone! The numberless mouths of the Rhone, all gone! The church of the Three Maries, built on the spot where the three holy women are said to have landed a short time after our Saviour's death, gone! Martigues, the Venice of Provence, gone! Marseilles, its harbor, its forts, its churches, its bastidos, all gone! Servadac began to fear that he should never see again one single point of continental Europe that had borne the name of France.

Not that he easily surrendered all hope. Often when the direction of the coast changed a little northwards, he confidently expected to be soon able to catch a glimpse of some part of the French soil that had escaped the disaster. But, vain hope! Whether the new line was long or short, it afforded no glimpse whatever of what had been till lately the wonderfully beautiful coast of Provence. When it was not the new coast that covered the old line, it was the waters of this strange Mediterranean that flowed over it always, always, mercilessly, remorselessly.

22*   R

Is all the old land of France indeed gone? the Captain asked himself. Does nothing remain of all the
French territory, except that shred of Algeria, the little
Isle of Gourbi? Must there not be something behind
that crystal wall? In spite of the strongest evidence
to the contrary, may we not be still inhabitants of the
old Earth and not of the new Gallia! If so, must not
France be there, and Germany, and Russia, and the
most of Europe? Can we not find some means of
scaling these frowning steeps and thus obtaining some
knowledge of what they conceal from view? Can't
we land somewhere, Count? Can't we land anywhere,
Lieutenant?

No landing was possible. No creek afforded shelter.
Not even a rock appeared large enough to set foot on
Its direction this coast changed occasionally, but its old
character never. Its base, as before, was smooth,
slippery, perpendicular, and never less than two or
three hundred feet high. Its summit, as before, was
a vast fantastic forest of crystallized peaks, needles,
blocks, pillars, obelisks, monoliths, serrated crags, now
red and dazzling in the rising sun, now black as ink
in the gloomy shade. The description on the first day
would do for every day. As the Captain said, it had
been all cast in the same mould.

The *Dobryna* still headed eastwardly with full steam

on. The weather was fine and singularly clear. The atmosphere was almost too cool to retain vapor. A few clouds, streaking the sky here and there, formed gauze veils of almost perfect transparency. The sun, however, our travellers could not help noticing, was getting visibly smaller and his light less brilliant. The stars, on the contrary, were brighter than ever. Some planets, indeed, were gradually fading away. Mercury had disappeared altogether. Venus gave only a feeble glimmer. A new planet — Procopius called it the Earth, and the Captain tried to persuade himself that it was its enormous disc he had seen that night on the Sheliff — was fast losing her former splendor. Even Mars, latterly such an attractive object, and so near that his satellites, never before suspected, could now be easily seen, began to grow less dazzling in his blaze. Jupiter, on the contrary, and Saturn grew larger, more radiant, more beautiful every day. Even Uranus, usually invisible without a very good telescope, could be detected by a sharp eye. Procopius explained all this by saying that Gallia, retreating from the centre of attraction, was plunging deeper and deeper into the boundless realms of solar space; and his companions did not undertake to contradict him.

Coasting along what was once the winding shore of the department of Var, and seeking in vain for

Toulon, the delightful islands of Hyēres, the Gulf of Saint Tropez large enough for the evolutions of a war fleet, Fréjus with its Roman remains, Cannes with its enchanting position, the Lérins Islands, recalling the Man in the Iron Mask, the *Dobryna* found herself, on the twenty-fourth of February, sailing over the Gulf of Jouan, and approaching the spot till lately occupied by the little fortified city of Antibes.

Here, to the extreme surprise but also to the profound satisfaction of our explorers, a narrow, perpendicular fissure was seen cutting the enormous cliff from base to summit. On its left side, a few feet above the water, a little stretch of beach extended, where a boat could easily effect a landing.

"At last!" cried Captain Hector, hardly able to contain his joy. His companions were hardly less excited at this unexpected prospect of some immediate discovery. Through the opening they could see a rugged slope gradually ascending, like the dry bed of a mountain torrent. By following this natural staircase might they not succeed in reaching the top of the cliff? And once there could they not get a view, if not of the French territory, at least of the strange country that had replaced it?

Landing at seven o'clock in the morning, their attention was immediately attracted by some relics

UP THE CRYSTAL MOUNTAINS.

of the former coast: namely, those concrete lime peb-
bles of a yellow color that are so frequently found on
the Provençal shores.   But these, souvenirs of a former
state of things, though highly interesting in themselves,
could not delay our explorers longer than a few minutes
from hurriedly ascending the ravine which they were
desirous to examine.

This ravine was quite dry, and it had evidently never
been the bed of a roaring torrent.   The rocks forming
its floor, as well as those lining its steep sides, presented
the same metallic, laminated texture so far noticed
everywhere else, and they showed none of the effects
of ordinary disintegration.   A geologist would probably experience little difficulty in assigning them their
proper rank in a lithological scale, but none of our
explorers knew enough either of geology or mineralogy
to speak with sufficient accuracy regarding their precise
nature.

Though still perfectly dry, it was, however, easy to
see that, in case of change of climate, this ravine might
one day become the outlet of a considerable quantity
of water.   Already even little caps of snow glittered
here and there on the tops of the pillars and in the
niches of the slopes; and the greater the altitude of
the road, the broader, thicker, and more numerous
these caps became.   It was quite possible that the

mountain valleys, and even the whole country lying beyond this wall, would disappear altogether under the white shroud of great enveloping glaciers.

"This snow is the first trace of fresh water I have seen so far on Gallia," said Procopius.

"Yes, and, if this cold keeps on, we shall soon find not only snow but plenty of thick solid ice too," said the Count.

"This cold must continue," said Procopius. "Remember we are here in the arctic regions of Gallia where the solar rays, coming only very slantingly, cannot impart much heat. Here, it is true, we can never have real night, as the sun is always vertical to the equator. But in time the cold, even on the equator, must be exceedingly great if Gallia's orbit carries her a considerable distance from the centre of the solar system."

"Lieutenant," asked the Count, "is there no danger of the cold becoming so excessive on Gallia's surface that no living creature could endure it?"

"To that question," replied Procopius, "Fourier, an illustrious French physicist, would answer decidedly, No!—his experiments having convinced him that the temperature of interstellar space, that is, space entirely deprived of air, never falls much below 60 or 70 Fahrenheit below zero."

" 70 below zero ! " exclaimed the Count; "why, even in St. Petersburg we cannot endure that ! "

"But other and later authorities," continued Procopius, "notably Pouillet and Sir John Herschel, would answer decidedly, Yes ! — their experiments having convinced them that the temperature of space may sink as low as 220 or 230 Fahrenheit below zero."

"Excuse me, gentlemen, for interrupting this interesting conversation," said the Captain, "but really I must stop a little to catch my breath."

Yielding to his usual impetuosity, he had run ahead of his companions, and was of course the first to experience the effects of the rarity of the atmosphere usual at great altitudes. The rest was very grateful to all, for though they had as yet risen no more than five or six hundred feet, they began to feel a very great difficulty in breathing. They soon recovered, but thought proper to resume the journey a little more slowly; the road, however, was unobstructed, and, though they stopped every now and then to accommodate their lungs to the increasing rarity, in about two hours they reached the ridge of the cliffs.

The Captain was the first to touch the summit. His companions saw him look eagerly to the north, and then heard his mournful cry of despair.

France was not there ! No country was there !

Rocks rose behind rocks, peaks behind peaks, crests behind crests, high into the northern sky, and all along the horizon from east to west! Moraines, leaden-gray icy seas, glaciers, icebergs, cairns, serrated crags, black straight walls, and snow-streaked mountains were mingled together in bewildering confusion, and yet not without a kind of strange uniformity. It was all an enormous agglomeration of matter that had crystallized in the shape of hexagonal prisms. Gallia appeared to be the production of a single mineral formation unique and unknown. If the coast bordering on the Mediterranean did not always present the same uniformity of pinnacles in its upper portion as prevailed in the interior of the continent, it was because the occurrence of some other phenomenon at the moment of the cataclysm — probably that to which the presence of the ocean was due — had perhaps somewhat modified the peculiarity of the general texture.

Nowhere the slightest trace of a European land! Everywhere the ancient soil replaced by the new! In vain did the Captain's eye seek for the lovely landscapes of Provence: its citron and orange gardens rising in stone-faced terraces over the blue waves; its olive groves of sea-green foliage; its majestic avenues of pepper-trees, nettle-trees, mimosas, palms, and eucalyptuses; its odoriferous thickets of gigantic geraniums, sprinkled here and there with brilliant bean-trees and long-stemmed aloes; its foreground of rust-stained rocks; its magnificent back ground of dark mountains bristling with forests of pine.

Nowhere the slightest trace of vegetable — in such stony soil even the snow lichens, the hardiest of the polar plants, could not find sustenance! Nowhere the slightest trace of vegetable — even a petrel of the arctic regions could not live here a single day!

Everywhere mineral — mineral in all its aridity, desolation and horror!

Servadac, overwhelmed by an emotion of which he had not considered himself capable, stood motionless on the summit of a frozen rock. In vain his moistened eyes made a last effort to catch some glimpse of his dear France in the dreary region before him. His heart was sinking low, but with an expiring effort he roused himself to a new hope.

"No!" he cried wildly; "in spite of experience, in spite of my own eyes, in spite of your calculations, I cannot believe it! France still exists! We cannot yet have reached the Maritime Alps! That this crystal continent has suddenly sprung up out of the waves, I don't deny. But it has not destroyed France! Beyond it she still lives! Come, dear friends, let

23

us cross this icy territory! Let us explore more carefully —"

He had gone some yards ahead of his companions
in his eagerness to discover some path through this
impenetrable jungle of hexagonal pillars. Suddenly
he stopped. His foot had kicked something from
under the snow. It was a bit of cut stone differing
too much in shape and color from the surrounding
rocks not to attract instant attention. Hastily picking
it up, he found it to be a fragment of yellow marble
covered all over with traces of some inscription. He
showed it to his companions, who examined it with
much interest, though for some time they could not
make out a single letter. At last they read VIL —

"Villa!" cried the Captain suddenly and in such
surprise that the slab slipped out of his nerveless grasp
and was instantly broken into countless fragments.

Was this indeed all that remained of some of the gor-
geous marine villas that crowned the slopes of Cape
Garoupe, the most lovely site on earth for pavilion,
palace or château? Well did the three explorers remember the pleasant summer evenings they had once
spent in the Hotel du Golfe built on this very spot,
when the sun setting behind the Var mountains turned
the Gulf of Jouan into a living sea of fretted gold.
On the north extended the splendid panorama of the

A MORSEL OF OLD EARTH.

snow-crowned Alps from Draguignan on the west by
Grasse, Nice, Monaco, Vintimiglia, to Bordighera, the
home of the palms, the last point visible on the Cornice
Road in the extreme east. Southward heaved the blue
waters of the Mediterranean, whilst in the south-east
the mountains of Corsica, piercing the azure, showed
white and rosy like the glorious city of a golden dream!

A dream indeed our explorers now felt it to be, and
a most gloomy one, in the presence of the stern reality
all around them. The Captain was particularly despond-
ent. His last hope had vanished. The frightful stony
desert that surrounded them seemed to crush his life
out.

"Dante!" he cried, "never did your phantasm-
haunted imagination conjure up vision more dismal
than the reality now environing us! The grim face
of yonder rocks is just the spot to carve the appalling
words of your shriek of despair:

'Lasciate ogni speranza voi che 'ntrate!' "

"No hope! No hope!" he cried, sitting down and
holding his head in his hands, unable to stand any
longer.

"Dear friend," said the Count endeavoring to console
him, "things are really no worse now than they were
before the discovery of the slab. We must not sin

against hope.   Despair is even worse than presumption.
Did you not know some members of the Hope family
in England?"

"Yes," said the Captain almost mechanically.

"You remember their motto?"

"No."

"It is:

Orbe fracto, spes illæsa!
'Hope soars over a crumbled universe!'"

"You're right, Count!" said the Captain, rising
with renewed animation.   "It's a better motto than
Dante's.   Henceforward let it be ours!"

CHAPTER XVII.

WHAT WAS LEFT OF ITALY.

W HITHER now, friends?" asked the Count of his companions once more assembled on the deck of the *Dobryna*.

"To the Isle of Gourbi!" cried the Captain. "It seems to be the only part of the old Earth now left to us — not to mention," he added with a deprecating smile, "that to me it is almost a portion of my dear France!"

"Captain," said Procopius, "before returning to your island, which in my opinion we must do pretty soon in any case, allow me to remind you that a portion even of the limited coast of the new Mediterranean is still unexplored. As yet we know nothing of the region lying between Antibes and that western opening of the narrow strait by which we escaped into the waters of Gibraltar. And we also know nothing of what lies between the Gulf of Cabes and the eastern opening of the same strait. We have followed the old line of the African coast, but not the new one. Who

can say that every issue to the south is closed? May
not some fertile oasis of the Algerian Sahara have
escaped the general catastrophe? Besides, Italy, Sicily,
the Balearic Islands, Corsica or Sardinia may still be
left. It would certainly be worth our while to try."

"I think you are right, Lieutenant," said the Captain; "the first thing to be done is perhaps to complete
our survey of the new Mediterranean."

"Unless that could be done after revisiting the
island," suggested the Count.

"Father," observed Procopius, "our time for exploring will not last long. We must make the most
of the little left us."

"What do you mean, Procopius?" asked the Count.

"Our temperature," was the reply, "is steadily
diminishing; Gallia is following a line that removes
her further and further from the sun; the time can't be
far off when we must experience very severe cold. Of
course, the sea then congeals, navigation becomes impossible, and difficult exploration over ice-fields is the
only resource left us. Would it not therefore be better
to continue our exploration while the sea is still open?"

"You are right again, Lieutenant," said the Captain. "Let us satisfy ourselves that, even if there is no
discovery to be made, we have done our best to make
one."

"It is quite possible, after all, that some poor human beings may have temporarily escaped the terrible calamity," said the Count warmly. "We should never forgive ourselves if we afterwards found out that even one of our race had perished for want of timely succor."

"Count," exclaimed the Captain, "you are more than right! Whatever human creature we might pick up, were it even the most miserable specimen of humanity possible, we should and would regard as our brother — a survivor of our dear old mother Earth!"

"Besides," added the matter-of-fact Procopius, "we should need all the help we may get. If we are never to return to the old Earth we must make the new Earth as comfortable as possible!"

On the twenty-fifth of February, the *Dobryna* was again sailing eastwardly, following the crystal coast on her left as closely as safety permitted. A brisk breeze blew from the west and the cold began to bite. The thermometer was as low as two or three degrees below freezing-point, but fortunately salt water is not so readily frozen as fresh. The *Dobryna* was therefore still free, though not a moment was to be lost.

The nights were now most lovely. The gradually cooling layers of the atmosphere becoming drier and drier, the clouds grew thinner and thinner, and finally

disappeared altogether. The constellations blazed out
with incomparable splendor. How happy would an
astronomer have considered himself if placed in a
position so favorable for sounding the mysterious
depths of the starry heavens! Our friends were not
astronomers, but they gazed on the spangled plains of
night with something of the sense of happiness induced
by reviving hope.

On the night of the 26th, they had a new experience. They suddenly found themselves in the midst of
a display of fireworks, in comparison to which the most
magnificent bouquet of rockets ever let off by Ruggieri
would be no more than a box of matches set on fire
by accident. A hail-storm of shooting-stars streaked
the black sky. They all seemed to start from Algol,
the Demon star of Perseus, and flared through Gallia's
atmosphere with the intensity of sulphur burning in
oxygen and with the white, dazzling glare of an electric lamp. The rocks of the crystal coast, reflecting
the glittering radiance from innumerable points, looked
like the magnificent diamond palace of an Arabian tale.
The phosphoric sea blazed with the silvery radiance,
and its heaving billows sparkled and coruscated like
countless mirrors of polished steel.

The Gallia in fact was now passing through the
meteoric ring that lies between Mars and Jupiter, **and**

METEORS.

is almost concentric with the Earth's orbit. Were these millions of shooting-stars the sole remains of some planet that had come to a premature end through a catastrophe somewhat resembling that which had just befallen the Earth? Was Gallia herself no more than one of these meteors, only on a larger scale, and following a more eccentric orbit? These questions our explorers could not answer, but of one fact they were soon fully assured. Gallia was moving onwards with enormous rapidity, for the grand meteoric display hardly lasted twenty-four hours.

For some time lately the *Dobryna's* eastern course had been stopped by a long projection of the coast, running southwards as far as the extremity of the former island of Corsica. Of this famous island the slightest trace could not now be seen. Nor of the Straits of Bonifacio which till lately had separated Corsica from Sardinia. Nothing but a vast sea, bare, black and gloomy.

Early on the morning of February 26, the cry of "Land ahead!" brought our explorers rapidly on deck. A black spot was easily seen some miles to the south-east; it was evidently an island and, unless of recent origin, should be the remains of Maddalena, Caprera or some other of the little islands north of

S

Sardinia. As for Sardinia itself, it was no more visible than Corsica.

In less than another hour our three explorers were rapidly approaching the islet. To their great satisfaction, it presented none of the terrific crystal formation to which of late they had been so much accustomed. It rose gently from the water with a smooth slope covered with rich green grass. Here and there a little thicket of myrtles and mastics could be seen. Elsewhere a grove or two of old olives showed themselves. On the whole scene the travellers' eyes rested for some time with unalloyed delight. But they looked around in vain for some sign of a human being or of a human habitation. Neither could be seen. Ascending a little eminence whence the ocean could be discerned in, all directions, the explorers found, to their great disappointment, that the islet was very small, containing no more than a few acres at most, and giving no sign whatever of the abode of a human creature.

They were returning with heavy hearts to the little creek where they had left the boat, when their ears were suddenly greeted by the bleating of some domestic animal, and their eyes were as suddenly greeted by the sight of a beautiful little pet goat looking at

NINA AND MARZY.

them through the thicket and unmistakably signalling them to approach !

"That goat is not alone, you may be sure!" cried the Captain, running towards the mastic thicket, closely followed by his companions.

Peering through the branches, they saw that they themselves had been seen, and were now timidly examined by two large black eyes belonging to a little girl seven or eight years old, of the pure Italian type, and pretty as one of Murillo's angels in the Assumption.

Having eagerly scanned her discoverers for a minute or two, her eyes gradually began to express reassurance, and her lips at last broke into a sweet confiding smile. Starting up suddenly, she ran towards them without hesitation, stretched out her little hands, and exclaimed in accents as charming as her country's lovely language :

"I signori non sono cattivi! No mi faranno male! No bisogna ch' io abbia paura !"

(The gentlemen are not wicked! They will not hurt me! I must not be afraid, must I?)

"No! figliuolina mia!" said the Count, also in Italian. "Siamo amici! Ti amaremo carissamente!"

(No, my dear child. We are friends. We shall love you very dearly !)

He took her hand gently and rubbed it for a little while to give her confidence.

"Come si chiama carina mia?" he asked.

(What's your name, my dear?)

"Nina," was the ready reply.

"Nina, pote Ella dirci dove siamo?" asked the Count again.

"A Maddalena," she replied. "Là stava io quando tutto tutto si cangiò subitamente!"

(At Maddalena. At least I was there when everything changed all of a sudden!)

A few more questions, answered by very intelligent replies, informed the explorers that little Nina was all alone in the island, that, her father and mother being dead, she had been tending goats for a neighboring farmer when all at once everything suddenly disappeared all around her except the bit of land on which they now stood, that herself and her goat Marzy had been the only survivors of the earthquake, that she had been terribly frightened, but, soon recovering courage, that she had knelt down and thanked the dear good God for having made the earth stop shaking, and that then she had done the best she could to keep herself and her only friend Marzy alive. Very fortunately she had been supplied that same day with a small stock of provisions which had lasted so far; she had prayed every morning and evening for a boat to come and take her away. She had seen the boat coming, but was too much afraid at first to let herself or Marzy be seen. She was not afraid, however, to go now with the good gentlemen if they would only take poor Marzy too along. The poor animal would surely die if left alone on the island, and how could Nina then ever restore Marzy to Marzy's owner?

Nina's proposition was unconditionally accepted. Captain Hector loved the gentle creature already almost as dearly as his own little sister. Marzy offered no objection to the general arrangement, and in less than half an hour afterwards the *Dobryna* received this most unexpected addition to her crew with the heartiest welcome. The sailors, in particular, were overjoyed at their good fortune in finding the child. It was a most lucky sign, they said ; they called her their good angel, and almost imagined that she had wings. From the very first day among them she went by no other name than *The Little Madonna.*

In a few hours all that remained of Maddalena was completely lost from view. The *Dobryna,* starting on a northeast course, soon found herself once more as close as she could venture to the crystal coast, which now ran somewhat parallel to the old Italian shore, but more than a hundred miles farther seaward. Near the 42d parallel, that of Rome, a vast gulf had been formed, which, how·

ever, as a hasty examination soon convinced our explorers, retreated as far back as to cover up the site of
the Eternal City, but afforded no farther outlet.   At the
latitude of Naples the new coast nearly coincided with
the old, that of Lower Calabria at the extreme toe of
the boot.   But no more Lipari Islands; no more Straits
of Messina; no more Sicily; no more Etna even, though
that enormous volcano had once lifted its smoking summit to a height of nearly eleven thousand feet above the
level of the sea.

About a hundred and fifty miles farther south, the
Dobryna found herself once more at the west entrance
of the strait which had so providentially given her
refuge during the frightful storm of the sixteenth of
February, and the eastern end of which opened into
the sea of Gibraltar.

The coast directly south of this point having been
already examined, further exploration in this direction
was evidently useless.   Procopius, therefore, turning
directly south-west, followed that course as far as parallel 34, where, on the third of March, he found himself once more close to the crystal coast, and very near
the point where they had first discovered it.

Here therefore the *Dobryna* turned directly west and
followed the new coast as far as what once was the oasis
of Ziban, south of the centre of the Province of Con-

stantina. Making a sharp turn at this point, the coast ran south to the 32d parallel, the boundary of Beled el Jerid. It soon, however, turned north-west, thus forming a deep, irregular, triangular-shaped gulf, everywhere framed by the everlasting mineral formation. Following its new course for about four hundred miles, it crossed the Algerian Sahara, and rejoined the old coast at a point between Oran and Mostaganem.

But this point reached, no Oran, no Marocco even. Instead of going west the coast took a sharp and sudden turn southwardly, and soon disappeared in the distance. No discovery evidently was possible by following this coast any longer.

At this very point, however, a discovery *was* made which surprised our explorers considerably for the moment, and which, as they afterwards found, proved to be one of supreme importance.

Just as they rounded the point to their left, they caught sight of a black mountain, rising almost directly out of the sea to a height of probably three thousand feet. It was a volcano in full activity, for its summit was belching forth vast clouds of dark smoke occasionally livid with flame.

"Gallia, therefore, must have a red hot interior!" cried Captain Servadac, much astonished at this new phenomenon.

"Why not, Captain?" asked the Count. "Gallia being but a fragment of the Earth, she is just as likely to have carried off a portion of the Earth's central fire as of the Earth's atmosphere, seas and continents."

"A very small portion of the continents!" observed Servadac, "though, upon second thought, perhaps more than is enough for our present population."

"Talking of population reminds me of our English friends at Gibraltar," observed the Count. "Before returning to Gourbi, which now can hardly be a day's sail away, what do you think of landing at the Rock and telling them about everything that we have since discovered?"

"What would be the use?" answered the Captain without the least hesitation. "Those English fellows would not believe us. They know very well where Gourbi lies, and can reach it whenever they think proper. They are not poor suffering creatures, destitute of resources. On the contrary, they have enough and for long enough. Gibraltar is little more than three hundred miles distant from our island, and, once the sea is frozen, they can sled over to us as often as ever they please. We had no particular reason to be overjoyed at our reception, and, when they pay us a visit, we shall have a splendid opportunity for retaliating —"

"By giving them such a welcome as to make them ashamed of themselves," interrupted Timascheff.

"Exactly so, Count," replied the Captain. "Here in Gallia, as in the United States of America, there is no such thing as a Frenchman, a Russian, an Italian, an Englishman —"

"There I can't agree with you, Captain!" interrupted the Count, shaking his head. "An Englishman, unless caught young, is untamable. Once an Englishman, forever an Englishman!"

The English were therefore left to their fate for the present, though in any case a visit to Gibraltar just then was probably out of question. The cold was increasing so decidedly that Procopius began to be afraid of the vessel getting suddenly caught in the ice. The coal too was getting low and would soon give out. Gibraltar, therefore, and all further explorations southwardly were deferred to a future and more favorable occasion. On the fifth of March the *Dobryna's* head faced Gourbi, where they could easily arrive during the course of the day.

"My poor Ben Zouf!" said the Captain, with eye to glass, "how glad I shall be to see you! I hope nothing unpleasant has befallen you during our absence!"

The run, short as it was, was not to be made with-

out an incident. The explorers were fortunate enough
to come across a second notice from the mysterious
astronomer who, having already calculated Gallia's
elements, was now carefully following her course day
by day.

About an hour after starting, a floating object was
signalled a mile or so on the larboard bow, and soon
fished up. This time it was a pickle-jar, but it was
carefully sealed as before and bore the same initials:
P. R.

The paper was quite uninjured and contained the
following:

Gallia?
Ab sole, au 1 mars, dist.: 78,000,000 l. !
Chemin parcouru de fév. à mars: 59,000,000 l. !
Va bene ! All right! *Nil desperandum !*
Enchanté !
(*Gallia ? From the sun, on March* 1, *distant* 78 *million leagues !
Distance travelled from February to March,* 59 *million leagues ! It
goes well ! All right ! Never despair ! Delighted !*)

"Again no address or signature!" exclaimed the
Captain with some impatience. "Can it be somebody
fooling us?"

"If it be," answered the Count, "he must be giving
himself more trouble than the sport is worth! He must
be raining cases and jars into the sea. We have already
received two !"

"But why this silly concealment of his name and address? Where do you think he can be concealing himself?"

Natural and reasonable questions, but very difficult to answer. Could the writer of these singular documents be the inhabitant of some islet spared by the catastrophe and missed by the *Dobryna?* Could he be on board some vessel that could sail against wind and tide and disappear at pleasure, like the Flying Dutchman? No one could tell.

"In any case," observed Procopius, "if these documents are serious, and in my opinion the figures are really so beyond all doubt, they give occasion for two important remarks. First, Gallia's velocity has diminished twenty-three millions of leagues in one month — from 82 to 59. Second, Gallia's distance from the sun has increased in two weeks nineteen millions of leagues. Therefore, the greater her distance from the sun the less her velocity — a fact in perfect correspondence with all the laws of celestial mechanics."

"Your inference from these observations, Procopius?" asked the Count.

"We are following an orbit which is probably elliptic, but the eccentricity of which at present cannot be calculated."

"Before we are done with this subject, gentlemen,'

said the Count, "and while I think of it, I move we adopt for our planet, at least temporarily, the name *Gallia* proposed by our unknown friend, and that we also call the waters all around the *Gallian Sea.*"

The motion was carried unanimously.

"I shall also make a proposition," said the Captain. "To show a proper appreciation of our astronomer's pluck, and his untiring devotion to science under the present appalling circumstances, I move that we henceforward make every effort to imitate him (applause). Let us begin to do so by adopting his motto as our own, on all occasions and under all circumstances: NIL DESPERANDUM!"

"NIL DESPERANDUM!" shouted his companions approvingly.

"Land to nor'-east!" sang the watch on the foredeck.

At the same moment a voice from the mast-head cried out:

"The Isle of Gourbi in sight!"

CHAPTER XVIII.

VISITORS.

THE *Dobryna* had started on her exploration trip on the thirty-first of January, and she now returned to Gourbi on the fifth of March. The journey had, therefore, lasted thirty-five days (it was leap year) old calendar, or seventy days Gallian, the sun having crossed the Gourbi mountains seventy separate times.

It is needless to say that the Captain experienced much emotion as he drew nearer and nearer to the only fragment of Algerian ground that had escaped destruction. Many a time he had asked himself and his companions if they were ever to see it again. Might it not have sunk in the waves, like everything else on this unstable surface of Gallia? And if so, what could have become of his faithful follower and friend, Ben Zouf?

Such fears had, fortunately, no foundation. There lay the island now before them, safe and sound as when they had left it. What a beautiful green did the slopes of its mountains present! And, contrasted with the terrible crystal coast, how charming seemed even the rust-stained cliffs and the sandy shore! But look! What black cloud was that which rose and fell in turns, strangely, automatically as it were, immediately over the island? The Captain and his companions were at first a little startled at the puzzling phenomei.on; but a nearer approach showed it to be no cloud at all. It was a vast throng of birds pressed closely together in the air, like a shoal of herrings in the water. It was soon heard to give forth a confused noise of discordant cries, varied every now and then by what sounded like the distant discharge of a gun.

The *Dobryna* announced her approach by firing off her cannon, and was not long coming to anchor in the little harbor of the Sheliff. As the Captain and the Count were being rapidly rowed ashore, they caught sight of a man, gun in hand, rushing down the cliffs and jumping from rock to rock wildly towards the landing-place. Even the Count had no difficulty in recognizing Ben Zouf.

As they landed they found him standing motionless in the position of "present arms!" ten or twelve yards distant from the water. His countenance showed an expression in which the most profound respect struggled so comically with the most exuberant joy as to be perfectly irresistible. The Captain and the Count shouted with laughter. Ben held out pretty well for a few seconds, but no longer. Throwing aside his gun, he rushed up to his old master, caught his hands, shook them and kissed them, laughing, whining, and dancing around him with every demonstration of delight.

"Oh, my dear Captain!" he exclaimed at last, "how happy I am to see you back again! I thought you would never return! How miserable I have often been during your absence! But it's all right now! Monsieur the Count too! I am delighted to welcome him once more to the Island! Everything is ready for you all! How well you both look!" etc., etc.

But even in the very midst of these exclamations, so very natural and so perfectly intelligible, the Captain and the Count soon began to notice others which were anything but either natural or intelligible.

"You're both as brown as berries!" he went on. "The beggars! Let me only get a crack at them! — Captain, you're gone five old weeks to-day! The longest five weeks I ever spent! — The brigands! The plundering robbers! You're not come an instant too soon, Captain! Days and nights all the same! The pirates! The Thugs! The Corsairs never give me a moment's rest!"

He stopped to take breath and the Captain cut in like lightning.

"What do you mean, Ben Zouf, by pirates and Thugs?

You don't want us to believe that a band of plundering Arabs has invaded the island?''

"Arabs?" cried Ben, "I wish they were Arabs! Arabs can be put an end to! Kill an Arab — good-by! he gives you no more trouble. But these bandits! — the more you kill of them the more you bring to life! Have n't I killed at least a thousand a day for the last two weeks? It's all no use! They're more numerous than ever! Captain, if you don't contrive some plan to exterminate the whole tribe, you'll not be left a grain of corn on your island! Kabyles are bad enough, Captain, but they are nothing in comparison with these thieving birds! We had a splendid harvest, but if something is not done to kill off these depredators pretty soon we shall have all to go fishing."

The Captain now understood the singular appearance presented by the birds when the *Dobryna* was nearing the island. He also comprehended why they flocked in such enormous numbers to Gourbi. It must really be the only spot on all Gallia where the starving creatures could find fields, meadows, fresh water, corn and refuge in general. But, of course, if their subsistence was incompatible with that of the human inhabitants of Gourbi, something should be done to effectually oppose the invasion.

He said so to Ben Zouf after learning further particulars, and dismissed the matter for the present by assuring him that it should have his earliest possible attention.

" All right, Captain ! " said Ben, rapidly changing the subject. " How did you leave the boys in Africa ? Jolly as ever, of course, though no doubt a little dumbfounded at the look of things ? "

" The boys in Africa," said the Captain gravely, " are still in Africa."

" Good ! Captain. Glad to hear it. Long live the boys ! "

" Only Africa, Ben Zouf, is no longer in existence."

" No Africa any more, Captain ? You 're joking, are n't you ? " said Ben, with a face as long as his arm.

" No Africa any more, Ben Zouf."

" But France, Captain ! France is on hand, as usual ? " he asked in a voice tinged with misgiving.

" Ah ! France, France — is far, far away, Ben Zouf."

" And Mont — Mont — Montmartre, Captain ? "

The poor fellow could hardly pronounce the words. It was the cry of the heart forcing itself through the lips. The Captain at first could give no answer. In fact, he did not know what to say. At last he tried to explain to Ben in a few words what appeared to have really taken place. How a fragment of the

Earth had been exploded into the sky, carrying with
it little bits of Africa and of Europe, but much of
the Mediterranean. How Montmartre, and with Montmartre Paris, and with Paris all France, and with
France all Europe, and with Europe the whole Earth,
were now about two hundred millions of miles distant
from their Island of Gourbi. Consequently all hope
of ever seeing Montmartre again had better be given
up, as most unlikely to be ever realized.

Ben's face had at first borne a look of extreme de-
jection. But as he listened to the Captain's explanation of matters so difficult of comprehension, it was
easy to see that he grew only more puzzled and perplexed. The astounding intelligence was evidently
too much for his matter-of-fact head. By degrees,
however, his look of bewilderment wore away and
began to give place to an expression of amused incre-
dulity. He was even smiling gayly when the Captain
had got through, and it was almost with a laugh that
he exclaimed with a knowing shrug of the shoulders:

"All right, Captain! Of course, one has a perfect right to believe these things, if one feels like it!
But I should rather be excused! That's not the kind
of a fellow Laurence, commonly called Ben Zouf, considers himself to be. That astronomer is probably an
escaped lunatic! The Earth exploded like an old

steam-boiler, and we're riding about on one of the fragments! Shot up like a plug out of a pop-gun! Excuse me, Captain! I'm not learned man enough to swallow any such ideas! Too thin! as the boys used to say. Yes, Captain, with the greatest respect for your superior knowledge, learning and information, I must say the story is either too thin or my skull a great deal too thick!"

The Captain endeavored to make his language more comprehensible, but Ben would not listen.

"No, no, Captain," he would exclaim with a pleasant smile and touching his cap every moment with the back of his hand, "learned men, book men, like the Count and yourself and the astronomer, may believe such things or think they do. But for Montmartre hard-headed fellows like Ben Zouf, these stories are too thin! I can't agree with you, Captain, but I'm sure poor old France is all right, and especially Montmartre!"

"Very well, Ben Zouf," answered the Captain, in perfect good-humor. "Have it all your own way! Believe what you please and disbelieve what you please. Hope on, hope ever! *Never despair!*—the motto, by the by, of no less than the astronomer himself, against whom you appear to be unreasonably prejudiced. But enough of this for the present. The first thing to be done is to prepare the Isle of Gourbi for a place of residence. I think we shall be likely to make a good long stay here."

Procopius, little Nina and her goat Marzy now joined the group, and all started together for the *gourbi*. They soon arrived there, Ben carrying Nina, the child taking a great liking to him at once and calling him her friend Zuffo. Everything was in perfect order, the *gourbi* being completely restored and the old guard-house made very comfortable. Zephyr and Galette, in splendid condition, neighed aloud and commenced capering to testify their joy at the Captain's return. Poultry in immense numbers and of all kinds came running up to Ben with loud cries, demanding their regular meal. Great stacks of corn and ricks of hay, well protected against sun, rain, and birds, lay in the immediate neighborhood, and more were seen in the adjoining plains. In short, the *gourbi*, instead of being as formerly a mere military outpost for two men, had now, thanks to Ben's incessant industry, attained the appearance of being the abode of a highly intelligent, provident, successful, and even wealthy farmer. How Ben managed to bring about these wonderful results will shortly appear.

The proper compliments had been paid to Ben, who, however, was so very busy welcoming his guests that he hardly appeared to hear them; the sumptuous din-

ner, which he took an incredibly short time to prepare, had been disposed of with a good deal of cheerfulness and even fun, considering the state in which
our adventurers now found themselves; Nina and
Marzy had been put away in a little recess hastily
arranged by Ben, and were now fast asleep; even
Ben himself, the indefatigable, had showed signs of fa-
tigue and had either gone out or retired for the night
after preparing three comfortable beds for the gentlemen.

But our friends did not feel sleepy. Sipping their
wine and smoking their cigars they sat far into the
night, or at least the darkness, discussing the situation and revolving over plans for the future.

What was the first thing to be done? Evidently to
make instant provision for every immediate and pressing danger. First of all, how to prepare for the terrible cold that Gallia was certain to encounter in a
few days and which was to last for a time nobody
knew how long? Fuel, water, and food were evidently the three chief and indispensable requisites.
Now, fuel was by no means abundant. Coal there
was none. Trees were comparatively few, and even
of them the growth would be checked if not killed
during the long cold period. What was to be done
to meet this fearful eventuality? Some expedient

should be devised, and that too with the briefest possible delay.

The other two requisites of life, water and food, were abundant enough. Wells and springs were numerous, and the great tanks were full. Besides, in a short time, the Gallian Sea would freeze, and the ice would furnish a sufficiency of water comparatively fresh, sea ice, as is well known, containing very little salt. As for food, properly so-called, that is the nitrogenized substance indispensable to the nourishment of man, there was a plentiful supply of it, and for a long time. In the first place, the cereals, in spite of the birds, were still in the greatest abundance; and in the second, the flocks and herds of domestic animals scattered over the island were very numerous and in a most flourishing condition. It was not forgotten, of course, that during the great cold period the soil would remain unproductive and that even forage for the animals could not be renewed. Too many of these, therefore, could not be retained. How many were too many? An exact answer to this question, though depending evidently on the length of the hibernation — a problem deferred for the present — did not present any great difficulty. The real trouble was the fuel question, and with a promise to give it careful consideration, the friends at last retired for the night.

Next morning, after a copious breakfast, the council of war was resumed. What was the actual population of Gallia, as far as known? The Captain pulled out his memorandum-book, and began jotting down the items. Leaving out for the present the thirteen Englishmen of Gibraltar, there were eight Russians, two Frenchmen, and the little Italian girl — total, eleven.

"That makes altogether a population of eleven souls," said the Captain, "depending on Gourbi for support."

"Beg pardon, Captain," suddenly interrupted Ben, who was busy clearing off the table; "sorry to contradict you, Captain; but your total is not quite right."

"What do you mean, Ben Zouf?"

"I mean that, instead of eleven, there are twenty-three of us."

"On this island?"

"Yes, Captain; on this island."

"Won't you have the kindness to explain yourself, Ben Zouf?" cried the Captain impatiently, whilst the Count and Procopius looked from one to the other with glances of the greatest surprise.

"The reason I did not mention it sooner, gentlemen," said Ben deprecatingly, "was simply because I wanted you all to get a little rest after your long journey. During your absence, Captain, I have had some visitors."

" Visitors ! "

" Certainly visitors, and helpers too. Yesterday you remarked the great quantity of corn stacked and of hay saved around here. Of course, you could not have imagined that my two arms alone had made such a harvest."

"Of course not!" said the Captain. "I could not understand it myself, but I was fully intended to ask all about it at the first opportunity."

"We are all very much surprised indeed," said the Russians.

"Suppose we start now, gentlemen, to see our visitors," said Ben. "You will not have far to go — hardly a mile and a half — but be sure to bring your guns along."

"To defend ourselves?" asked the Captain.

"Yes," said Ben, "but only against the birds."

Not knowing what to make of all this, the Captain and his companions followed Ben, leaving Nina playing with her goat at the *gourbi*.

"Now, gentlemen, use your guns as soon as you please," cried Ben, pointing to the birds that were soon fluttering in thousands overhead, or were spread in countless numbers on the corn-fields. They were of all kinds and sizes, but chiefly wild ducks, snipes, swallows, crows, ravens, gulls, quails, partridges, wood cocks, etc., etc., many of them mere nuisances, but many more furnishing delicate and wholesome food. For an hour or so our friends turned themselves into merciless sportsmen. But it was not exactly sport — it was a war of extermination waged against a horde of plundering invaders.

When Ben considered they had done sufficient execution for the present, he quitted the sea-shore and led his party obliquely across the plain to the south-east. In less than ten minutes, thanks to diminished gravity, the Captain and his companions found themselves near a dense grove of sycamore and eucalyptus trees picturesquely climbing a hill of moderate elevation. Here Ben stopped and looked around in all directions.

He was fully twenty yards ahead, but his companions could easily hear him exclaiming, in no measured terms: "Oh, the drones! the slugs! the lazy thieves!"

"Birds again, Ben Zouf?" asked the Captain. "Shall we fire?"

"No, Captain," answered Ben, pointing to a lot of rakes, reaping-hooks, scythes, and other agricultural implements thrown carelessly here and there all around, "not birds this time! Though I should not be sorry to see you take a pop at the lazy rascals that I can never keep at their work! Just hear how the rogues enjoy themselves while they think I am talking to you at the *gourbi!*"

The Captain and his companions were now more mystified than ever.

"Ben Zouf!" cried Servadac, sharply; "I'm tempted to take a pop at *you* first, if you don't explain pretty quickly the meaning of all this."

"Only keep quiet a little while, Captain," observed Ben, "and you'll soon understand it without further explanation. Listen, gentlemen. I thought I should catch them at it!"

The Captain and his companions, obeying orders, listened with some attention; and they could soon distinguish the mingled sounds of a voice singing, a guitar thrumming, and castanets rattling, all in perfect tune and harmony.

"Spaniards!" exclaimed the Captain, hardly able to credit his ears.

"Spaniards! who else?" said Ben. "These fellows would think nothing of castanetting at the cannon's mouth!"

"But, Ben Zouf, won't you —"

"Listen again, Captain and gentlemen," interrupted Ben. "That's Methuselah!"

A harsh, grating voice was now heard, talking very angrily, if not actually scolding and cursing. But it was soon drowned in shouts of derisive laughter.

Our party had by this time approached near enough

to catch the Spanish words, which the Captain and the Russians understood very well.

The song, with guitar and castanet accompaniment, was immediately resumed :

> "Tu sandunga, un cigarro
> Y una caña de Jerez,
> Mi jamelgo y un trabuco,
> Que mas gloria puede haver?"

(Thy beauty, a cigar, a glass of sherry, my horse, and a blunder-buss — what greater glory can be found?)

"Mi dinero! mi dinero!" cried the grating voice. "No quereis pagarmi lo que debeis honradamente, majos miserables?" (My money, my money! Won't you pay your honest debts, you miserable pretenders?)

Once more the song :

> "Para Alcarrazas, La Chiclana,
> Para trigo, Trebujena,
> Para niñas muy bonitas
> San Lucar de Barrameda."

(For earthen pitchers Chiclana is famous; for wheat, Trebujena; but for very pretty girls, San Lucar de Barrameda.)

"Si! si! mi pagareis mi deuda, ladrones!" the rasping voice was heard again exclaiming, in spite of song, guitar and castanets; "milo pagareis, por el padre Abrahan!" (Yes, you shall pay me, you bandits! You shall, s' help me Father Abraham!)

"A Jew, by all that's wonderful!" cried Servadac.

"Better than that, Captain, a Dutch Jew," said Ben, who, quite as much as his master at that time, detested everything German.

They were making for an entrance through the under-wood into the open part of the grove, when the sight of a strange spectacle suddenly stopped them.

The Spaniards began to dance their national fandango, but, Gallia not being Spain, every dancer rose in the air to a height of forty or fifty feet. Nothing could be more comical than the sight of the Spaniards bobbing up and down, as they appeared and disappeared behind the tops of the highest trees. Shouts, claps, and en-couraging cries of "Ole salero!" greeted every new success. But a new feature in the dance soon raised the applause to absolute frenzy. Four muscular Spaniards, holding an old man by the hands in spite of himself, were seen to rise and fall in the air, swinging half round, back again, and performing pirouettes, shuffles, and all kinds of fancy steps. Laughing, yelling, and screaming with delight, they would even throw the old man from one to the other, and catch him before he touched the ground. The most accomplished Japanese athletes never did anything so wonderful. They seemed to move about in the air more easily and gracefully than swimmers in enchanted waters. But it was the vicious resistance and

the comical terror of the old man that created the greatest fun. The louder he shrieked, and cursed, and swore,
and appealed to his Father Abraham, the louder and
more joyous was the laughing chorus of his tormentors.
The more wildly he kicked and struggled, the more
clamorously twanged the guitar, and the more dinningly
rattled the castanets.

The Captain and his companions, desiring to put an
end to this ridiculous scene, hastily entered the opening. In the cleared part of the grove they saw the
musician, the castanet player and five other Spaniards
in different attitudes of supreme enjoyment, as, roaring with laughter, they rapturously applauded the dancers.

At the instant, however, that they caught sight of the
strangers, they became mute as statues; the music
ceased at once; and the dancers, handling their victim
a little less roughly, landed him quietly on his feet, but
torn, bruised, perspiring and hardly able to catch his
breath. But no sooner did he see the Captain than he
ran towards him eagerly and, probably recognizing him
by his military dress, cried out in good French but with
a strong German accent:

"Oh! Monsieur Governor General! These rogues
have stolen my property, they have, s' help me Father
Abraham! But you'll do me justice, won't you?"

Before replying, the Captain asked Ben in a low voice what was the meaning of this title?

"It's all right, Captain!" whispered Ben; "you're our Governor General. I have made all the arrangements."

The Jew, having lodged his complaint, took off his old cap, bent his head, crossed his arms, and waited patiently for the Governor General's decision.

In the meantime the Captain had taken a good look at him, and soon knew his man.

About fifty years of age, but looking old enough to be sixty, he was small of stature and unhealthy of look. Eyes that glittered with cunning, nose sharp and hooked, stubbly beard of a dirty yellow, matted hair, feet clumsy and shambling, hands all fingers, like an eagle's talons — all pointed him out as one of a class well known in every quarter of Europe — the Dutch Jew. He was moreover one of the worst of the type— a usurer, supple of backbone, cold of heart, voluble of tongue, the gold-clipper, the skinflint, the lickpenny, the muckworm in all its ugly deformity. He scented money as unerringly as a hound scents blood, and heaven or earth could not throw him off the track. A veritable Shylock, he would take nothing less than his sixteen ounces of flesh. But his worst trait was hypocrisy. Though of Jewish parentage and continually in-

DUTCH ISAAC.

voking Father Abraham, he could be a Turk with the Turks, and even a Chinaman with the Chinese if there was any money in it.

A few questions soon put the Captain in possession of his main story. His name was Isaac Hakhabut; his birthplace, Cologne; his profession, coast-trader on the Mediterranean. In his tartan of one or two hundred tons burden, a regular floating country grocery store, he had everything for sale, from a box of matches for a penny to a roll of Lyons silk at ten dollars a yard. In fact this tartan, the *Hansa*, was his only place of abode. Without wife or children, it amply supplied all his wants. A crew of four, a captain and three deck hands, easily managed to take good care of the light vessel on its regular rounds to Algeria, Tunis, Turkey, Greece and the Levantine cities. Well supplied with coffee, sugar, rice, tobacco, textile fabrics, gunpowder, etc., Isaac sometimes sold, sometimes exchanged, sometimes bought, but always made money. The *Hansa* happened to be at Ceuta, on the African coast opposite Gibraltar, at the moment of the catastrophe. The four men composing the crew spent the night on shore, and of course disappeared with all the rest. But the extreme northern point of Ceuta had been spared — the reader may kindly remember that it had been visited by the two English officers — and with it eleven Spaniards, who never seemed to have an exact idea of what was taking place around them.

These jovial Andalusian peasants, loving fun as much as they hated work, extremely obliging and good-natured, and as slow to give an insult as they were quick to avenge it, had formed a kind of club or trades'-union for self-defence, putting at its head one of themselves, Negrete by name, who knew a little more than the others because he had run around a little more. When they found themselves that memorable morning alone and abandoned on the rocks of Ceuta, their embarrassment and terror were equally great. At first, they did not know what in the world to do. But the sight of the *Hansa* lying a short distance from the shore soon inspired them with the idea of seizing it, and sailing back in it to Spain. One part of the idea was put into instant execution — they were not the kind of men who upon all occasions never forget the difference between *meum* and *tuum*. But the second part of the idea hung fire — there was not a sailor among them.

It was while they were still in a state of great perplexity as to what was the best course to pursue in these difficult circumstances that the two English officers arrived and held a secret conference with Negrete. What took place on this occasion Isaac could not tell. All he knew was that, as soon as the Englishmen had taken their departure, Negrete compelled him, Isaac, to set sail for the nearest point of the African shore. This he had done, unwillingly of course, but partly because he could not help it and partly because the Spaniards had faithfully promised to pay him the full amount of the passage-money. They started on February the third and, the wind being west, they had found handling the sails and steering to be the easiest work in the world. The vessel took them of her own accord and without their ever knowing anything about it, to the only point on the whole globe where they could find refuge.

Here Isaac's testimony coming to an end, Ben Zouf stepped forward to complete the story.

He began by saying how astonished he had been one fine morning at seeing a ship, not the *Dobryna*, approaching the island in full sail and coming to anchorage in the port of the Sheliff. Boarding it immediately, he soon learned the circumstances of the case from Dutch Isaac (Isaco el Tudesco), as the others called him. The Spaniards he had found very jolly, but quite amenable, and the cargo entirely uninjured. This cargo, Ben volunteered his opinion, should be seized at once for the common stock, whether the Jew was willing or not to come to terms. Suitable terms, of course, might be offered to him, for the fulfilment of which he should take his chances; at present one thing was certain — the Jew could never expect to sell these goods either at a profit or otherwise. As to the trouble regarding the passage-money, Ben went on to say, he had not been able to make the parties come to anything like a settlement — Isaac demanding the full price, no abatement, and the Spaniards positively refusing to pay him a single sou. After several days wasted in listening to arguments on each side, he had determined to give himself no further trouble in the matter and told them to leave it all in the hands of his Excellency the Governor General, at that time occupied in going his "Rounds of Inspection."

During the course of Ben's narrative, the Captain could not help exchanging an occasional smile with the Count and Procopius, at his Orderly's readiness in comprehending the claims of the emergency, and at the official style and dignity of his language.

When he had concluded, his Excellency the Governor General thanked him gravely for his presence of mind, ability, and general energy, in a responsible position; then, turning to Isaac, he dismissed him with a few quiet words, promising that his case would be immediately looked into, and justice done to everybody.

By this time the Spaniards were thoroughly tired of standing around and listening to a long story, of which they did not understand a syllable. Negrete, therefore, whispered Ben, that they were all desirous to return to their work with his Excellency's permission. This being readily granted, the Spaniards, nine full-grown stalwart men and one young boy named Pablo, gave three rousing cheers, by way of welcome to their Governor General, and quietly returned to their work in the fields outside the clearing. Isaac also retired, mumbling blessings on his Excellency and protesting that he was a poor old man, not worth a single centavo, "s' help him Father Abraham!"

"How can that old miser expect to be paid?" asked the Count, some hours afterwards, when all were quietly strolling back to the *gourbi*. "These poor Spaniards can have no money."

"Beg pardon, Count Timascheff," answered Ben, "these Spaniards have plenty of money."

"Spaniards of their class with money!" observed the Count. "Unless you know it for a certainty, I should say it was very unlikely."

"I do know it, Count, for a perfect certainty," said Ben, respectfully. "I have seen it — plenty of English sovereigns. I know them well!"

"Ah!" exclaimed Servadac, suddenly recalling the

visit made to Ceuta by the English officers. "Well —
but no matter just now — we shall settle this question
hereafter. But, Count, changing the subject, our Gallian population is improving in variety, as well as in
number. We can boast of a good many specimens of
the nationalities of old Europe."

"Yes," answered the Count, "our fragment of the
old world can show natives of France, of Russia, of
Italy, of Spain, of England, of —"

"Of Germany too," added Procopius, seeing the
Count hesitate.

"Well, yes, of Germany too," continued the Count,
"though I hardly think, Captain, that the great German
nation is well represented by Dutch Isaac."

"I do!" answered the Captain, angrily flushing up.
"I think grasping, greedy, heartless, treacherous, lying
Dutch Isaac is the best possible representative of the
modern German Empire!"

The Count, seeing the dangerous ground he had trod-
den upon, hastily turned the conversation.

"Let us go look at the *Hansa!*" he exclaimed, suddenly.

His proposition met with a ready response.

CHAPTER XIX.

A STIFF-NECKED CHARACTER.

THE Count's sudden thought was a most happy one. They had not yet seen Isaac's vessel; it lay in a little creek north of the island, and the *Dobryna* had arrived by the south.

On their way they quietly discussed the situation in all its aspects. They had now a pretty good idea of how things actually were. Of the old world there remained but five points: Gourbi, a portion of Algeria; Gibraltar, in possession of the British; Ceuta, abandoned by the Spaniards; Maddalena, where Nina had been found; and St. Louis's tomb, on the shores of Tunis. All around these points extended the Gallian Sea, comprising about half the old Mediterranean and completely encircled by a crystal coast of composition and origin alike unknown.

Of these five points only two were inhabited: the Rock of Gibraltar, where the thirteen Englishmen seemed to have provisions in abundance for many years to come; and the fertile Isle of Gourbi, containing at

present a population of twenty-two. Likely enough
also, another survivor of the old world still existed on
some unknown island — the mysterious astronomer who
had sent the strange documents. Total: thirty-six inhabitants in the new asteroid.

In case the whole thirty-six should be collected
together at some future period on the Isle of Gourbi,
would its nine hundred acres of good soil, at present
under cultivation, well managed and well tilled, be
sufficient for their support? The answer was still what
it so far had been. It depended altogether on the
length of time elapsing until her soil had recovered its
reproductive power; that is, until the period when
Gallia, once more free from the colds of starry space,
would receive heat enough from the sun to start anew
her vegetative capacity in full vigor. When this approach to the centre of light and heat might be expected
still depended on two problems extremely difficult of
solution: (1) Did Gallia follow an orbit certain to bring
her back to the sun — that is, an elliptic curve? (2) If
so, what was the value of this curve's eccentricity?
These problems being for the present totally beyond the
capacity of the Gallians, no time should evidently be
wasted in considering them. Better do what could be
done, which was, first of all, to take an inventory of
the actual state of their provisions. The sugar, wine,

brandy, flour, preserved meats, etc., at present on board the *Dobryna*, and which the Count surrendered at once and unconditionally as his contribution towards the common stock, might possibly last two months. The *Hansa's* cargo, still untouched and which Isaac could be compelled in case of necessity to hand over for general consumption, was quite sufficient to last for twelve or fifteen months. Finally, the vegetable productions and the animals of the island were abundant enough, under an economical management, to assure the population plenty of food for at least six or seven years.

In the midst of the conversation, another idea suddenly struck the Count.

"By the by, Captain," said he, "I just remember that you are looked upon by our population as Governor of the island. I sincerely hope you will not think of declining the position. Every reunion of humanity, however small, requires a head. You are just the man for the position. You are French, and the island is yours since it is all that remains of a French colony. As long as we are here, I and my people shall always consider it both as a pleasure and a duty to recognize you as Commander-in-chief."

"Count Timascheff and Lieutenant Procopius," said Servadac, "I have been already thinking seriously over this matter, and I can say without hesitation that I accept at once the position with all its responsibility. Without vanity I can promise that we shall always have a good understanding with each other, and that I shall never attempt any measure that is not strictly for the general good. We are all, it is true, in a situation of extreme difficulty and of a most marvellous nature, but it seems to me that the worst is already passed. What we have now to do, if it can be done, is to keep ourselves alive till the period comes, if it ever comes, when we shall once more have an opportunity of beholding the familiar aspect of old Mother Earth, from whom we have been so suddenly and strangely separated. In every attempt of mine for this purpose I must rely on your cordial co-operation, and my experience so far, dear friends, has been of a nature to convince me that no co-operation could be more reliable, earnest, or capable.''

This little speech, an unusually long one for the Captain, was spoken with a hesitancy and diffidence that showed decided emotion. At its conclusion he extended his hands warmly to the Count and Procopius, who pressed them with much earnestness and even affection. All three kept their hands united for a few seconds, as if silently registering a solemn compact for life and death.

This affair settled all resumed their walk in the direction of the *Hansa.*

"I have been debating with myself for some time," said the Captain, taking up the conversation, "whether we ought to acquaint our friends the Spaniards with the true situation of affairs."

"I hope, Governor, you won't do anything of the kind!" quickly answered Ben Zouf, who, fully appreciating his own difficulty in realizing how matters stood, considered every attempt at explaining such things to ignorant Spaniards as mere waste of words. "They could never understand you, Governor, and, if they did, so much the worse! They would abandon themselves at once to despair, and we should never be able to get a stroke of work out of them!"

"Yes," said Procopius, "these poor peasants are probably so ignorant that your explanation would be either entirely thrown away on them or so misapprehended that it would do more harm than good."

"In my opinion, Lieutenant," said the Captain, "it would make very little difference to them whether they understood me or not. From what I know of Spaniards, they are not the kind of people that surrender themselves lightly to despair. Quite the contrary! Give a Spaniard his guitar, a pair of castanets, and room enough to dance his fandango, and there is no happier mortal breathing. What do you think of the question, Count?"

"Tell your Spaniards the whole truth, Captain, as I have told it to my Russians."

"You are right, Count," answered Captain Hector. "I think with you that we should never conceal our danger from those participating in it. Our Spaniards are not so ignorant as not to have observed the new and obvious modifications of physical phenomena, such as the shortening of the days, the new path of the sun, and the diminution of gravity. Starting with this as a foundation, I don't think we shall have much difficulty in showing them that we are no longer on the Earth, but on a small fragment of it, called Gallia, which was suddenly shot into space little more than two months ago."

Ben had the good sense not to say another word on the subject, but he mentally promised himself some good sport at the sight of "Dutch Isaac's" long face on learning that he was now many millions of miles away from the Earth, where he had, no doubt, left many a debtor behind him. He chuckled audibly at the idea, and almost rubbed the skin off his hands with delight as, looking over his shoulder, he saw the Jew, grumbling and growling to himself as he stealthily followed the party at a distance of forty or fifty paces.

It must be acknowledged that Ben had taken a very

great dislike to this poor descendant of Abraham, and he did not even attempt to conceal it. German, Jewish (in the objectionable sense of the term), miserly, cowardly, sneaky, mean, hard-hearted, Isaac did not possess in Ben's eyes a single quality entitling him to the slightest regard beyond the ordinary rights of humanity. Often kind and even brotherly to some poor Spaniard that would lose his spirits now and then, Ben was never kind or even civil to Isaac, who was always in the lowest spirits possible. But, strange to say, the Jew seemed to have conceived a special liking for Ben. He always had a comparatively pleasant word for him, appeared to take particular pleasure in his company, and never failed to treat him with the greatest attention and respect. All this, however, was completely lost on Ben. He never called the old man by his right name. To his simplest question he would never return a serious answer. His most innocent observation would always draw forth some sarcastic reply, the wit of which must have hugely pleased Ben himself, for he always greeted it with a noisy laugh.

"The new days are only half as long as the old, Signor Ben Zhouf!" Isaac would say, trying to draw Ben into conversation.

"That'll make you at least two hundred years old when you kick the bucket, Jeremiah!" Ben would answer with a merry giggle.

"Ah, Signor Ben Zhouf! the weight of so many years —"

"Can't ever be a heavy burden, Judas! The diminution of gravity has fixed all that!" Another peal.

"And the moon too, Signor Ben! The moon gone away!"

"Why are you so alarmed about the moon? Judas, you surely can't have lent money on her!" A new roar.

"Ah! Signor Zhouf! You laugh much! You be a very merry gentleman! But the sun rising in the west—"

"The sun likes a change in his old days, Potiphar. Profit by his example!"

"You are a very nice gentleman indeed, Signor Ben Zhouf! But I comprehend not —"

"Not comprehend, Noah! Well for you the Governor General is not listening! Comprehend or die! is his motto."

"The Governor General is also a very nice gentleman, Signor Ben Zhouf! He will not pillage my properties!"

"Pillage your property, Cain! Not he! He would be satisfied with confiscating it!"

Here Ben would get tired of laughing at his own wit, and, suddenly running off on pretence of some business, leave Isaac taking what consolation he could out of what he had learned, and trying to decide as to whether he desired the Governor's arrival or not.

In the meantime the Captain and his companions had reached the shore, and were inspecting the *Hansa*. Her dangerous situation instantly struck them. She was moored in a little creek so utterly unprotected on one side that even a tolerably brisk gale from the north-west would inevitably dash her to pieces on the rocks. Here, therefore, she should not be allowed to remain a moment longer than was necessary for making a hasty inventory of her contents. This inventory the Captain and Procopius undertook to make in an hour or so, and in the meantime the Count and Ben Zouf, returning to the Spaniards, could explain to them the necessity of assembling as soon as possible at the *gourbi*.

The *Hansa*, interiorly as well as exteriorly, was in perfect order. A glance was enough to show that. Descending into the hold and comparing what they saw there with Isaac's papers, which Ben had surrendered with all other important documents very ceremoniously into the Captain's hands, they readily discovered that the cargo had not suffered the slightest injury. Sugar-loaves by hundreds, chests of tea, bags of coffee, hogs-heads of tobacco, pipes of brandy, casks of wine, kegs of beer, barrels of dried fish, bales of cotton, woollen,

and silken goods, boxes of shoes for all feet and hats
for all heads, agricultural and domestic utensils, pottery
and china ware, writing and letter paper, ink, matches,
salt, pepper and allspice, Holland cheese, almanacs,
cheap novels, thread, needles, soap, candles, etc. —
the whole cargo was probably worth from twenty-five
to thirty thousand dollars. It had been renewed at
Marseilles only a few weeks prior to the catastrophe,
with the intention of exchanging it for good hard gold
at almost every point on the African coast between
Ceuta and Tripoli.

"A splendid cargo!" said Captain Hector, hastily
checking off the items.

"A perfect mine!" said Procopius. "Of course you
will make a requisition —"

"Not exactly, Lieutenant," said the Captain. "The
owner, though a German, will not be treated in the
German style. He must be paid for his goods. Only,
as soon as he finds himself in a new world and very
unlikely ever to see the old one again, he will probably
be willing to part with them at a reasonable price."

"Perhaps he may, Captain," said Procopius doubt-
ingly. "But whether he will or not," he continued,
"one thing is certain — the *Hansa* should not be left
here an hour longer. Not to talk of a storm which may
spring up any moment, she could never resist the pres-

THE EXPLANATION.

sure of the ice, and the sea may be frozen solid within twenty-four hours."

" All right, Lieutenant. Order your crew to take her to the port of the Sheliff as soon as you please."

" It shall be done to-morrow, Captain, the first thing."

An hour afterwards they found the rest of the inhabitants of the island assembled in the large room of the old guard-house. One of the Spaniards, the Captain was delighted to observe, the boy called Pablo, a very lively little fellow, was already on the best terms with Nina, who seemed quite rejoiced at having a suitable companion.

The instant the Captain appeared, the Spaniards ceased their merry chattering and at once assumed every appearance of respectful attention. The Captain began at once. In a few clear sentences, Spanish of course, he told them that they and he and all were just then in a very serious situation, which required all their courage, devotion, industry, and obedience. These he asked of them, and these he was confident that he should obtain.

The Spaniards listened quietly and made no reply, but Negrete their chief, speaking in their name, told the Governor that the gentlemen, before pledging themselves to anything, would first like to know at what time he proposed taking them back to Spain?

"Take them back to Spain!" interrupted Isaac in a hot, angry tone but in very good French. "The Signor Governor General will not do anything of the kind until they pay their passage-money! The buccaneers promised twenty reals apiece to be taken from Ceuta. There's ten of them — the boy Pablo was ten years old last month and must therefore pay full fare — that makes two hundred reals — a lawful debt and too much for a poor man to lose, s' help me Fa—"

"Keep still, old Benjamin!" cried Ben Zouf. "If you interrupt the Governor you shall be shot!"

"Isaac," said Servadac quietly, "your claims will be investigated and, if found just, shall be paid to the last maravedi."

"Found just!" exclaimed Isaac. "S' help me Father Abraham, if my claim is not just nothing is just! The good Governor General will see this himself and will make these Spanish filibusters pay me my lawful debt! And if the good Russian lord will only lend me two or three of his sailors to take my tartan to Algeria —"

"Algeria!" roared out Ben, unable to contain himself, "why, old Balaam, are you ignorant enough not to know —"

"Keep silent a little, Ben Zouf," interrupted the Captain, "while I tell these good people what they are at present profoundly ignorant of, but what it is absolutely necessary that they should know."

Then resuming in Spanish :

"My friends," said he, "a very strange phenomenon, which so far none of us has been able to explain, has separated us from Spain, from Italy, from France, in a word, from all Europe. Even of Africa nothing remains except the little island where you have found refuge. Of the other continents we know nothing and can learn nothing. In fact, we are no longer on the Earth at all, but probably on one of its fragments. This fragment is at present carrying us farther and farther into space, and it is now really impossible to say that we shall ever return to the old world again."

Did the Spaniards understand this speech? Hardly. They looked at each other with faces so blank and so utterly void of every expression except that of bewilderment that Negrete, speaking for them all, asked the Governor General to have the kindness to repeat what he had just said.

The Captain readily complied and, by taking very particular pains with his language, using for this purpose whatever terms, phrases and comparisons he judged to be most familiar to the Spaniards, he at last, perhaps, succeeded in making them realize their situation. They gathered round Negrete and at once commenced a very animated palaver, though it was carried on in low respectful tones. By degrees, the faces of most of them

brightened; some even laughed; a few crossed themselves, and looked serious; but, in general, they seemed
to accept the state of things with wonderful resignation
if not with absolute indifference. So at least the Captain was assured by Negrete when, after a few kind
encouraging words, he broke up the meeting and sent
the Spaniards back to their work.

Old Isaac did not follow them. To the Captain's
explanation he had listened with extreme attention,
never uttering a word. But his eyes twinkled now and
then with a gleam of malicious cunning, and his thin
lips pressed themselves knowingly together as if to prevent a smile. When the Captain, seeing him still
lingering behind, asked him if he still thought of taking his vessel to Algiers, he sniggered and grinned and,
turning to the Count, said to him in Russian, loud
enough to be heard by the sailors:

"Ne pravda-li, moy blagorodni Russki kneyas? Ego
Prevoskhodeytelstvo General Goobernator lubeet puskat
svoy nebolshie ostroti!" (Is it not so, my noble
Russian lords? His Excellency the Governor General
likes his little joke!)

The Count, turned on his heel, disdaining to reply.

Isaac then, approaching the Captain and pointing
over his shoulder with a leering expression at the retiring Spaniards, said in French:

"Such stories, Signor Governor General, may do very well for ignorant Spaniards. They're even too good for such swine. But you can't expect to catch an old bird like me with such chaff!"

On his way to the door, he saw little Nina kissing her hand to Pablo, and telling him to come early to-morrow.

"Non e vero, carina mia?" said Isaac, as he passed her. "Isaco il Tedesco e un viaggiatore troppo vecchio per essere burlato cosi!" (Isn't it so, my dear? Dutch Isaac is too old a traveller to play any such tricks as these on!)

"That old Bedouin knows all the languages of the universe, I believe!" cried Ben Zouf, sufficiently recovered from his surprise at the whole scene to be at last able to speak.

"No, Ben Zouf, you're wrong," said the Captain quietly. "That old Bedouin, as you call him, knows but one language. The words he may change as much as he pleases, but his language is always the *Dutch Isaac!*"

CHAPTER XX.

THE first thing done next morning was the removal of the *Hansa* by Procopius and his men from its dangerous position on the north coast of the island to the port of the Sheliff. Isaac made no objection beyond a growl or two; for, in the first place, the proceeding put his vessel in a place of safety; and, in the second, it would facilitate his acquaintance with the Russian sailors, two or three of whom he was pretty certain to be able to seduce from the Count's service by the bribe of higher wages. With their assistance, what was to prevent him from slipping cable some fine morning, himself and his *Hansa*, and starting for Algiers or some other well-known point?

The next item in order was immediate preparation for the severe winter now close at hand. The extensive works contemplated for that purpose the Captain confidently expected to be rendered comparatively light, by the great muscular force which the diminution of gravity would enable the laborers to develop.

324

The Spaniards showed themselves to be quite as active as the Russians in commencing operations. Up to this time they had slept in a kind of shanty constructed in the woods under the direction of Ben Zouf, but now the *gourbi* and the station-house were to be the general headquarters. In a short time both were put in perfect order for this purpose. Here all were to take their meals and here the Spaniards slept, but the Russians passed the night in the *Dobryna* and Isaac in the *Hansa.*

Ships or even stone houses could, of course, be now no more than mere provisional habitations. Abodes of a very different nature would be required for protection against the fierce colds of interplanetary space. They should be warm of themselves since, for want of coal or other combustible, they could not possibly be heated. The only abodes of this kind that could offer a safe refuge to the Gourbians were *silos*, the Spanish name for underground dwellings, somewhat of the same kind as those used by the Samoieds and northern Siberians. The surface of Gallia once covered by a thick coating of ice and snow, both bad conductors of heat, the temperature of these silos might be reasonably expected to remain at a supportable degree of warmth. Living in them would be anything but comfortable or healthy; perhaps it would be even unendurable; but there was

no choice left.   Silos or death were the sole alterna·
tives.

Fortunately the Gourbians were more favorably cir-
cumstanced than whalers or other explorers obliged
to winter in the Arctic regions.   They had at least
the solid earth underneath them.   They were not
obliged to fight the icy blasts in ships or snow-huts
on the surface of the frozen ocean, where proper protection from extreme cold is almost impossible.   By
digging out excavations twenty or thirty yards in
depth, they had every reason to expect to reach a
point where, as on the old Earth, the thermometer
never varied from year's end to year's end.

All set to work at once in the best spirits.   Shovels,
spades, pickaxes, barrows, drills, implements of all
kinds, as we know already, were numerous enough
in the *gourbi*.   Ben distributed them around; Procopius drew the plans; the Captain and the Count
staked off the lines; while the Russian sailors and
the Spanish peasants seemed to vie with each other as
to who would do the most and best work.

All went on very well for awhile; then a difficulty
occurred which at once stopped the workmen and puzzled the engineers.   Digging, shovelling, blasting, and
carting off, to active and healthy laborers presented
little or no difficulty.   But once arrived at an average

DIGGING THE SILO.

depth of eight feet below the surface, they could get no farther. There they found themselves endeavoring to penetrate a strange hard mineral substance that resisted all their efforts, breaking even their best steel drills.

This substance, the Captain, the Count, and Procopius recognized at once as the material composing the crystal coast and the bottom of the sea. It must therefore form the undercrust of all Gallia. Gun-powder had no effect on it. Even dynamite, if they had such a thing, would have probably failed in fracturing its adamantine grain.

"Shall we never escape this accursed thing?" exclaimed the Captain angrily. "How does it get here? As well as I can remember there was never anything like it in the old world!"

"Your impatience is quite natural, my dear Captain," said the Count, "but, I'm sorry to say, quite useless. Remember our motto: a silo or death! There's not an instant to be lost!"

The Count was only too right, as the Captain himself knew perfectly well. It was only that very morning that he had exchanged a few calculations with Procopius regarding the fast diminishing temperature. Gallia, at the present time, could not be less than 250 millions of miles distant from the sun, that is, nearly three times farther than the Earth ever is from the centre of our system. From this you can judge how much the light and the heat must have been diminished. Fortunately, Gourbi lying on Gallia's equator and the equator itself coinciding with the ecliptic, the sun was always vertical at noon and therefore imparted all the light and heat possible at such a distance. But the distance was too great, and the thermometer was steadily getting lower and lower. Little Nina, to her great surprise and joy, had already discovered some ice here and there among the rocks, and the moment was rapidly approaching when the whole sea would be frozen solid.

The temperature was now never higher than 21° Fahrenheit. The fresh water rills and streams over the country were ice-bound. A roaring fire, kept up in the great stove of the guard-house day and night, hardly made headquarters comfortable. But how would it be when after awhile the thermometer would sink to two or three hundred below zero, when the mercury itself would freeze, and when perhaps even alcohol could not stand the deadly chill? Competent shelter could not come an instant too soon. Silos or death!

As to the *Dobryna* and the *Hansa*, they not only could not be sufficiently heated but would be even in great danger of being crushed to pieces by the ice-blocks that would be piled up all around them. What then was to be done? Silos or death! Wooden houses, useless. Stone houses, useless. Ships, useless. Silos or death! No alternative. Every instant the moments became more and more valuable. The sun, already small enough, was growing smaller. As long as he was in the zenith, he certainly imparted some heat; but as soon as he sank below the horizon the cold was already quite sharp and biting. Silos or death!

But where to dig the silos? The Captain and the Count, mounted on Zephyr and Galette, searched all parts of the island for some spot that could be sufficiently excavated. The horses flew as if winged, and the hurried exploration was soon made. But it was all in vain. Here, there, elsewhere, the soil was carefully probed. Everywhere without exception the same hard crystal formation was found, in some case even only two or three feet below the surface. Silos were impossible!

What then should be done? Prepare for an immediate and cruel death? Not yet awhile! Not until the extreme moment comes! Fight it off as long as possible; then surrender with submission and resignation. Defend the *gourbi* and the guard-house as carefully against the cold as could be done, and hold out there as long as a breath could be drawn!

"Collect all the wood at once, dry or green, that can be found in the island!" was the Captain's order to Ben Zouf. "Detail a squad of your men to cut down at once all the trees growing in the low lands! Not an instant can be lost!"

"Ay, ay, sir!" cried Ben, rapidly comprehending the meaning of the order and as rapidly starting off his men for its execution.

All that day and the next the fuel came in abundantly. Great piles of fire-wood were made in the immediate neighborhood. Even the *gourbi* and the guard-house were covered with a coating of chopped wood five or six feet in thickness. Timber being a bad conductor of heat, this coating would afford at least temporary relief against the approaching deadly cold.

Yes! at best it would be but temporary. All this fuel and ten times as much would soon be exhausted. What then? The sure end, if some better expedient were not soon hit upon. The Captain and his friends racked their brains day and night in search of this expedient, but all to no purpose.

"An idea?" said the half-distracted Captain one day to Ben. "Oh, Ben Zouf, give me an idea!"

"I wish we were at Montmartre!" said Ben simply.

"Montmartre! What has Montmartre to do with our present difficulties?"

"The quarries and caverns at Montmartre would be just the thing we want."

"Quarries and caverns! — Well! That's an idea certainly. It may lead to something, though at present I'm blest if I know what it is!"

"Lieutenant," said the Captain that evening to Procopius, "let us examine the south-west portion of the island a little. The Count and myself have been everywhere else. I have a faint recollection of seeing some quarries or caverns in that direction, which might be turned to some account."

Off they both started at once for the point agreed on, and during the walk they conversed very earnestly on the all-engrossing subject — how to protect the colony against the deadly cold now so close at hand? Differing very decidedly as to the best means to be employed for the purpose, their discussion soon became quite warm. The Captain, full of hope and burning with eagerness, insisted that there *was* a way, extremely simple and practical, only that he could not then say exactly what that way was. Procopius, on the contrary, insisted that the only proper mode of facing the terrible trial before them was not to weaken the mind in useless attempts to guess at something new, but to devote all its energies towards making the most of the advantages already in their possession. With this idea constantly in view, he had applied himself carefully to the solution of the question. The result was that he had already invented fuel-saving stoves of different kinds but all founded on the same principle, namely —

"Hello! What's that?" interrupted the Captain, suddenly stopping and putting the glass to his eyes.

They had now reached the summit of a very high ridge running east and west through the island and therefore affording a wide prospect over the ocean that washed the southern coast. In the foreground lay the *Dobryna* and *Hansa* securely moored.

"What's what?" asked Procopius, looking in the direction in which the Captain pointed, but seeing nothing save a horizon of indigo blue.

"A light! as sure as I exist!" answered the Captain.

"A light! Where?" asked Procopius, much excited and now using his glass.

"A light most decidedly!" answered the Captain. "A very brilliant speck on the horizon! over the *Dobryna's* mast, but a little to the left!"

"I see it clearly!" said Procopius. "What can it be?"

"A ship on fire probably," answered the Captain. "No mere signal light could be visible at such a distance."

"It is getting brighter and brighter as night comes on," observed Procopius. "Besides it never changes its place."

"Can it be a lighthouse?" asked the Captain.

"No!" answered Procopius promptly. "Yon light lies exactly in the course by which we returned in the *Dobryna,* and had a lighthouse been there we should have seen it."

"Procopius!" cried the Captain, as if inspired. "It's the VOLCANO!"

Procopius said nothing, but examined the light with redoubled care.

But the Captain hurriedly closed his glasses, and, putting them away in the case, prepared to return to the gourbi. He was flushed with excitement and could hardly speak without pausing to take breath.

"That's the very spot we're looking for, Procopius!" he exclaimed in high, unnatural tones. "There is where Nature saves us the trouble and supply of fuel! Yonder burning lava is inexhaustible! We can do what we please with it! Ah! the good kind Providence does not forget us! Come, Procopius, let's hurry back to the Count! To-morrow we visit yonder mountain! There we shall find heat enough to last us as long as we are inhabitants of Gallia!"

Whilst the Captain was rapidly exclaiming with all

the ardor of his enthusiastic nature, Procopius was quietly thinking. Yes; there was no doubt of a volcano existing in that very direction. They had all seen it from the *Dobryna* on the western side of a long promontory on the former site of the Oran mountains. At that time its summit was covered with smoke; but this smoke must have yielded to an eruption of flames or red-hot lava; it was this eruption that was now lighting up the horizon and that was strongly reflected from the dark evening clouds above.

"Captain," said Procopius at last, "you must be right! That is certainly the volcano, and we shall explore it to-morrow!"

On hearing of the discovery, the Count became almost as enthusiastic as the Captain.

"I shall start along with you!" said he. "Procopius, have the *Dobryna* ready without a moment's delay!"

"Father," said Procopius, "for such a short distance the *Dobryna* is hardly necessary. The coast, besides, is unknown and dangerous. The little steam-sloop will answer every purpose."

"Arrange all that as you please, Procopius," answered the Count. "Only let us start to-morrow at daybreak."

Like most of those expensive and luxurious steam-yachts of the day, the *Dobryna* had been provided with

THE VOLCANO.

a little steam-sloop set in motion by a powerful donkey engine of the Oriolle patent. It was got ready at once and without commotion, not even Ben Zouf being admitted into the secret. He could hardly believe his eyes next morning, March 11, when he saw it disappearing over the southern horizon. But, like the prudent superintendent he was, he made no remarks on the subject, and after breakfast had all his men hard as ever at work, collecting wood, sawing it, sorting it, and making it up into great piles around the gourbi.

A rapid run of three or four hours brought the explorers close under the volcano. Its summit was all in flames, and the eruption was evidently one of considerable violence. What had caused this eruption? The oxygen lately transported from Earth by Gallia and now coming in contact with explosive material in the mountain interior? Or, more probably, did this volcano resemble the volcanoes of the Moon and supply its own oxygen?

After half an hour's exploration of the coast, the little sloop came to anchor in a sort of natural harbor formed by a semicircular line of rocks. This ready-made harbor, though small, was large enough to afford, in case of need, pretty safe mooring-ground to even the *Dobryna* and *Hansa*.

Our travellers, landing without difficulty, began to

ascend the slopes of the volcano on its western side. Though it was by the eastern side and northern side that the lava torrents made their way to the sea, a change of temperature was immediately noticed by the explorers and gratefully appreciated. It was a good omen. Perhaps, after all, their enthusiastic expectations were realizable! Perhaps, by carefully exploring this enormous mountain rock, they might meet some caverns where the Gallians might find shelter from the deadly danger that otherwise surely awaited them.

Up they started the steep mountain slopes, therefore, carefully on the lookout for every favorable turn, scaling rocks, climbing precipices, crawling over the rough strata, jumping from point to point with all the nimbleness and almost all the surefooting of chamois, but never meeting with any substance except the omnipresent and everlasting hexagon-prismed metallic material with which they were by this time so unpleasantly familiar.

For an hour or so they saw nothing to encourage them. But they persevered. They could not believe their researches were to be useless.

They were struggling along the side of the mountain at an elevation of eighty or ninety feet over the sea, when they approached a great pile of rock, towering like a vast pyramid into the sky. Behind this they suddenly discovered a narrow gallery or rather crooked shaft tunnelled into the mountain side. It was high enough to admit their entrance, and into it they immediately plunged.

After a little while everything around them was as dark as pitch. But that they did not mind. They might break their necks by falling down some frightful precipice. But such a contingency never seemed to occur to them. One apprehension troubled them and one only — they might suddenly meet with a solid wall which barred all further progress. Only such an obstacle as that could make them afraid or uneasy. Groping their way, therefore, with hand and foot equally on the alert, keeping closely together, and rapidly communicating mutual experiences, on they crawled in very good spirits for at least half an hour. They had as yet seen nothing, but their hopes were rising higher and higher; the temperature was certainly growing warmer.

Suddenly the Captain stopped.

"Hist!" said he. "Do you hear nothing, my friends?"

"I hear something like the distant roar of a great cataract," said the Count.

"I hear something like the far-off rumbling of a thunder-storm in the mountains!" said Procopius.

" Exactly ! '' cried the Captain, " but you both know very well that it is the bellowing of the great central vent of our volcano ! We can't be very far from it now ! Where there's a chimney there's a chimney hearth ! It's all right, dear friends ! Mother Nature does the whole business ! By Jove, we shall be all as warm as toast without ever burning a stick of wood ! Lieutenant, strike a light and examine the thermometer ! ''

" Sixty degrees, Fahrenheit, Captain,''

" How did it stand at the mouth of the tunnel? ''

" At twenty-five ! ''

" You see, gentlemen, we are on the right track ! Onwards ! ''

Procopius tried to guide his steps by a burning match, but it went out immediately and he was too impatient to light another. For ten or fifteen minutes longer they groped on through pitchy darkness. But the roaring grew louder, and the temperature warmer; in five minutes more the wall around and the floor beneath grew so warm that the heat began to feel somewhat oppressive.

" The material of this mountain must be metallic,'' said the Captain; " it conducts heat so well. Let us push on a little farther. We shall see the furnace presently ! ''

CENTRAL HALL.

Even as he spoke, the sides of the tunnel began to grow visible by a lurid reflected light, every moment growing stronger. The roar could now be distinctly heard, and the heat made them perspire profusely.

"Eighty degrees, Fahrenheit!" said Procopius, this time without striking a ·match.

The roar of the flames was soon so loud as to drown their voices, and a sudden turn brought our explorers in presence of an awful sight. The gallery which they had followed here ended in an enormous cavern so high that the roof was invisible, but the red glare of its sides was almost brilliant enough to dazzle the eye. It was a Hall of Eblis without its Afrits, its Spectres, or its Despair! At the far end of this mighty grotto was an opening through which the eye could see a cataract of white hot lava rushing down furiously on its way to the ocean. It was the Falls of Niagara viewed from the Cave of the Winds, only the shooting columns of water had been suddenly changed into hissing, sparkling, crackling, roaring pillars of white hot iron!

"Oh most gracious Heaven!" cried Servadac, falling on his knees and humbly taking off his cap. "Our heartiest gratitude for such mercy! This is more than we could ever expect!"

The three friends remained for a few moments in silent prayer.

CHAPTER XXI.

THE CHANGE OF DOMICILE.

OUR friends had every reason to feel grateful. In fact, under the circumstances, no better habitation could be devised for the little Gallian colony. Well heated, well lighted, and sufficiently spacious, it would afford very comfortable quarters not only to the Governor and his "subjects" as Ben called them, but also to the horses and even a considerable number of other domestic animals during the whole course of the long and dreary winter — that is, if this long and dreary winter was ever to come to an end.

The enormous cavern itself, as our explorers soon discovered, was simply a great Central Hall, into which some twenty or thirty other tunnels conducted after ramifying different portions of the mountains. The air in all of them, though remarkably pure, was very warm, the metallic walls being excellent conductors of heat.

"Locked in the arms of these lofty chambers," said the Captain proudly to his companions as they traversed them, "thoroughly sheltered from all the rigors of a more than Arctic climate, knowing little or nothing of the colds of space no matter how low they may go, every single animated being of our new asteroid can here find sure refuge as long as —"

"As the eruption lasts!" said the Count, seeing the Captain hesitate. "Which," he went on to say, "it is likely to do for years, if not for ages, to come. You have remarked that it is the only volcano so far discovered on the shores of the Gallian Sea. Being, therefore, in all probability, the only vent for Gallia's interior fires, the eruption is likely to last quite as long as the asteroid herself remains in existence."

"Nothing can be more correct than that remark of yours, Father," said Procopius very decidedly but rather hurriedly. "Captain, I must congratulate you on your sagacity and ourselves on our extraordinary good fortune in finding such a place of refuge. But remember, we have no time to lose. While we are speaking here the sea may be freezing outside! If so, our 'moving' from Gourbi would be attended with endless difficulty!"

"Right, Lieutenant," said the Captain. "We start immediately for Gourbi Island. Our 'moving' commences to-morrow, when the *Dobryna* shall land her first instalment here. By the by, what name shall we give this promontory so opportune and so friendly in every respect?"

"*Terra Calida* (Hot Land)," suggested Procopius.

"A good name," said the Captain, "but, in honor of our Spaniards, the most numerous nationality of our little colony, I would change its form to *Tierra Caliente.*"

"My amendment is still better," said the Count. "In honor of the French nation, one of whom, our worthy Governor, is the discoverer of this happy winter haven, I suggest that the final form of the term be *Terre Chaude!*"

"Carried by acclamation!" said Procopius inscrib ing the name in his note-book. "*Terre Chaude* it is!"

We shall not attempt to describe the joy with which the members of the little colony received the news of the wonderful discovery. Not that they by any means fully comprehended its great importance. It was only the Captain himself and, of course, the Count and Procopius, that had a clear idea either of the nature of the long and terrible winter in store for them, or of the careful precautions necessary in order to be prepared for it. The Spaniards and even the Russians never dreamed that it must be infinitely worse than the six months of awful darkness and winter to be endured by the dauntless navigators of the high polar seas. These simple creatures never thought of asking themselves if the moment could ever come for Gallia to be once more free from the death-grip of ice-fetters? Or whether her orbit followed a reëntering curve to take her back finally to the sun, or an open curve to carry her off for-ever through the boundless regions of stellar space?

Such questions, of course, never perplexed these art-less souls. But they had their eyes wide open to every-thing going on all around them. They saw the sun every day getting smaller and smaller; the sky every day getting darker and darker; the ground every day getting harder and harder; and, what frightened these simple children of nature most of all, they saw the coun-. tenances of the three good men, in whom they had reposed the most unbounded confidence, getting every day gloomier and gloomier. All this portended the approach of some terrible calamity, which the three leaders, in spite of their best efforts, did not seem likely to be able to avert.

But the news regarding Terre Chaude, seeming to please the Captain and his companions, should there-fore be good news. Dispersing at once all the gloomy forebodings of the colony, it was hailed with an ex-travagant joy which, as already observed, we must not attempt to describe. Suffice it to say that when they heard it, the Spaniards threw themselves at once on their knees, improvised a *Te Deum*, and ended the proceedings with a lively dance. The Russians, not knowing any sacred hymn and unable to improvise one, chanted a *Song to the Czar* which, in spite of its words, being sincerely addressed to a Greater Being, in all probability answered its purpose quite as well as the most successful effort of the most devoted poet. Little Nina, who said her prayers regularly every night and morning, remained longer than ever on her knees that evening, thanking the good DOMENIDDIO for making her friends happy, particularly her beloved Padrone, the Russian Count, the Ship-master, and her dear Benni Zufo. Even for Isaaco il Tedesco, the poor cross old man who was always mumbling to himself because he had no friend to talk with, the kind little creature contrived to offer a prayer or two.

It took the colony three days' hard work to get through the "moving." The *Dobryna*, loaded to her bulwarks, could make but one trip a day. Her first cargo was all the grain, hay, straw and other stores of the kind, that she could carry; it arrived safely, and was carefully stowed away in the galleries destined for its reception. Next day, March 15, the rocky caverns received those domestic animals, cattle, sheep, hogs, etc., whose species it had been determined to preserve — about fifty or sixty altogether. The others, as they could not be kept alive, were slaughtered, the bodies butchered, and the meat packed away carefully for future use. This furnished a supply of provisions at once immense and safe, as such cold was always sure to keep them perfectly fresh and sweet.

Whilst Procopius superintended the loading and the discharging of the cargoes, the Captain and the Count saw that the goods were properly stowed away in the vaults. In performing this important duty they displayed much ingenuity and were attended with great success. New explorations discovered new galleries ramifying almost without end, so that the mountain resembled a vast beehive full of honeycombs. Here the bees, that is to say the Gallians, could find plenty of heat to warm themselves with, plenty of food to feed themselves with, plenty of sleep to refresh themselves with, and plenty of company to amuse themselves with. What more could the most industrious bee desire? It was with this idea in his mind, and also in honor of the Italian girl, their little Madonna, that the Captain named the new dwelling-place *Alveario di Nina* (The Nina Beehive).

It was soon clear enough that the great lava torrent, though a powerful engine for imparting general heat, would be of very little use for the other daily wants of the colony unless some plan was hit upon for utilizing it

to the best advantage. To this object one of the Captain's first engineering labors was directed, and with
Procopius's intelligent aid he soon completely succeeded.
By closer exploration they discovered here and there
smaller winding galleries opening out on the great Falls.
As long as both ends of these galleries were open, the
heat in them though great was not insupportable. By
stopping up the outer end, however, and thus cutting off
the rush of cold air from outside, each little gallery was
at once turned into a perfect oven. The cooking-range
of the *Dobryna* being brought into one of these galleries, it was so readily heated by the irradiating lava
that Mochel the head cook at once declared he had
never found anything so convenient in all his life. In
fact, he really felt himself far more comfortable at the
closed end of his little lava channel than he had ever
been in the stifling, roasting steam kitchen of the
yacht.

"Hey, Mochel!" cried Ben, one day seeing him
quietly superintending the cooking of a new soup he
had just invented, called *Potage à la Volcano*, "hey!
Chef, what do you think of our new heating apparatus?
When we get back to the Old World, we're going to
take out a patent for the idea! We shall begin by
laying pipes from Vesuvius for southern Europe, and
from Hecla for northern! . Fact, I assure you. I heard

the Governor telling your Old Man all about it ! They have already decided on the name of their pamphlet — I saw it myself ! It is called : FUEL SUPERSEDED ! COAL MONOPOLY CRUSHED ! *Every man his own volcano at a penny a day !* ''

The great cavern in which most of the galleries ended was to be the Central Hall for general use. It was accordingly made as comfortable as possible by a supply of the chief articles of furniture from the gourbi and the *Dobryna.* The great sails, also taken down and brought in, served here for screens and a variety of other important purposes. Here too the Count's fine library, well supplied with Russian, French, German, Italian and Spanish books, naturally found its place. Plenty of tables, lamps, chairs and cushions made everything quite cosy, and even the bare metallic walls were quite relieved by some valuable paintings that the Count was afraid might get injured if left on board the *Dobryna.*

The lava torrent, which was continually falling at a distance of thirty or forty feet from the great opening of the Central Hall, was here, as has been already mentioned, the great source of light and heat. By tracing the course of this torrent a little further down, which was done after awhile by exploring the mountain on the outside, the Captain discovered that it plunged

hissing and smoking into a kind of vast lake surrounded
on all sides by rocks and therefore probably completely
cut off from the rest of the Gallian Sea. This was
another most fortunate discovery. Might not the
waters of this lake remain in a liquid state in spite
of the severest rigor of a Gallian winter ?

A pretty large recess, opening on the left out of the
Central Hall, became the chamber especially reserved
for the Captain and the Count. Another corresponding opening on the right was occupied by Procopius
and Ben Zouf. A little nook quite close to this, a
charming boudoir Ben called it, was turned by his
taste and care into a very pleasant sleeping apartment
for Nina. The Russians and Spaniards arranged their
dormitories as well as they could in the different galleries opening into the Central Hall and rendered perfectly comfortable by its light and heat.

Such was Alveario di Nina — The Nina Beehive. Here
the little colony could wait without much uneasiness for
the long and terrible winter which should soon rage
in every other part of Gallia. And even in case the
asteroid should follow an orbit carrying her as far as
Jupiter and therefore be subjected to a degree of cold
twenty-five times lower than the mean temperature of
the Earth, there was every reason to hope that the Gallians could brave it with perfect impunity.

But what was to become of old Isaac? Was he to be left behind in disgust to perish of cold and hunger? Not exactly; he was not to be left behind though, to tell the truth, he tried the patience and humanity of the Gallians so sorely that many of them wanted never to see his foxy face again, and swore that to leave him behind would be serving him quite right.

In fact, the misbelieving old miser, deaf as a post to every argument, reason and proof which the Captain, the Count or Procopius through motives of pure humanity showered upon him, never quitted the *Hansa* a minute. There he stuck day and night, rambling up and down from deck to hold and from hold to deck. starting at every noise as at a robber's footstep, growling at the thieving Spaniards that would not pay their fare, scanning the lonely horizon for some ship with news from Europe, and continually on the watch for a chance to bribe two or three of the Russian sailors. But this chance he waited for in vain. Having declared formally to Captain Hector that he would not part with a single dollar's worth of his goods without cash down — gold too, none of your rags for him — the Captain, by way of reprisal, had issued positive orders that no one should either buy of Dutch Isaac, sell to him, or take anything from him on any account. In case of pressing necessity, they might *give* him what he wanted if they liked to do so, but on no account should they *take* anything from him, or, in short, hold communication with him any further.

But this embargo, except that for the moment it "blocked his little game," as Ben said, of corrupting the Russians, did not appear to give the old miser the smallest concern. What did he care whether they spoke to him or not? He was not to be frightened by bugbears! He was no such jackass as, like those Russian boors or those Spanish buffoons, to be imposed upon by every cock and a bull story! Not on the Earth any longer! On a block blown off it, like a bung out of a beer barrel! Flying through space like a broken kite on a windy day! No, no! Old Dutch Isaac had had his eye-teeth cut long ago! That something very strange had happened, he did not deny. An earthquake or some other physical catastrophe had certainly considerably modified the ordinary condition of things. But the disturbance was entirely local. He would soon be able to get away from this accursed spot and once more resume his traffic with the simple natives of the African shore. These Frenchmen and Russians were no doubt hatching some conspiracy to deprive him of his goods. But they should find their match! He, Isaac, had dealt with as smart people as ever they were, and had not come off second best!

There was nothing green about him, etc., etc. After scolding and grumbling this way for an hour or two, he would start up suddenly, clap to his eye an old telescope patched all over and as rusty as a worn-out stovepipe, and sweep the horizon once more for the ship that was to bring news from Europe with perhaps a merchant with plenty of red gold in his purse to be exchanged for the contents of the *Hansa.*

Ship and merchant he sought in vain, but he could see very clearly that something unusual was taking place in Gourbi Island. What was up? Preparing to remove into winter-quarters? Not a bit of it! Some new dodge of these Frenchmen and Russians to do him out of his property! But it was to be a miserable failure, like all the others!

But when he saw the *Dobryna,* laden down to her very last water-mark, make two separate trips to the south and return for a third, he began to entertain some misgivings regarding the justice of his conclusions. Was Captain Servadac really determined to transport the whole colony from the Isle of Gourbi? He certainly looked like it. In fact, there could be no doubt about it. Here certainly Isaac had to acknowledge to himself that he had been altogether in the wrong. But might he not be quite as wrong in all the other points? What if what he called a cock and a bull story were after all perfectly true? What if he were really on an asteroid instead of on the Earth? On the Gallian Sea instead of the Mediterranean? What if he were never again to see his dear Germany, or, what was infinitely worse, if he should never again have a chance of selling his goods at 300 per cent. profit to the simpletons of Tunis and Tripoli? Such thoughts were actually distraction, and in a quarter of an hour he made up his mind to endure the suspense no longer.

Hastily quitting the *Hansa*, he soon found himself in the midst of the Russians and Spaniards, all as busy as bees, getting everything ready for their last trip from Gourbi Island.

He noticed that Ben Zouf was watching him like a hawk, but that did not disconcert him.

"Oh! my dear Signor Ben Zhouf!" he cried, running up and presenting his greasy old snuff-box. "Won't you take a pinch this morning? It is the best snuff the *Hansa* can offer, but it is not half good enough for Signor Ben Zhouf!"

"No, thank you, Pharaoh!" replied Ben. "Nothing from you! That's our orders. You can eat up, drink up, and snuff up the whole *Hansa* if you like, old Nabuco!"

"S' help me Father Abraham!" persisted Isaac, "this snuff is perfumed with attar of the roses of Ghazipour ! It was manufactured expressly for the Khedive of Egypt, but he found it too dear and could not take it. I bought some of it for such good gentlemen as Signor Ben Zhouf. Try a pinch ! "

"You'll be put in irons for tempting me to disobey orders, Nehemiah ! " said Ben. "But look ! " he added hastily, pointing at the Captain. "There's the Governor General himself! Try your snuff on him ! "

Servadac was very busy at the moment, but, seeing Isaac shuffling up to him, he waited to hear what he had to say.

"Has Signor the Governor General really and truly ordered the people to remove?" he asked with nervous earnestness.

"The Governor General has done so really and truly," answered the Captain; "if you're coming along you had better hurry up ! "

"S'help me Father Abraham ! " cried Isaac, very much perplexed, "I don't know what is best to be done ! "

"Don't you want two or three good men to take the *Hansa* to Terre Chaude?" asked the Captain.

"I want two or three good men to take the *Hansa* to Algiers ! " was Isaac's truthful reply.

"But Algiers isn't there ! You have been told so a thousand times ! "

"Holy Father Abraham! ' Is it possible?"

"Isaac, I ask you for the last time, are you willing or
not to follow us with your vessel to Terre Chaude, where
we expect to be able to pass a long and terrible winter
with perfect safety?"

"Don't ask me to move, Signor Governor; it would
ruin my goods!"

"You are not willing then? Well, I must now tell
you that, with your consent or without it, we shall put
the *Hansa* in a secure position."

"Without my consent, Signor Governor?"

"Yes, even without your consent. Such a precious
cargo must not be lost through your stupid pigheaded-
ness."

"S' help me Father Abraham, the Governor wants to
ruin me!"

"I am strongly tempted to abandon you to your fate,
you stubborn Dutch boor!" cried Servadac, hurrying
away in a towering passion very unbecoming in a Governor, who, no matter what the provocation, should never
forget his manners.

Every preparation being completed that evening, the
general departure from the Isle of Gourbi was fixed for
next morning, March 20. The thermometer was now as
low as 18° Fahrenheit, and every particle of exposed
fresh water was of course solidly frozen. The *Hansa*

was to accompany the *Dobryna*. She would never be able to resist the pressure of the ice in the port of the Sheliff. In the little harbor of Terre Chaude she would be better protected every way, and even in case of disaster her valuable cargo would be likely to be saved.

The embarkation was quietly and safely effected. A little after sunrise all were on board the *Dobryna*, except the four Russian sailors detailed by Procopius to conduct the *Hansa* to her winter-quarters. With what invectives Isaac welcomed these sailors on board, how often he told them that they were no better than burglars, that he did not require their aid, that all he wanted was to be let alone, that even the Governor General had no authority to invade the rights of a poor unoffending man, that he should pay dearly for it if justice were to be found any more in the world, etc., etc., cannot here be told. In the midst of his bitter tears, however, and his loudest lamentations and wildest fits of passion, a close observer could easily catch a cool gleam flashing every now and then out of his cunning eyes that showed him clearly, in spite of all his apparent excitement, to be the most self-possessed man on board and one from whose notice in reality nothing was allowed to escape. Three or four hours afterwards, when he saw his vessel comfortably and securely cradled in a little inlet not far from the *Dobryna,* the same observer would have caught glances

of very unequivocal satisfaction beaming from his countenance every moment he thought he was not watched.
He would also see his lips moving as if angrily and hear
his voice grumbling as if muttering imprecations, but,
if close enough, he could have heard expressions of deep
fierce joy:

" For nothing!   The numskulls have n't charged me
a cent!   S' help me Father Abraham, it would be dog
cheap at ten dollars!   But the asses ask no pay!   They
work hard and work well, and do it all for nothing!
For nothing!!"

The Captain and his companions took possession of
Terre Chaude with some pretension to formality and
order.   The Spaniards and Russians were highly delighted with Alveario di Nina, warmly extolled its interior arrangements, and congratulated each other on
their warm and comfortable winter-quarters.   The only
man who did not answer his name that evening before
supper in the Central Hall was old Isaac.   Ben Zouf
reported him as still on board his vessel, which he positively refused to leave on any account.   " He 's probably afraid," added Ben, " of being charged for his
board.   But wait awhile!   The old fox will soon be
glad enough to get his nose in here!"

The supper was a great success.   Mochel's lava steaks
and volcano chops were universally and loudly com-

mended. Wine — some of the best French brands, thanks to the Count's generosity — flowed pretty freely, and everybody was soon decidedly gay and happy. Songs were sung, speeches made, toasts to the Governor General and his Cabinet drunk with enthusiasm, and Ben Zouf, who drank everybody's health in sparkling Clos Vougeot, made such lively and characteristic sallies as set the company in roars. The Spaniards, jumping up, danced a national dance with extraordinary spirit and abandon. While taking breath, they asked Ben for a touch of his famous *Zouave Chorus* which, though often promised, he had always put off on some pretext or other. Description of its execution would be labor lost. To get some idea of it, you should have it done by a master like Ben Zouf — no one else should attempt it. His rendition of the following doggerel, mostly untranslatable, was inimitable :

> Misti goth dar dar tire lyre !
> Flic ! floc ! flac ! lirette, lira !
>   Far la rira
>   Tour tala rire
>   Tour la Ribaud,
>   Ricardeau,
> Sans repos, répit, répit repos, ris pot, ripette !
>   Si vous attrapez mon refrain,
>   Fameux vous êtes.

When the wild enthusiasm that greeted the *Zouave's*

Chorus had subsided, the Spaniards started off again
with another of the graceful sarabands of the country.
The Russians treated the company to some of the
most popular national dances and sailors' hornpipes.
Then the vaults rang with cries for "Ben Zouf! Ben
Zouf!" Ben, nothing loath, took the floor and entranced the company with a *Pas seul* of the kind so
well known at the Salle Barthelemi or the Closerie de
Lilas, executed in a style that even a virtuoso would
pronounce unsurpassable out of Paris.

At nine o'clock the inauguration ball came to a close,
but, before retiring, the Captain suggested the propriety
of all going outside for a few moments to take the air.
The wine, the lights, the dancing and the heat, had
raised the temperature of the blood somewhat too high,
and a little cooling off was advisable.

In a few moments Central Hall was completely
deserted except by the Captain and his two friends,
who had remained a little behind to exchange a few
words on the events of the day. They were proceeding leisurely towards the outward opening when they
were suddenly startled by a general cry outside expressive at once of surprise, joy and triumph. Not knowing
what to make of it and imagining worlds of strange
conjectures, they hurried with all speed out of the
gallery. They found the entrance blocked up by their

A PAS SEUL.

people, very much excited and still shouting with all the power of their lungs. Ben Zouf in particular was remarkable for the loudness of his cheering and the violence of his joyous gesticulations.

"Oh! Governor General!" he cried as soon as he caught sight of the Captain. "Oh! Monseigneur, come out here quick!"

"What is it, Ben Zouf?" asked the Captain, hurrying forward.

"The Moon!" exclaimed Ben, pointing to the western horizon.

And sure enough, there was a little moon working her way up out of the mists of night and moving slowly for the first time over the Gallian sky!

CHAPTER XXII.

LIFE AT TERRE CHAUDE.

THE Moon! If the Moon, why had she been so long absent? And if she now reappeared, whence could she have come? So far, no satellite whatever had accompanied Gallia; had the faithless goddess of night abandoned old Earth to transfer her affections to the young asteroid?

Procopius scouted the idea. The Moon! Impossible! She was still at her post, ruling the nights of old Earth, and now many millions of miles away!

"I don't feel quite so sure about that, Lieutenant," said the Captain, who still had his doubts regarding the correctness of the Procopian theory. "Why could not the Moon have lately succumbed to Gallia's attractions and so become her satellite?"

"Such a supposition is altogether inadmissible, Captain," said Procopius.

"Why so, Lieutenant?" asked Servadac; "could not the same explosion that blew us off have blown the Moon off too? Wandering about then in solar space, might she not at last have fallen —"

"No, my dear Captain," answered Procopius. "The Moon could not have fallen within the sphere of Gallia's attraction for the very good and sufficient reason that, her mass being far superior to Gallia's, our little asteroid would have become the Moon's satellite instead of the Moon becoming ours."

"Very true, Lieutenant," said the Captain, who, being very much puzzled himself, naturally took a malicious pleasure in puzzling Procopius, "but how do we know that such is not really the case? May we not be the Moon's moon? How do we know that the Earth has not been launched on a new orbit, and that we are not still accompanying her in her journey through planetary space?"

"Do you really expect an argument in reply to this new theory of yours, Captain?" asked Procopius, who in spite of the cold air was beginning to feel a little heated.

"Not at all, my dear Lieutenant," said the Captain, smiling, and feeling that the discussion had gone far enough. "I see the simplicity of my question now, and can answer it readily enough. If Gallia were a secondary satellite, she would not take three months to make a half turn around her primary. Consequently, if there was anything in my new theory, we should not be now looking at the old Moon for

the first time since the catastrophe. Let us examine
the new one!''

A glance or two from their telescopes showed the
stranger not to be the old Moon certainly, whatever
else she was. Though evidently much nearer, she
was also much smaller. Though full, she had not the
tenth part of the lunar surface, and she reflected the
sunlight so feebly as scarcely to extinguish a star of
the eighth magnitude. She showed none of the
''seas'' or ''craters'' or ''mountains'' or ''rills''
or other characteristics that give such peculiarity to
our ordinary maps of the Moon. In short, the new
comer had not the slightest claim to be considered
the ''Chaste Diana'' of the poets, the ''Silver Goddess of Night,'' the ''Queen of the Golden Stars.''

What was she then? A special moon in all proba
bility, as the Count suggested, a little asteroid captured
by Gallia as she flew through the zone of the telescopic
planets. Many of these asteroids are well known to be
so small that a good walker could easily get round one
of them in twenty-four hours. It was not at all improbable, therefore, that, being so much inferior in
mass to Gallia, one of them should have become her
satellite.

Long before this point was settled, the unscientific
portion of the colony, Ben Zouf included, had grown

tired of admiring the little moon, and, withdrawing to their quarters, were soon fast asleep. The first night at Alveario di Nina passed without further incident, and next morning the general mode of living was regularly organized. The Captain, justly regarding idleness as the source of every vice, gave every man some occupation, and took care that all should have plenty of work. The care of the domestic animals, in the first place, demanded great attention. Then preparing preserved food; fishing, while the sea was still open; clearing the galleries, many of which were very much obstructed; and thousands of other details furnished employment enough to keep every hand continually busy.

The very best understanding existed all through the little colony. The Russians and Spaniards were the best of friends, and soon began to talk to each other a little in French, the official language. Pablo and Nina went to school every day to the Captain, who found them very interesting pupils from their intelligence and docility. Amusing them was one of Ben Zouf's numerous occupations. He taught them rhymes without number and tricks without end. He always wound up his lecture by the description of a beautiful and famous city that he would take them to as soon as they should return to old Earth. It was built at

the foot of a mountain still more beautiful and famous
that had not its equal in the world and was in fact
a perfect land of enchantment.   The city's name, the
Professor said, commenced with a P, and the mountain's with an M.

"Isn't it all true, Monseigneur?" he asked the
Captain, who happened to pass by one day while Ben
was amusing the children with his wonderful stories.

"Ben Zouf!" answered the Captain impatiently;
"how often have I told you that I do not wish to be
designated by any such title?"

"Ten times at least, Monseigneur!"

"Well—?"

"I shall do so no more, Monseigneur!"

"I want you to have done with it at once—now—
do you understand?"

"Certainly, Monseigneur!"

"Why—you don't want to call me nicknames, do
you?"

"Certainly not, Monseigneur!"

"That's precisely what you are doing!"

"How's that, Monseigneur?"

"Do you know the exact meaning of the word?"

"I can't say that I do, Monseigneur!"

"*Mon* means *my*, and *seigneur* is French for *senior*
the Latin for *old man*. So in titling me monseigneur

you are simply calling your Captain 'my old man.' Is that showing a proper respect for your commanding officer ? "

" It is not, Mon — I mean Captain ! Excuse me this time and I promise I shall never call you ' my old man ' again as long as I live, Mon — that, is Governor ! "

And he kept his promise.

Meantime the second half of March was passing rapidly away and still the extraordinary cold so long expected did not make its appearance. The Captain, therefore, and his companions did not house themselves very closely. They even attempted a few excursions along the western shore of the new continent, and ventured a little into its interior to a distance of five or six miles from the volcano. It was still the same terrible rocky desert without the slightest sign of vegetation. A few threads of ice and here and there a few lumps of snow announced already the appearance of water on its surface. But how many ages and ages should elapse before a river would be powerful enough to scoop out of this rocky soil the channel in which it might roll its united waters to the ocean ! And as to this Terre Chaude itself — what was it ? A continent ? an island ? did it extend to the South Pole ? An answer could not be given to these questions until

such time—apparently distant enough now—as an expedition over these metallic crystallizations was possible.

A bird's-eye glance over this dreary region, however,
would be possible, in a limited way, from the summit
of the volcano which could not be less than three or four
thousand feet over the level of the sea. This bird's-
eye view the Captain and the Count determined to
obtain. The volcano itself was an enormous solid lava
block, of a pretty regular shape, somewhat resembling
a truncated cone. Its crater was rather narrow in
dimensions, and a dense canopy of black vapor covered it like a cap.

To climb such a mountain even in Italy would have
been a difficult feat. Its steep slopes and slippery
declivities would have offered little foothold to the
most enterprising member of the Alpine Club. If
success was at all attained, it would be only after an
extraordinary expenditure of pluck, energy and time.
But the diminution of gravity rendered the ascent of
the Terre Chaude mountain a task of little or no difficulty. Indeed the Captain and the Count found it
rather a delightful pastime rather than a severe piece
of toil. Chamois could not have bounded more lightly
from rock to rock ; eagles could not have floated more
gracefully over the bottomless abysses. They hardly
took an hour to scale a mountain between three and four

thousand feet high ; and even when they stood on
the edge of the crater they were no more fatigued
than if they had walked no more than a few miles
on a level plain. Decidedly if Gallia possessed some
inconveniences as a place of residence, she had also
her advantages.

From their lofty pinnacle, the two explorers, glass to
eye, soon saw that, in whatever direction they looked,
they could learn nothing new. To the north stretched
the cold liquid plains of the Gallian Sea, without a
ripple, smooth as a mirror, the very breezes of heaven
seeming to be frozen into stillness. A small black speck
nor'-east by north, doubtless an ocular delusion due to
refraction, showed the position of Gourbi Island. To
the south, endlessly and hopelessly extended the inhospitable regions of Terre Chaude, shaped somewhat like
a triangle, the volcano being the vertex, and the base
lying on the other side of the horizon. Even when
examined from this high point, which of course should
soften off all asperities, the surface of the unknown
territory seemed totally impracticable. Bristling with
millions of hexagonal crystals, sharp as steel, hard as
adamant, and rising here and there into ridges of immense height, it presented, except for a short distance,
an obstacle absolutely and completely impervious to
mortal foot.

" Wings alone or a balloon," said the Captain, "would enable us to explore such a craggy, spiky, spiny territory! We can now gaze, Count, on a chemical formation the like of which has never been exposed in any of the museums of Earth."

"Very true, Captain," said the Count. "You have also remarked how easily we can detect Gallia's convexity from this vantage ground. See what a comparatively short distance separates us from the horizon!"

"Yes, Count; I have often witnessed that effect from the cliffs of Gourbi. From a height of four thousand feet on our old Earth a horizon nearly eighty miles off could be easily seen. Here the horizon can be hardly more than one-third of that distance."

"Yes, Gallia is quite a small place when compared with our Earth," observed the Count.

"Small as it is, however," replied the Captain, "it is large enough for its population. Remark besides, its productive portion is strictly confined to the cultivable portions of Gourbi."

" Productive," observed the Count, " for two or three months in summer. Unproductive—a desert, for a winter of perhaps thousands of years' duration."

" Well, Count," replied the Captain cheerfully, " we were not consulted when they started on this journey through planetary space, and we must only try to make the best of it. A philosophical turn of mind is a wonderful help to a man in difficulties!''

"A grateful turn of mind is still better," said the Count gravely. " Let us not forget the Heavenly Hand that built this volcanic pillar, and filled its interior with lava. Without this vent for Gallia's internal fires we should have been undone ! ''

"I am profoundly grateful," said the Captain, lifting his cap, ''and hopeful too. These fires will not give out before the end."

''What end, Captain?''

"Whatever end, my dear Count, God has in store for us! He alone knows it. Welcome be His holy will ! ''

After a few moments spent in silent recollection they thought of descending, but first wished to cast a glance at the crater of the volcano. The chief peculiarity that struck them was its singular calmness. None of that stunning commotion, of that ear-splitting thunder by which ordinary volcanic eruptions are always attended. The profound silence here was really wonderful. There was not even a bubbling of the lava. This liquid substance, white hot, rose gradually in the crater, as in a sheltered lake, broad and deep, and fed at one end by a noiseless stream. As the Captain phrased it, the crater was no pot, heated so much by a brisk fire as to boil over with gas, steam, noise and smoke; it was rather a basin, filled to the brim and a little more, so as to trickle over without sound, almost without motion. Nothing therefore escaped but pure incandescent lava. None of those flying masses of molten rock; none of those enormous clouds of burning cinders that make other volcanoes look at times like a gigantic fire fountain. Accordingly therefore the base of the mountain was perfectly free from blocks of pumice, slag, obsidian and other rocks of Plutonic origin that usually strew the approaches to a volcano either active or extinct. No depositing glacier having yet begun to exist, it is hardly necessary to say that no boulders were visible. All "these peculiarities," observed the Count as they began descending, "are good signs that our volcano is not one of the intermittent kind. Violent effort, in the physical as well as in the moral world, must be of short duration. Furious storms, like furious passions, never last long. This liquid fire rises so regularly and overflows so calmly that its source is probably inexhaustible. You remember Niagara? The enormous body of water slips on so smoothly and moves on so grandly over the rocky channel that the thought never occurs to us of anything being ever able to interrupt its mighty flow. Here the effect is precisely the same. I really don't see why those brimming lava tides should not continue to flow on for untold ages."

"I am very glad you think so, Count," answered the Captain. "And now that our mind is at rest on one subject, what do you say to our being done with another?"

"What other?" asked the Count. "Do you mean the state of the sea?"

"Precisely," answered Servadac. "We are now quite ready for its freezing. Once solid, the surface of the Gallian Sea would open up easy communication with Gourbi, besides giving our people plenty of healthy and amusing exercise."

"It is now certainly cold enough to freeze," said the Count. "Why the sea has not frozen is due I suppose to its perfect immobility."

"Yes," said the Captain, "you see the slightest breath of air does not ripple its surface. In such a condition it can bear a very considerable degree of cold without solidifying. But give it the slightest disturbance — Crack!"

"Let us start it this evening," said the Count.

That evening, by the Captain's order, the whole colony was assembled on a rocky ledge at the extreme point of Terre Chaude, commanding a broad and uninterrupted view of the Gallian Sea. He wished them all to be witnesses of a curious physical phenom enon.

"Dear Nina," said he to the child, "I want to see how far you can fling a lump of ice into the ocean."

"Signor Ettore," answered Nina, she always called him by that name, "I can't throw it far, but you should see how far Pablo can throw it."

"You throw it now, little pet," said the Captain, putting a piece of ice into her hand; "we shall try your friend Pablo another time."

"Watch carefully, Pablo," he added turning to the little Spaniard. "You will soon see what a wonderful witch our little Nina is. She can command the elements. Come, darling. Throw when I give the signal. One. Two. Three!"

Away went the lump of ice whirling out of the child's hand. In a second it touched the smooth water. Instantly a slight crackling, shrivelling, shivering, quivering, jarring, rustling sound was distinctly heard flying in all directions as far as the horizon.

In less than another second the Gallian Sea was frozen solid!

"FLING!" SAID THE CAPTAIN.

CHAPTER XXIII.

ON THE TRACK AT LAST.

THREE hours after sunset on the twenty-third of March the little moon rose in the west, and the Gallians could see that she was now nearing her last quarter. In four days, therefore, she had passed from opposition to quadrature, which gave her about a week of visibility and fifteen or sixteen days for a lunation. The lunar months were thus, like the solar days, diminished by half.

Three days afterwards she entered into conjunction with the sun and, of course, disappeared in his irradiation.

"Will she ever come back?" asked Ben Zouf, naturally interested in her reappearance, but too much astounded at the late cosmical events to have great confidence in the stability of anything.

The sky being now very clear and cold, the mercury fell to 10° Fahrenheit.

How far was Gallia now from the sun? What orbit had she followed since the date given in the last docu-

ment? No one could tell. The sun's diameter **was**
of course still getting smaller and smaller, but that
told nothing definite. What had become of the astronomer?

"Cases, barrels, and bottles can serve his purpose no
longer," said the Captain, "now that the sea is as
hard as steel. But I should like dearly to hear from
him again."

"Hard as steel" was no exaggeration in describing
the surface of the sea. The Captain might have added
"and smooth as a piece of plate-glass." It had become frozen in magnificent weather and at a moment
when not a breath of air played on its surface. Accordingly it had not a single break, crevice, crack, or
the slightest bit of roughness. It was a splendid
mirror, extending in every direction, without flaw
blur, or fault of any kind.

"How different it is from what we saw in the Pola
seas, Procopius," observed the Count as they were
talking together one evening. "There, nothing but
icebergs, hammocks, ice packs, ice blocks, ice fringes,
ice feet, ice ridges, ice tables, ice cliffs, flues, glaciers
and what not! all thrown together in the wildest confusion, in the most fantastic attitudes, and often rising
to most astounding heights!"

"Yes," answered Procopius, "I remember our 'ice-

fields' well. Nothing was firm on them, nothing unchangeable. A slight variation of temperature, a faint
blast of wind, and everything was transformed! It
was fairy-land with ice decorations. Here, on the
contrary, everything is solid, more stable even than
the land. For smoothness and extent our plains surpass anything that the old world could ever show.
The plateaux of the Sahara, the steppes of Russia are
nothing in comparison. And this icy armor will go
on getting thicker and thicker as the temperature becomes colder and colder until thaw time comes — if
indeed a thaw time *is* ever to visit Gallia.''

The Russians, though already accustomed to almost
every form of congelation, looked on the Gallian Sea
at first with great surprise, but soon also with delight.
It offered the most splendid skating-ground that could
be imagined. The *Dobryna*, in her character as a
yacht prepared for every climate and every temperature, possessed a fine assortment of skates of all sizes
and patterns. These the Count generously distributed
to everybody willing to use them. His generosity was
duly appreciated. Every Gallian was soon on the ice.
The Spaniards, dancers *par excellence*, under the in-
struction of their friends the Russians soon became
excellent skaters. Nina and Pablo were quite as apt
as the rest. The Captain likewise soon did honor

to his professor the Count. But it was Ben Zouf who most astonished the little world by the ease, grace and audacity of his style.

"Where did you learn your skatesmanship?" asked the Captain one day, lost in admiration of Ben's super-fine skill.

"In the Montmartre Basin, Captain," replied Ben. "Where else? It's quite a sea, you know!"

But though Ben could cut up shines on the ice and perform such tricks as no one else could attempt, he was no match for Procopius at a steady piece of hard work. The Lieutenant, on several occasions, went the round trip to Gourbi and back, on ice, a distance of fifty or sixty miles, in little more than two hours.

"Skating is a good substitute for railroads," said the Captain one day, trying to be epigrammatical. "Indeed I may call it a flying railroad. The skate is the rail smooth and hard, diminutive indeed in size, but compensating for this by its mobility!"

In the meantime the cold kept on steadily increasing and the sunlight steadily diminishing. The sun's disc at midday gave no more light now than he had often given on Earth during the moments of a partial eclipse. A kind of gloomy lurid tinge began to fall on every object. Against the depressing effect of this on the spirits it was necessary to take action. It would never do to let these poor exiles of humanity begin to brood over a solitude that was to last perhaps forever. How could they forget that their dear old Mother Earth was already left at an infinite distance behind them, and that this distance was becoming greater and greater every day? How could they suppose they would ever see her again, plunging as they were on the wild wings of that flying block deeper and deeper into the soundless depths of interplanetary space? What reason had they even for flattering themselves that Gallia would not finally abandon altogether interplanetary space and run the endless rounds of the starry universe in search of another sun and of a more congenial centre of attraction?

Though such thoughts as these were certainly too deep for the simple Russian sailors and the merry Spaniards, the Captain and his friends could not help noticing every now and then a shade of sorrow crossing their faces and an expression of regret stealing involuntarily from their eyes. But every symptom of this sorrow or this regret, the Captain, the Count, Procopius, and Ben Zouf set themselves resolutely and upon all occasions to banish at once. Without allowing their efforts to be noticed, they did everything to cheer up their poor companions and to make their life as pleasant as possible. They taught them reading and writing, they set them to work, they gave them time for amusement and encouraged them in their fun; they hardly left them an idle moment. Skating, the principal *pièce de résistance*, was of immense advantage as an exercise at once recreative, exhilarative, most successful in dispelling monotony and cheering up the spirits.

In any of these labors, lessons, or amusements, it need hardly be said that old Isaac took no part. In fact, he had never showed himself to any one since his compulsory arrival at Terre Chaude. But he was not dead. A little smoke, continually ascending from a funnel of the *Hansa*, showed him to be still alive and as usual watching his property. The fuel and food of course, must have cost him some bitter regrets, considering that he could have his board and lodging free at the Nina Hive. But he preferred incurring this terrible expense to being obliged to leave the *Hansa*. In his absence what might not befall his precious cargo?

The *Hansa* moreover seemed to be perfectly secured. Both vessels had been so disposed of as to be able to withstand every hardship of a long winter. Procopius was an old hand at such business. By levelling the ice under the hull, as is done by winterers in the Arctic seas, he allowed it to meet under the keel, thus relieving the sides of the vessel from all danger of being crushed together by the tremendous pressure. With the rise of the ice-field, the *Dobryna* and the *Hansa* would thus also rise; and when thaw-time would come, it was expected to be not a very difficult matter to enable them to reach their respective water-lines without incurring great danger.

The whole Gallian Sea was now, as far as the sight could reach, a solid mass of ice in every direction — except one. This was the lake at the mountain foot already referred to, separated by a rocky reef from the rest of the ocean, and receiving the overflow of the incandescent lava. There the water remained entirely in a liquid state; even on the outer edges a tendency towards the formation of ice-cakes was overcome by the neighboring fire. Loud hissings of water, wild shrieks of steam, and dense clouds of smoke showed the line of immediate contact between the two elements, but the whole surface of the lake was continually boiling, bubbling, seething, fermenting, and enveloped in a fleece of mist.

In the early part of April the weather changed a little; clouds darkened the sky, without, however, producing a corresponding increase of cold. This showed that the altitude of the mercury depended no longer on any particular condition of the atmosphere, or as to its being more or less saturated with moisture. Gallia, therefore, no longer imitated the circumpolar regions of the Earth which are always considerably affected by atmospheric influences, especially the sudden shifting of the winds. The thermometer had now no maximum, no minimum; the altitude never rose beyond a certain degree, which kept on steadily diminishing as the asteroid kept steadily withdrawing from the great source of light and heat. And this action of the thermometric column would still keep on, steadily sinking until it should attain the limit assigned by Pouillet to the temperature of interplanetary space — about 250° below zero Fahrenheit.

The darkening of the sky, however, was soon followed by a tremendous storm, not of rain of course, or snow, but wind alone. As long as it lasted, the little colony could not venture outside; even inside, the storm produced very strange effects by its action on the screen of white hot lava that closed one end of Central Hall. Generally, like an immense fan-blower, it blew some of the lava inwards in great sparks, and saturated the rest so much with oxygen as to render the galleries disagreeably hot and even dangerous to life. But very often its violence was great enough to tear an opening through the sheet of flame and fill the halls with currents of ice-cold air which, by reducing the temperature, were generally oftener welcomed as highly advantageous than otherwise.

On the fourth of April the little moon had so far dis-
engaged herself from the solar irradiations as to be once
more visible — to the Gallians' great delight. Ben
Zouf in particular, the first discoverer, hailed her reappearance with particular interest. He was continually
begging every one to notice how the little thing did
her duty with just the same regularity in revolving
around Gallia as the old Moon had ever displayed in
revolving around Mother Earth.

One cause of disorder — the birds — still troubled
Alveario di Nina, and was not got rid of without
considerable difficulty. The gracious reader no doubt
remembers that the disappearance of cultivatable land
in Gallia had driven them in great numbers to Gourbi
Island. There, all, excepting the comparatively few
that had fallen victims to the war of extermination
waged on them by Ben Zouf and the others, had found
pretty safe refuge as long as the fine weather lasted.
But the great colds bringing snow and ice, and snow
and ice covering the soil with a crust impenetrable to
beak or claw, an immense emigration to Terre Chaude
was the sure consequence — though seemingly for nc
other reason than the company of man. Far from
being afraid of their old enemy, the poor creatures now
took every opportunity to seek his society. The gar-
bage and refuse of the little colony thrown out every

day from the galleries, they instantly gobbled up; many
of them even, impelled as much by cold as by hunger,
were daring enough to force their way into the tunnel
and to install themselves in the warm galleries of Alveario di Nina.

In self-defence these desperate intruders had to be
driven away, and at this task the colonists did not spare
themselves. At first, indeed, far from being alarmed,
they had taken pleasure in protecting their winged guests
and admiring a tameness that allowed them to take bits
of foo l out of their hands. But the numbers increased so
rapidly as soon to become a regular invasion. Instead
of waiting for the food to be offered to them, the starving creatures boldly snatched it off the dining-tables of
Central Hall. Then " Repel or Exterminate ! " became
the watchword of the day. Stones, sticks, guns, every
kind of offensive weapon was employed. No mercy
was granted, no quarter shown, except now and then in
sparing a pair to preserve the species, and yet the final
success was anything but complete. Ben was commander-in-chief. What a profound strategist he was !
The Count said he could give lessons to Von Moltke.
And when the decisive moment of execution had come,
when to tremble was destruction and retreat ruin, how
grandly he rose with the occasion ! How gallantly he
led the charge ! How scathingly he rebuked the skulk-

ers! How he encouraged the timid, restrained the rash, rallied the repulsed, reviled the enemy, and finally led on to a glorious victory! All this we must leave to the kind reader's imagination, as well as the style in which he afterwards cooked all the dead that were edible, and especially the fabulous number of a certain kind of canvas-back ducks that he contrived to put away in what he called his *garde-manger*.

The invaders at last, after an immense loss in killed and wounded, appearing to think they had got enough of it, drew off all their forces in pretty good order, with the exception of a few unconquerables that took refuge in nooks and crevices through the galleries, from which it seemed almost impossible to dislodge them. At least, the Gallians did not attempt to do so. Rendered magnanimous by victory, or, more probably, heartily sick of such a dragging warfare, they made no immediate attempt to renew the attack. The consequence was that in less than a week the few hundred birds that had managed to stand their ground soon began to consider themselves tenants in fee, and, as such, deemed it their bounden duty to keep out all other intruders whatsoever. It must be said that this duty they faithfully performed. Woe to the luckless fowl that had strayed into the interior of the Nina Hive! He was immediately set upon by hundreds of beaks and killed or expelled without mercy.

All this led to a curious incident.

On the morning of April 15, little Nina's voice was suddenly heard crying "Accor'uomo!" (Help! Help!)

Ben, recognizing the voice, started in the direction, but he was soon passed by Pablo, also running to help his little friend.

"Presto! Presto!" they heard her shrieking; "Mi ucciden!" (Quick! quick! they are killing me!)

Pablo, dashing into the opening, saw half a dozen of the largest and fiercest gulls flying wildly around the little girl and fiercely attacking something that she endeavored to defend.

Hastily picking up a stick, the boy instantly attacked and soon dispersed these daring sea-birds, though not without receiving a severe peck or two.

"What's the matter, Nina?" he asked.

"Oh! look, Pablo!" she cried, showing him a bird nestling on her breast and half covered by her folding arms.

"A pigeon!" cried Ben, now rushing in, "and what's more surprising, a carrier pigeon! And, by all the saints of Montmartre, it has a little bag around its neck!"

A few minutes afterwards, the fluttering little stranger,

THE RESCUE.

tenderly held in the Captain's hands, was the centre of attraction to a council of war assembled around the chief table in Central Hall.

"News from our astronomer of course!" said he as he opened the little bag, which had been somewhat injured in the struggle. "The sea being no longer free, he despatched this pigeon, which naturally came here, seeing there was nowhere else to go. I hope he has sent his name and address this time!"

The notice, like its predecessors, was short and laconic:

"Gallia.
Chemin parcouru du 1er Mars au 1er avril: 39,000,000 l.!
Distance du soleil: 110,000,000 l.!
Capté Nerina en passant.
Vivres vont manquer, et —"
(*Gallia.*
Distance travelled from the first of March to the first of April.
39,000,000 leagues.
Distance from the sun: 110,000,000 *leagues!*
Captured Nerina on the road.
Provisions giving out, and —)

Here the paper abruptly ended, the rest having been torn off by the sea-gulls.

"What hard luck!" cried the Captain in despair. "The name and address, the very thing we most wanted, is exactly what these accursed birds have destroyed! It's all written in French this time and in all probability it's a Frenchman that wrote it. And now not to be able to give the unfortunate man any assistance!"

Timascheff and Procopius hastened back immediately to the scene of the contest, hoping to pick up some scrap of paper that might put them on the right track. But they returned empty handed, and the Captain was disconsolate.

"Alas!" he cried, "shall we never know where to look for this last and most important survivor of the Earth?"

"Oh!" suddenly exclaimed the joyous tones of little Nina standing by. "Benni Zufo, look here!" and she pointed to something she had just discovered under the bird's left wing. It was a postage stamp, bearing on its face one written word — but that one was enough:

"FORMENTERA."

CHAPTER XXIV.

A WILD RIDE.

FORMENTERA!

The word had a world of meaning for the Captain and his friends. This little island then, the most southern of the Balearics, was the spot whence the astronomer had launched his dispatches. It was even in its neighborhood that two of them had been picked up. He was certainly alive two weeks ago. Was he alive now? This last dispatch was without a single comforting expression that denoted cheerfulness or satisfaction. No more *Va bene's* or *All right's* or *Nil desperandum's.* It was crabbedly written all in French, and the last words "*Provisions giving out*" affected every listener profoundly. They were the last cry of despair!

"We may be in time yet!" cried the Captain, "if we start at once for the relief of the poor sufferer!"

"The poor sufferers more likely," replied the Count. "Captain, I am ready to accompany you!"

"We passed by the site of the Balearics," observed Procopius, referring to his chart, "without seeing any sign of them.   You may have some trouble in finding all that remains of Formentera."

"We shall find it, Lieutenant," cried the Captain, "if it can be found!   How far is it from here?"

"Between three and four hundred miles, Captain. How do you propose reaching it?"

"On skates of course.   The quickest way, now that the sea is solid.   Don't you think so, Count?"

"I'm ready to go whatever way you like, Captain," answered the Count, who never hesitated when a question of humanity was under discussion.

"Skates won't do," said Procopius quietly.

"Why not?" asked his companions.

"The cold is excessive, in the first place," replied the Lieutenant, pointing to the external minimum thermometer, "as I have just ascertained, being seven or eight degrees below zero Fahrenheit.   In the second, a brisk wind from the south-west renders this cold absolutely intolerable for any length of time.   In the third, supposing you were able to endure a hundred miles a day, it would take you more than three days to reach Formentera.   In the fourth, this would require a considerable quantity of provisions, not only for yourselves, but also for the man or men whom you are going to relieve —"

"We shall start with our knapsacks!" interrupted

Servadac, chafed at the methodical Lieutenant's way of laying down the impossibilities of the expedition.

"You may do so," continued Procopius calmly, "but every now and then you shall need rest. The ice being perfectly flat, you can find no hummock behind the shelter of which you might have chance of snatching an hour's repose."

"We shall travel night and day!" cried the exasperated Captain; "instead of three days we shall take but two, perhaps but one, to reach Formentera!"

"Suppose you do, Captain," resumed Procopius, "admitting for the sake of argument that you had arrived there in one day, what relief could you afford to those you might find dying of hunger and thirst? If you ever undertook to bring them here, it would be corpses, not living beings, that would arrive in Terre Chaude!"

"At moments like the present, words are useless, Lieutenant!" said the Captain, who really could not reply to Procopius's cold logic; "all I can say is that poor human creatures like ourselves are dying this moment of hunger, cold and misery. Can we abandon them, Count?"

"We cannot!" replied Timascheff. "Procopius, is there no way besides skating by which we can reach Formentera? If there is, let us hear it at once!"

"There is, Father," answered Procopius slowly, and almost lost in thought. "I have no doubt there is! There must be! I have not hit on it yet, but I'm thinking over it."

"If we only had a sledge!" suggested Ben Zouf.

Procopius started and his eyes flashed, but he said nothing.

"A sledge is easily made," said the Count; "but how could we run it?"

"Ice-shoe the horses!" said Ben.

"They could never endure the cold," said the Count.

"No matter!" exclaimed the Captain, with decision; "it is our last resource! Let us have a sledge made as quickly —"

"It's already made!" interrupted Procopius rapidly, and as if inspired. "And the horses are ready too! They are even harnessed and can start in an instant! Not Zephyr and Galette though," he added, seeing that all were looking at him with eyes full of inquiry. "To drag a sledge in a storm over a smooth ice-field when the temperature is below zero, horse-flesh is but a poor *motor*. We have one swifter, surer, and in all respects safer!"

"Which is — ?" they all asked.

"The wind!" answered Procopius.

Certainly the wind. Why not think of it before? The Captain had often heard of the famous American ice-yachts. The Count had actually seen one in action. Starting from West Point on the Hudson, it had made New York, a distance of at least fifty miles, in less than an hour. The wind was now fortunately blowing a pretty stiff gale exactly from the right point. It was therefore possible to reach Formentera by means of an ice-yacht within a period of at most ten or twelve hours.

An ice-yacht they were not long in constructing — in fact, one was already on hand. The *Dobryna's* little sailboat, about twelve feet long, could easily contain five or six persons. By mounting it on a pair of steel sledrunners, plenty of which were to be found among the ship's stores, could not a perfect ice-yacht be got ready in a few hours? Besides, when decked over by a sort of wooden roof and carefully covered with three or four folds of sail-cloth, would it not afford complete shelter not only to the explorers themselves but also those whom they were to bring back? Sheltered in a vehicle of this kind well provided with furs, eatables of different kinds, cordials and other restoratives, besides a little portable stove heated by alcohol, the travellers should have very little difficulty either in reaching the island or returning.

Returning? Unless the wind changed, how were
they to return?

"Never mind about that just now!" cried the Captain, feverish with impatience. "The chief point at
present is to get there!"

Besides, as Procopius observed, even against an ad-
verse wind, the ice-yacht, though not protected by a
rudder against leeway like ordinary boats, could make
some headway by judicious tacking, the sharp edges of
its steel runners giving it grip enough on the ice to prevent too much drift.

The engineer of the *Dobryna*, assisted by a few handy
men, went to work at once and accomplished his task
after about half a day's labor. The ice-yacht, maintained in a horizontal position by means of a false keel
mounted on a pair of steel runners belonging to the
Count's own sledge, covered over by a light roof, and
even equipped with a long, light, metallic scull to protect it against lurching, and well supplied with provisions, tools, and warm clothing, was soon ready to
start on her all-important trip.

Procopius, however, now insisted on taking the
Count's place. More than two should not go — there
was no telling how many were to return, when crowd-
ing would be particularly unadvisable. Besides, the
management of the sails and the steering required a

sailor's hand. The Captain, moreover, reminded the Count that he was really the proper man to be Vice Governor; that the passage was dangerous, a sudden squall easily bringing on a fatal accident; that the people at Terre Chaude could not be left to themselves; that he, the Captain, would surrender his place with pleasure only that, the astronomer being a Frenchman, it was the duty of a French officer to be the first to fly to his relief.

Yielding to these observations, though much against his will, the Count at last consented to forego the pleasure of flying at once to the succor of suffering humanity.

At first light on the morning of the 16th of April, Servadac and Procopius made their way to the ice-yacht, surrounded by every member of the little colony, all shaking their hands and bidding them God-speed on their dangerous but humane voyage. Ben Zouf shed tears bitterly, as likewise did little Nina and Pablo; even the Captain himself showed considerable emotion as he warmly embraced his friend the Count. But time was precious. In a few minutes everything was ready for the start; in a few more, the ice-yacht was fast disappearing on the northern horizon.

Her rig consisted of a mainsail and a jib as large as was safe to carry. Her velocity was therefore very great, probably forty or fifty miles an hour. Through a thickly glazed aperture in front of the little cabin, Procopius could easily keep a good look-out and by means of his compass steer in almost a bee-line for Formentera.

Her motion was extremely smooth: no car on the best-appointed railroad could approach it. Much lighter than she would have been on Earth, her friction was almost reduced to zero; she glided on without rocking, rolling or pitching, and at least four or five times faster than any wind-impelled ship had ever moved through water. Her passengers sometimes could hardly detect any motion at all; at other times they felt themselves as if lifted up into the air by some powerful balloon; it was only by looking back that they could convince themselves that they were still on the ice-field. But they could not look back very far. For one moment only could a glimpse be caught of the white streaks made by the runners; in another they were enveloped in thick clouds of flying snow-dust.

It was now easy to remark that the frozen sea presented everywhere the same unvarying aspect. Nowhere could a living being of any kind be seen to enliven its dreary solitudes. Yet in spite of its dispiriting effect the dreadful loneliness of the scene was not without its poetic side. Even Procopius's cold eye of science kindled with a gloomy enthusiasm over this materialized realization of his wildest calculations.

But the Captain's artistic sense actually revelled in spite of himself in the contemplation of horrors which, far from depressing his imagination and emotion, actually enkindled both. Perhaps it was the maddening sense of terrific velocity that raised our friends to a high pitch of excitement; perhaps it was a sense of utter dependence amid the weird surroundings of such a novel scene that drew them more closely together. The red sun, dropping from a black sky, set in a sea of solid fire on the right. The yacht's gigantic shadow tore madly after her on the left. Even in the dark our friends could almost hear its shrieks of agony at the idea of being left all alone in such a land of desolation. Then the pitchy sky instantly flashed out in millions of golden stars glittering with supernatural brilliancy. But, seated in the little cabin, the two friends required no light to know each other's place. As if obeying an involuntary attraction, they drew closely together; their hands unconsciously sought each other, and a silent pressure said infinitely more than mere words could express.

An occasional glance at the new Polaris was sufficient guide through this exciting night. With wind a-beam and the course almost directly north, steering was a comparatively easy matter in spite of the yacht's tremendous velocity.

This gave Procopius an opportunity to reflect on another subject that still kept obtruding itself on his attention. Gallia's velocity had diminished twenty millions of leagues during the month of March, strictly in accordance with Kepler's second law. But her distance from the sun having increased by thirty-two millions of leagues in the meantime, she now found herself among the Minor Planets that lie between Mars and Jupiter. One of these, Nerina, she had passed even close enough to capture and carry off. So far the astronomer's calculations had proved themselves to be perfectly correct. Now was there not good reason to expect that he had also succeeded in calculating the exact orbit that Gallia was following, and that he could therefore tell them if she was ever to return to her starting-point? Even less important information than this, the Captain said he would be satisfied with for the present. For instance, when would Gallia be likely to reach her *aphelion* — in other words, how long was this fearful winter to last?

The sudden appearance of the sun on the left puts a premature end to this conversation, and suggests the propriety of a short consultation regarding the mode of prosecuting the remainder of the journey. At a rough calculation they must now be very near the object of their expedition, and a reconnoissance

LOOK! LOOK!

is therefore necessary. The yacht is laid to for a little while to take in a few reefs; when she starts again her speed is so reduced that in spite of the extreme cold the travellers can look around them a little.

The icy sea is as deserted as ever. Not a speck of any kind relieves the magnificent monotony.

"We're probably a little too far west for Formentera," suggests the Captain, examining the chart.

"Likely enough," answers Procopius, "for, exactly as I would have done at sea, I have kept to windward of the island. Let us turn a point or two eastwardly."

"All right," says the Captain, keeping a sharp look-out from the prow in spite of the cutting cold.

He does not waste his time looking for a trace of smoke in the sky — the poor astronomer is out of fuel as well as food. It is the black pinnacle of some rock emerging from the ice-field that his eye eagerly strains itself to catch on the horizon.

Suddenly he starts and puts the glass to his eye.

"Here! Procopius!" he cries as if in transport. "Come instantly! — Take this glass and look where I point! Don't you see something like framework twinkling against the sky!"

"Certainly!" answers Procopius. "It is the astronomer's watch-tower!"

Further doubt is impossible. The yacht's course, slightly modified, carries the travellers rapidly towards the signalled object. It grows larger and larger. It is a pile of rocks—surmounted by a framework of wood and iron—an observatory—something flutters from its summit—it is a rag of blue bunting—all that remains of the Tricolor!

A cry of agony breaks from the Captain.

No smoke rises from the rocks! No fire, and the cold intense! Are they hastening to a tomb?

The sails are dropped, the yacht's momentum giving force enough to make the rest of the distance.

On the top of the rocks, at the foot of the observatory, is a small framework cottage, the door closed and the windows shut air-tight.

To jump from the yacht, scale the rocks, and reach the cottage, costs the Captain a few seconds. He knocks loudly. No answer. He calls loudly. No reply.

He makes a signal to the Lieutenant. A vigorous push from both bursts open the worm-eaten door.

In the entry nothing visible but two doors, one on the right, the other on the left.

The left door is burst in, the chamber entered, the windows thrown open. Nothing visible, except figures, diagrams and drawings scratched on the bare walls.

IS IT TOO LATE?

The door on the right opens at a touch. Darkness, complete. Silence, absolute. He is either escaped, or dead !

Procopius, flinging open a shutter, admits the light.

Their eyes fall first on the hearth. Nothing there, save some white ashes, cold as ice.

In the dark corner to the right a bed. On the bed a human body.

"Open the other window, Procopius," whispers the Captain softly.

"Stiff as marble !" he moans in agony as he touches the body. "Frozen and starved! Frozen and starved!"

Procopius leans earnestly over the face, turns the clothes down a little, tries to feel for the pulsations of the heart.

A few moments pass — years of anguish and suspense!

"This man lives!" he cries suddenly. "Quick! Captain, give me the flask!"

With some trouble they succeed in pouring a few drops of a powerful restorative into the mouth of the unconscious sufferer.

For some seconds the silence of a midnight grave pervades the room. Then a faint sigh is heard — and the lips part as if trying to utter something !

Servadac and Procopius, stooping, listen intently.

"Gallia?" issues from the lips in a spent whisper.

"Gallia! Yes! Yes! Gallia!" replies the Captain eagerly. "What of Gallia?"

"Gallia's my comet — *mine!*" comes from the lips as faintly as the last words of a departing spirit.

That's all. These words uttered, the marble face resumes its rigidity, and the heart's pulsations are felt no more.

Wasting time in applying restoratives in this dreary freezing cabin is not to be thought of. The friends instantly form their resolution. In a few moments the body of the dying astronomer, his few philosophical and astronomical instruments, his clothes, papers and an old door that he has used as a blackboard, are all carefully stowed away in the ice-yacht. The wind has been slowly hauling round and is now in almost a favorable point. Taking advantage of the opportunity, the friends instantly set sail, but it is fully thirty-six hours later when the ice-yacht strikes the rocks of Terre Chaude.

The Gallians, headed by Ben Zouf, are drawn up in orderly array and impatiently await the Count's signal to burst into frantic cheers of welcome to the two bold companions. But a warning gesture of the Captain is well understood, and implicitly obeyed.

During the long return a block of marble could not have been more motionless than the astronomer's body. Is he living or dead? No one can say. Lifted carefully out of the yacht by the Captain and Procopius, he is gently carried up a practicable road that has been thoughtfully constructed by the Count during their absence. In front of the procession move quietly and silently Pablo and little Nina. On each side, in single file, march the Russians and the Italians, hats off, heads down, and lips moving as if in prayer for a departed soul. Torches illumine the dark walls of the galleries, guiding the footsteps securely through the devious labyrinth of the volcano.

Thus wound the solemn *cortége* into the heart of the mountain, reverent, mournful, slow, to the couch where they piously laid him.

END OF TO THE SUN? .